ALMOST REAL

A SWEET, SMALL TOWN, FAKE RELATIONSHIP ROMANCE

CLAIRE CAIN

Cover design by Emma Robinson

E-Book: 978-1-954005-25-9

Print: 978-1-954005-26-6

To the people who feel they must earn their worth: you are worthy, and you are loved.

CHAPTER ONE

Sadie

I made the grave and utterly irreversible mistake of looking up today.

This might not sound like a problem to a casual observer —doesn't everyone look up to see where they're walking or to avoid running into cabinets? And sure, yes, you bet they do. At least, I assume they do, or they'd all have bruised foreheads like I did last week after a run-in with a particularly pointy and aggressive cabinet door.

But today, I looked up from kneading a small batch loaf I've been experimenting with and gazed right out the glass panels that cover one long stretch of my new, gigantic industrial kitchen.

The glass that looks directly into Warrick Saint's gym, Grit.

Yes. *Him.* The Warrick Saint who used to play professional football. The pride and joy of Silverton, who'd come home with his head held high after a career-ending injury four years ago. The same Warrick Saint who'd just stripped off a sweaty shirt when his last client left and then proceeded to sit on a rowing machine and start another workout because, apparently, he was inexhaustible. That, and he had no awareness that his chest and arms and back and abs and—well, his *everything* made focusing on anything other than him while he pushed and pulled and worked himself into oblivion an absolute impossibility.

That said, I envied him.

Granted, envy was admittedly not the first feeling I had upon seeing the man. Not even close. Shirtless or zipped up in a puffy coat midwinter, a sixty-quart mixer's worth of emotions swarmed me every time—one of myriad reasons I didn't normally look up.

Generally, I did my best to block out the gym scene playing before me. Most of the time, I was nestled in my coffee shop and bakery's small kitchen, headphones on, scrambling through prep for the day, so I didn't have this front row seat to the insane people who spent their mornings exercising.

My scene—the actual one I created in Rise and Shine, my shop, and the one I sometimes let myself dream about when exhaustion hung too heavy around my shoulders—was something in between. Maybe a combination of both, really, though I couldn't imagine working out as hard as these people did so early. Yoga, maybe some jogging in decent weather, yes. Plus, I had no desire to sweat and groan and collapse into an exhausted heap in front of a dozen other people. Warrick's brand of workout seemed to be readying attendees for the zombie apocalypse with a side of fitness modeling.

But back to Warrick, who was still sprinting away on

the rower, every single muscle in his giant torso and arms on full display as he swooped forward, then stretched and pulled back, his legs extending out from the crouch of the forward motion.

Dear sweet cinnamon roll, the man had muscles previously undiscovered. I never thought of myself as a woman who liked that build, but having the parade of beautiful discipline on the other side of the glass every day had changed my mind about that quickly enough.

I chuckled and blew out a breath—honestly, he was too much. Too many muscles. Too much personality. Too much energy and social-butterfly charm. Too much... everything.

Essentially my opposite, where the opposite of too much was definitely *not enough*.

I shook myself from the view and focused on tucking in edges and nestling the loaves into their tins, where they'd rise until this afternoon.

A wisp of anticipation swept through me—this one would be good. A lemon blueberry loaf, it would hit the late spring feel of the week just right, if all went to plan. I hadn't made a new sweet bread in a while—just hadn't had the motivation. This wasn't anything revolutionary, but the edge-of-summer flavors made me happy, and I hoped they'd do the same for my customers.

I covered the loaves, cleaned my workspace, ran through the to-do list on my counter, all the while steadfastly keeping my eyes within the four feet of my typical visual bubble. Limiting what I took in helped control the slow creep of anxiety that spun out when the world got too big. Granted, that'd gotten so much better lately, but the old habit had stuck.

When my gaze clawed its way back up to look out the window that separated his part of the mill building from my kitchen, Warrick was zipping up a thin hooded sweatshirt and studying his phone as he scratched at his stubble-covered cheek. He'd been going longer between shaving, and I wondered if he had plans for a beard.

Then I gave myself a stern internal tsk because I did not need to be observing him so closely to develop thoughts and feelings about his facial hair. Obviously, I spent way too much time thinking about Warrick's face and body and general existence if I was over here considering the length of his hair.

Seconds later, Quinn Darling, Dahlia Price, Sarah James, and Callaway Rice, aka pop star Miss Mayhem, entered the gym. Warrick held up a bear paw of a hand to each of them, and somehow, they all knew just what to do in response. They swatted at his hand for a high five, and I imagined a loud *smack!* from the contact reverberating around the room with each slap of palms.

My chest twisted, and those confounded feelings knotted themselves into an unignorable ball. *I want that.*

The thought hit anytime I saw him with someone. I didn't need it to be *him*, not that I'd say no to him if he asked me for just about anything, really, but I wanted *that*. The easy way he had with people, the comfort and self-confidence that set everyone at ease when they entered his radius.

I'd seen him charm grumpy old men, coax shy kids out of their shells, and waylay the awestruck, lusty looks women and men alike gave him here at the gym by simply being so darn approachable, kind, and good at his job. He was flirty and fun and generous with his words and assistance and smiles with everyone.

Everyone but me.

It'd started in school well over a decade ago. Warrick

Saint was a legend on the football field and in the halls of Silverton High thanks to his size and skill on the field and his supreme likability. He was the hot, charismatic jock who was friends with *literally* everyone.

Not a huge shock when factoring in the size of the school—graduating class of one hundred fifty my year—and the small-town effect. Everyone already and always had known everyone else. For all of them, it must've been a kind of idyllic school experience.

For me? Not so much.

But I'd grown too used to that way of thinking as I grew up, and I'd worked for the last few years to combat it. The idea that everyone else's experience had been easier or better had snuck in through little cracks in my mind, and before I knew it, I felt like I was alone in my anxious, unsure little high school world. I used to feel guilty for being so far in my own head that I didn't see how many other people felt awkward and stressed and overwhelmed too, but I'd worked through that. Mostly. Sort of.

That I constantly failed to actually win the battle infuriated me more often than not, but better this than the quiet, stifling resignation that'd been a hallmark of most of my twenties.

A fluttering of hands and flashing white smiles broke my thought process, and my eyes focused enough to realize the small group at the far side of the gym could see me and was waving.

Nerves immediately took my stomach in hand and squeezed. My throat clogged up, and I couldn't swallow when I saw them walking toward the door. That one small, little portal between Warrick's world and mine. It was locked from my side, so I unstuck my feet and scuttled to it to flip the deadbolt. Without physically stuttering, though my mind had gone blank, I pulled it open to find them standing and smiling.

"Pretty sure this is the second time this door has ever been open," Warrick said, smiling one of his gigantic sunbeams of a smile while looking around at the pristine kitchen. "I feel like I'm walking on sacred ground or something."

"Is it okay that we're here? We won't touch anything, but I wanted to see your space. Warrick mentioned you'd taken the lease the other night at dinner and I got so excited."

Calla's smile shined bright, and her dark eyes really did seem genuinely thrilled to be looking at all the stainless steel surrounding me. If I didn't feel tight with nerves, the international pop star's awed expression at the sight of my kitchen would've made me laugh.

"Sure. Have a look. Not much to see just yet." The frog in my throat shrunk up a bit now that I'd spoken, so I pushed past it and my racing heart for more. "If you can swing by in a few hours, I'll have some blueberry lemon loaves. They won't be fresh for tomorrow, and I hate selling new recipes as day-olds."

Quinn, fellow local business owner and extremely talented musician, responded first. "Oh, I'm in. I'll circle back when I grab Cara from my mom's."

I couldn't imagine life as a single mom, especially at only a few years older than I was, but clearly my life and Quinn Darling's had taken rather different paths.

"I'll have to sample yours because I have a committee meeting, but thanks, Sadie." Dahlia looked genuinely regretful. I'd hardly ever seen the local florist without a smile on her face.

"I have a class, but if it wraps up early, I'll be by. If not,

I'm going to stalk Rise and Shine for when you have that one in store because it sounds amazing."

Sarah's kind words stroked that feeble part of me that craved adoration. I didn't know her well at all, so no idea what that class could be about, but anytime she'd been into the shop, she'd been chatty and nice.

Calla's face dropped too. "Shoot. I'm catching up with Wyatt, and we're heading back up to the ranch after a quick meeting in a few. We just stopped by to see the place, but I so wish I could come back because that sounds delicious. I love anything lemon."

Warrick cleared his throat lightly. "I can grab one for you and bring it with me when I come home, if you want. I know how you feel about Sadie's baked goods."

He glanced over like it was up to me to decide.

"Uh, sure."

Calla brightened. "Yes! Perfect. We'll have it for dessert." She hitched her purse over her shoulder, then turned back to me. "Also, we're doing lunch tomorrow afternoon. You should join us! I don't know what your Sunday work hours are, but if you can, we'll be at Guac at noon."

My mouth levered open unnaturally wide. Like, so wide, it didn't make sense. What word did one's mouth plan to make at that width? By the time I said, "Oh," the women no longer stood in front of me.

Calla had turned and taken a call after fluttering a friendly wave while mouthing, "Bye," and Quinn, Dahlia, and Sarah had echoed their agreement and followed her back into Warrick's part of the building.

And Warrick? He studied me with a frown. One of those looks that no one else saw, yet here it was, directed at me.

"You okay?" he asked in that deep, rich voice.

My mouth snapped shut. "Course."

He nodded. "Okaaay. Guess I'll see you this afternoon. Five too early?"

I shook my head, heart racing and still stunned by the lunch invite. "It's good."

He did one of those closed-lipped smile-frowns and widened his eyes. Maybe it meant *see you later*, or maybe it meant *your social skills suck*. Definitely an expression I hadn't seen him give anyone else—he'd have a cute retort or parting shot for them. Not for me, either because I'd clearly shut down or because he just couldn't be bothered with me.

I sank onto the stool sitting blessedly nearby and watched all of them retreat across the long space of the gym, my throat tight and dry, hands cramping into fists. I needed to funnel this churning pulse into something or I'd spin out.

I let out a ragged breath, willing my heart to slow, my mind to focus, and trying to figure out which of these things had shoved me so off-center and which one I dreaded most.

CHAPTER TWO

Warrick

Sadie Miller's face haunted my every step the rest of the day. Through my planning meeting before lunch, and then lunch itself. Knowing she'd returned to her kitchen and started baking again just before my last training session of the day caused a twinge between my shoulder blades.

Everyone in my four o'clock class applauded their hard work of the last hour, effectively shaking me from my space-out but not quite wresting the off feeling from my back. They'd pushed through barriers and a few people had hit PRs—they deserved to feel proud. They deserved my genuine encouragement, so I needed to buck up and do my job.

Normally, this was one of my favorite parts—the post-workout kudos for people who'd made progress, or for those who hadn't but showed up and did the work. This afternoon? Not so much. Because Sadie Miller's anxious eyes on me, and knowing I'd see her again later to get a loaf of her bread, had my mind bouncing around in my skull.

My buddy Pete wandered up, wiping his brow as he punched me in the arm a little too hard. People always assumed I liked a rougher approach, likely because of my size and history in the NFL, but nah. I liked it… sweet.

"Hey. Easy. I did shoulders yesterday, as you would know if you hadn't missed, ya slacker." I gave him a ridiculous, superior look I knew would annoy him.

Pete liked to pretend he was laid back, but he was actually even more anal-retentive than I was. Maybe that's why we got along so well.

"Shut it. My grandma needed help."

"Well, that's about the only legitimate excuse you could have," I said with a false glare and an inward wince against the grief that still nagged at me when I thought about my own grandmother's death a few years ago.

"So are you going to tell me what's up with you?" Pete raised both brows and crossed his arms.

"The ceiling?"

His brows dropped.

I huffed a little laugh at his lack of response to my lame joke. "Nothing's up."

He squinted. "Mm-hmm. Sure. You're just distracted and quiet 'cause that's always how you are, right? Good ol' Warrick Saint, shy, retiring, interior kind of guy."

I gave him a slow blink and flattened my lips to an unimpressed look. I wasn't about to admit to feeling way more off than I'd apparently been acting, though I hadn't realized I'd been quite so obviously out of it. In truth, I'd been off for a while, and this run in with Sadie had me in a tailspin I couldn't shake.

He waved me off just as Catherine walked up.

"Hey, great job today, Catherine." I summoned a smile, less challenging in the face of this woman's genuine joy than it had been seconds ago. She'd come so far and I really couldn't have been happier for her. When she'd started, she would hardly look me in the eye or speak—could barely stand to get feedback. In a matter of six weeks, she'd come out of her shell, and it was pretty darn glorious, if I did say so myself.

She grinned. "Thanks. I think I've gotten my squat deeper than ever."

"That you did. Nice work." And then, because I knew what progress it was for her to not only show up, do the work, and do it well, but also to talk to me so casually, I held up a hand for a high five. "Proud of you."

She beamed now and slapped my hand. "Thanks. Me too."

Next, I chatted with Cody and Charlotte, relative newlyweds who'd decided to spend more time together by working out at Grit since their schedules kept them so busy. They were sweet—kind of sickening if I watched their PDA show too closely, but I couldn't blame either one of them. Seeing them like this had been a long time coming.

A few more people came to talk or ask questions, all of them hopped up on endorphins and the accomplishment of a hard Saturday afternoon workout.

"Be good, kids! I'll see you bright and early tomorrow if you're not too scared. Remember, bravery is courage in the face of fear, not in the absence of it!" I sent them off with my typical taunt-slash-encouragement, enjoying their shaking heads and quips in response.

I'd never imagined the gym would grow this quickly, but I couldn't pretend I didn't love it. Seeing things grow and succeed fed my soul. Accomplishment was what I imagined a hit of cocaine felt like, assuming there was no downside to it and it didn't also destroy your mind and body. So not a drug so much as... what?

Well, not to be trite, but it felt like a touchdown. It was that same feeling as catching the ball from thirty yards out, running my route, and beating the opponent until I crossed that hallowed line and made it to the end zone.

I couldn't do the touchdown thing anymore, but success? Working my butt off until something clicked? I suppose I liked regular injections of that kind of rush.

"Warrick?"

I startled, way deeper into the football metaphor thoughts than I'd realized and knowing the voice immediately. I flipped around, anchoring myself into my hips, all the way down to my feet in my shoes on the slightly gummy mats below them like I had absolutely nowhere else to be. "Yeah?"

Aw, yeah. Look at that casual, calm response. No hint of the fact that she shoved me in a mental ditch just by talking to me earlier.

"Did you want to grab a loaf?" Sadie held one little brick out, already wrapped in wax paper and twisted at each end.

My stomach clenched. Whatever she'd made would sit in my car and the scent would cover every inch of airspace, and I'd be eating down the flavor without ever taking a bite. By the time I made it home, I'd be lucky if I hadn't either tossed it out the window or devoured the entire thing.

"I better, or Calla will kill me. Second to Wyatt, I've never seen her look at something so longingly." I added a cheesy grin like her standing in front of me, willingly talking to me, hadn't done things to my insides.

Plus, that wasn't a complete lie either. Calla loved her

some Sadie Miller baked goods. Honestly, I was about the only person in town who didn't.

And we all know what a crock that is.

I batted the thought away.

"That's nice. I hope she enjoys it."

She handed off the neatly wrapped package. A thin yellow-and-white twine crisscrossed over the loaf to hold the paper in place. I'd bet anything that shade of sunshine yellow matched the walls of Rise and Shine exactly.

"I'm sure she will."

Her gaze met mine, then dropped to just past my shoulder, like she couldn't stand to look me in the eye. Like she couldn't stand to be around me. Just like she'd always done.

My teeth set on edge as I waited for her to say something else, or turn and go, but she did neither. Her hands were clasped tight at her middle right overtop a pristine white apron and its double-wrapped strings.

I didn't actually have to see the strings to know they were wrapped once, twice around her tiny little waist. I'd seen her in an apron innumerable times over the last few years since I got back to Silverton, and sometimes thinking about it made my hands shake. Which was weird and stupid. Because, why would that even be a thing?

"Well... have a good one." I lingered another second, waiting for her eyes to meet mine again, but when they didn't, I assumed I'd been dismissed and turned in the other direction.

"Wait."

The word stopped me. Clipped and small, but clear— no mistaking it. I turned slowly to see her, somehow smaller there on the mat. She was more than a full foot shorter than my six feet six inches, and though I was no stranger to people being smaller than me, her tiny size made my insides twist. Always had.

"What's up?" I asked, still affecting casual, though no interaction I'd ever had with Sadie Miller had felt casual.

I tried not to notice the way her throat worked to swallow and how she crossed her arms and tucked them close to her body. Nervous energy spiraled up my spine.

"Um. Do you have a problem with me?" Her eyes jumped to mine, then away again as a bright red blush slipped up from the neck of her shirt.

I blinked a few times, waiting for something charming and easy to pop to mind to dispel the immediate unease that sliced through my gut at both her visible discomfort and words. Rare for me, but *no dice*. "Uhhh, no."

Yeah. *Real convincing*.

I forced myself to add, "What do you mean? Of course not."

Her cheeks flushed deeper red and made her eyes appear all the more blue when she did finally look at me again. "I don't mean to sound accusatory. It just feels like I've done something, or... *something*."

Her eyebrows pushed together, and my stomach dove off a cliff. First, I happened to have a bit of a thing for her eyebrows—they were like perfect little swoops that I'd had a mild obsession with in high school. Don't ask me why, but I'd wanted to trace the line of her brows with a finger and see her eyes flutter shut under the contact something fierce.

And second because... seriously? *Had she done something?* I huffed out a breath and looked left and right, like the answer might be found in the corners of the room. What was happening right now?

"Where's this coming from?" After knowing each other for something like twenty years, maybe more?

"Sorry, I just... I've always wondered."

Lead weights plunged into my gut. "*Always* wondered?"

"Since high school, honestly. But after that, we were both gone for a few years, so... whatever. But we've both been back for a while now, and working in the same building most days means we're interacting more often. I've just wondered if I owe you an apology, maybe."

"Uhhh—I—"

Did she owe me an apology? No. Not really. But did I find it impossible to act the same way I did with ninety-nine percent of people around her? Damn straight. Because she wasn't ninety-nine percent of people. Never had been. First, because I had been a little lovesick fool over her in high school, and second because she'd treated me like complete dirt.

That said, how do you tell someone you haven't actually had a conversation with in decades—not a real conversation anyway—that they kind of broke your heart by essentially pretending you didn't exist? By turning you down when you were at a vulnerable point in life, and then never speaking to you again unless under pressure for social niceties years later?

Answer: You don't. Because you're a grown man, and that's not a thing.

She'd never given any hint that she might think she'd done something wrong before. Or that she regretted rejecting me so cruelly. Where had this come from? "Why do you say that?"

She pressed her lips together and rolled them between her teeth, but after a beat, her blue eyes found mine again. "You're different with me."

Alarm shot through me. She couldn't know that, could she? "Different?"

"You're so nice to everyone. So friendly."

But not with me.

That was the thought she didn't say aloud, but it hung there between us like she'd tacked it up on an invisible corkboard.

I ran a hand through my hair and shifted on my feet. "I'm sorry. I haven't meant to treat you any differently than anyone else."

That was true. Wasn't it? I'd long since been over her. Obviously. *Right?*

"I know I'm not a person who people chat with. I don't have friends and I—I'm hard to get know. I get it." She shrugged.

"Don't say that," I said, though admittedly, it came out weakly.

She chuckled under her breath—actually *chuckled,* which was not a thing I'd ever imagined being able to make Sadie Miller do. Sixteen-year-old Warrick jogged by and gave me a fist bump.

"It's true. Nice of you to half-heartedly refute, but true."

Had someone slipped me the red pill today or something? "Sorry, I'm not sure I'm tracking. I just... what did you want?"

Her face, which had grown more open after that small moment of humor, locked up tight. "I'm sorry to waste your time. I shouldn't have said anything."

"No, it's fine, I'm just—"

"Really. Enjoy the bread, Warrick." She turned on her heel and walked at a just-shy-of-jogging pace back through the kitchen door, then closed it. She paused right inside for a few seconds, then continued her path to one of the steel tables.

And I stood there like an idiot, loaf of her bread in hand, unsure what I'd done to deserve a woman whose attention I'd wanted for more than a decade finally giving it to me, only to find out she thought I'd treated her badly.

Talk about a fumble.

CHAPTER THREE

Sadie

The memory of failing miserably at talking to Warrick plagued me consistently for the next twelve hours. I know this because I stayed awake for nearly all of them, despite the little incident happening at approximately six minutes after five p.m.

My mouth had run away with me, and that hadn't happened in... *ever*. Usually, jumpstarting my words proved to be the biggest challenge, not halting them or even choosing the right ones. But I'd been working up to this.

A little while ago, I'd started slipping into place in front of the register at Rise and Shine for ten-minute shifts when my regular employees were taking breaks just to practice helping customers—to practice speaking to people and not having a nervous breakdown.

And as hyperbolic as that might seem, the statement grew its roots from the fertile soil of historical evidence.

There was just no way around it: I had severe social anxiety.

Just thinking that inside my own head and not feeling a drowning wash of shame, guilt, fear, and despair was a process I'd worked through for the last ten years. This was not something I'd arrived at overnight. And in the last eighteen months, my therapist had suggested that we'd worked through the worst of the *severe* part of the diagnosis. But that didn't just disappear.

Nor did the desire to speak to Warrick Saint. It hadn't come out of nowhere, and it wouldn't go away, either. Sure, we'd interacted on and off for years, especially in the last few months since I'd taken a lease for the kitchen. We'd had to meet in person, and I'd signed a document becoming his tenant since he owned the entire mill building. He'd been more energetic than he often was with me, though he'd ultimately tamped down that vibrating energy nearly every time I saw him after the lease signing. Still, I'd gotten a little glimpse that day.

Since then, all interactions had been business-focused, short, and even on his side, relatively clipped. If he joked around with me, it was with a self-deprecating way that told me he expected me *not* to speak. And that never failed to stuff a sock down my throat and cause me to do exactly that. Basically just like every interaction I'd had with him from high school, until today.

But the combination of being generally intrigued by him, seeing him interact so easily with all kinds of people, witnessing Catherine's progress right before my very eyes, and being invited out to lunch by Calla had all dished up the inability to stop myself from talking, from being spontaneous and taking the plunge.

What I'd meant to do was ask him about how he did it—how did he manage to be so kind and warm to everyone?

And yet, what had I actually asked? Effectively, *why aren't you nice to* me? He normally acted subdued with me, but the man had seemed downright snuffed out even before I started babbling my nonsense. *Ugh.*

I groaned at my poor wording and timing and everything, pulled two trays from the double oven, then slid the last batch of loaves in and set three timers. Garrett, my regular morning employee, was great, but if he was busy, he'd miss the timers and burn the last batch.

Warrick had seemed so shocked by my question, so baffled. He'd claimed he didn't realize he treated me any differently, and based on his utterly shocked and appalled expression, I believed him.

How could he not realize that he directed all that warmth toward everyone but me?

That, ultimately, hadn't been the point, yet it'd been the one my traitor of a brain had attempted to make instead of seeking the information I actually needed. And, when faced with the giant, sweaty, frankly quite gorgeous man one-on-one, I'd cracked. Lost the words I'd planned on, spewed the wrong ones, and offended him in the process.

So... just another Saturday.

"Garrett, you're up. I'll see you tomorrow."

The tall redhead nodded, then turned back to the woman at the register. He'd worked for me since the day he graduated high school a few years back and was chipping away at school online so he still took the most hours of any of my employees. I currently had six, though several were super part-time or only worked the ski season when we were busiest.

Grabbing my small bag, I shuffled out the kitchen door,

along the path that led to the sidewalk, and around the corner to Elk Street. The walk between Rise and Shine and the mill building took between seven and eight minutes depending on my pace. And on a gorgeous, beaming May Sunday morning, the air still crisp and springy around me but promising a nice little warm up, there was almost nowhere else I'd rather be.

Although that wasn't quite true, because I was headed toward the place I'd rather be right now.

I tried to take shorter days on Sundays out of season. During some months, we closed on Mondays too, so that gave me a day off. But generally, I worked seven days a week from three thirty or four in the morning, depending on the menu I had planned, until about ten. By then, all the breads and pastries were well in hand, and often, I could even sneak out earlier, especially now that I'd hired two assistant bakers who could do quite a lot.

That was another thing—acknowledging my need for help, especially after Bel Paxton—er, now Morris—moved away and had less of a hand in things. She owned a quarter of the business, and though I could buy her out anytime now thanks to how well things were going, it felt nice to share it with someone. We weren't close by any means, but I trusted Bel.

"Morning," someone said as I passed Wallace Law Office and Cut. Next came a little smoothie and ice cream shop, Scoop, that was set to open next month. The flower shop was closed Sundays, but Bloom had quickly become one of my favorite new stores, and Dahlia seemed so nice whenever I went in there.

Thinking of Dahlia sent a little chill into my chest, especially as I passed Quinn's music shop, Pluck. I wouldn't go to lunch today, though so much of me wanted to. A personal invitation was exactly the kind of thing I'd hoped for without ever actually thinking it'd happen, but being locked into a full meal with four women I didn't actually know? Bridge too far for today.

I passed Keller Accountancy and waved at Cody Keller when he glanced up from kissing his new wife's cheek. Some stupid part of my Warrick-focused brain had me flashing to Warrick kissing my cheek, and I shook that thought right back into the trash where it belonged. No sense in getting wrapped around an idea like that, even if it did make my heart flip.

Last before the mill came the diner that'd been recently revitalized thanks to new ownership, including a facelift and total redesign inside, and then I finally made it to the little foot path that would take me to my entrance of the mill building.

Flipping on the lights, I eyed the various towel-covered baskets and bowls holding different bread starters and rising loaves. Excitement and anticipation made me hustle over to the hook where I hung my purse, then rush to the sink and scrub my hands. I wrapped an apron around my waist and knotted the strings tightly—I loved the secured, contained feeling of the knot at my waist. It settled me, the familiar pressure against my body a reminder I was home and in my element.

After peeking at several of my overnight rises, I got to work. Weekends were for experimenting, and I had all day to slip into the oblivion of my recipes and flavor combinations.

Sometime later, I startled when a bold knock banged on the door between the kitchen and gym. I wiped my hands on a towel I'd tucked into my apron and reached the door.

"Hey."

Warrick barged past me, his bright energy tumbling in after him today.

"Listen. I want to understand what you were saying yesterday, and I know you didn't say everything you wanted to. So. Lay it on me."

He slapped at his pecs, currently outlined by a shirt made of stretchy material designed to fit this man's chest with precision, and sat on the only stool in the kitchen, facing me.

"Um." I swallowed, entirely unprepared for this. That energy in my space or the sight of him in that shirt. "I'm sorry. I shouldn't have said anything."

But even after eking those words out, they burned my throat. Because they weren't true, and I'd worked on being honest with myself and others for years. Plus, I'd already taken that misstep yesterday; I couldn't back out now.

"What's that look for?" He tilted his head to the side in a boyish move that mismatched his very grown man body.

Something about that tilt made my stomach swoop low. The man was lethally handsome, but his sweet playfulness, that side I only saw from a distance, just hit me right in the chest. To have one of those grins directed at me? *Killer cute.*

Then I remembered he was waiting for me to speak. My eyes shot to his, and I firmed my resolve. "I lied. What I said yesterday is true, but it's not what I wanted to talk about. And now I feel weird for saying what I did because it's not the point."

His big brown eyes blinked once.

"Okaaay." He drew the word out.

I shut the door and inched closer to him so we stood about four feet apart. I exhaled slowly through my nose, working to calm my rioting heart with an internal countdown I often used when anxious. "I've been making changes in my life. And without going into too much boring detail, I want to say I admire your way with people."

He blinked at me again, and his brow furrowed, but then his phone went off. He pulled it out of his pocket like it might buy him time or give him the answer to a question I hadn't quite asked, then he held it out to me.

"It's for you."

"What?" I leaned forward and squinted at his screen. A message from "Rice Rice Baby" said, *"Can you please go ask Sadie if she's coming to lunch? Tell her she can be late, but we really want her to come."*

Warmth flooded my cheeks, a combo of both delight and embarrassment.

"They don't have your number."

"That's Calla?"

He nodded, a little half-smile tugging up one side of his beautiful mouth. "Yeah. Figured if my phone ever got hacked by some gossip site, it wouldn't be as obvious as her actual name."

"Sure. Yeah." Considerate with a side of humor—made sense that he was like that in all walks of life. It was one more thing that made him so completely appealing and overwhelming. His outsides matched his insides and they were both stunning.

"So?"

I raised my brows.

"Are you going to lunch? They aren't blowing smoke. They want you there in all your bread-baking, pastry-filling, magical-coffee-shop-running glory."

My mouth did that stupid thing it'd done yesterday—fell open but made no move to actually speak, though a laugh tumbled out inelegantly.

He ducked his head and gazed down at me—and it was definitely down because he was absolutely tree-like. And though you'd think he'd be sweaty and disgusting after training people and often participating in the workouts all day, he smelled like the outside and a hint of soapy, clean scent. Masculine and pure. I clamped my mouth shut. He was alluring enough that it derailed my foggy mess of a mind, and I had an insane vision of me walking into his space and pressing my face between the sloping curve of his pecs.

Mercifully, before I could get into real trouble, he spoke.

"You should go."

Remembering myself, I straightened and took a step back for good measure. "I can't."

"Busy?"

"No, I just—I can't."

He squinted at me, surveying the person in front of him. He was always so smooth and charming with others, but not with me. This focus and study felt heavy and warm and honestly delicious. I wondered whether it always felt like this to be caught in his gaze—a little like a spotlight, a little like a hug.

"Can't? Or won't?"

My face fell because, for some reason, I hadn't expected that. The words had no sharp edge, but they sliced at me all the same. I shook my head, unwilling to tell this tower of a man any details today. Maybe someday, if he'd sit down with me and let me ask him the questions I wanted to. If he'd give me more than a passing glance and quick comment.

But not now, when I felt suddenly flayed open by the question and all the insinuated feelings behind it.

I would've walked away, except he was in *my* space. I shifted side to side on my feet and studied my shoes—powder blue sneakers today.

"Sadie."

My head popped up because I couldn't ignore him saying my name, even if my heartbeat banged on the drum of my chest and my ears had started the whooshing sound. When I looked at his face, instead of censure or judgment, it was gentleness I saw there.

That same churning heart seemed to twist, then calm just a tick, and the cotton in my ears disintegrated.

He stepped forward. "I didn't mean that—shouldn't have said it like that. I don't know what's going on with you, but you should go to this lunch. Go for the last fifteen minutes. Eat some chips and salsa. Then make your excuses. Or call in a to-go order and sit at the table while they make it. You don't have to go for an hour."

My pulse raced. All those options sounded so surprisingly *possible*, and his suggesting them made me feel both energized and sluggish. A caffeinated heart inside a pancake-soaked body. "I'll think about it, thanks."

"Good." His eyes slipped down over me again, then darted around the kitchen before he held up a hand as he exited. "Let me know how it goes."

I braced myself against the counter as the door swung shut behind him, possibility a whirlwind circling me. Warrick had been... intense. A little more like I'd seen him with others, but less light and cheery and more focused. More butterfly inducing and, *oh this is not a good thing to be thinking*, sexy. Honestly, more than a little magnetic with those brown eyes and an awareness of me no one had ever shown. Truly, no one.

The cool metal grounded me to the space—a happy place I loved. My heart rate slowed as I practiced the breath work I used when I got scrambled like this. When I finally calmed completely, I gazed out the window separating our space, wishing for another glimpse of him. Wanting to reassure myself he'd actually come in here and made those suggestions like we were friends. Like he knew me, or wanted to try.

Oh, how I wanted him to try.

CHAPTER FOUR

Sadie

Shaking hands and knees, dry mouth, tingling fingers, mild lightheadedness—just me, walking into Guac like I knew what I was doing. I didn't normally get like this—not anymore. But between the terrible sleep last night, the encounter with Warrick, and overthinking the heck out of what I was about to do, I felt these symptoms like old neighbors.

Warrick's words had taken me by the shoulders and shaken me. They'd rattled all the resistance out of me, all my old excuses, and left only the reminder that if I wanted a different outcome, I had to try something new. How many times had my therapist and I had that exact conversation? I *had* made changes, but this was new territory.

His suggestion that I could order takeout or go late had been like someone opening a window in a crowded, too-small room. It was an option. A possibility.

Months ago, this exact group of women had been sitting down to lunch when I'd come to pick up a takeout order. Warrick had chased after me, suggesting I join them. *Why?* It'd made no sense. As much as I wanted him to treat me like everyone else, I'd never once understood why he did talk to me. Because I barely eked out words whenever he spoke to me, and that day, I'd only said something like "I can't," and ran away. When I'd heard him ask Garrett if I was in the kitchen—he'd actually followed me back to Rise and Shine!—I'd hustled out the back door and up the stairs to my apartment, mind whirling at why he'd come after me from the restaurant all the way over to my shop. *Why?*

That said, those times he'd tried to talk to me, even when I hadn't responded well, had been more fuel behind my desire to talk to him. To really talk to him. Remembering how he *had* tried, even if it came and went, had linked arms with my determination to make progress and, well, I'd done it. And though the first stab at it hadn't gone well at all, our earlier exchange had been something like progress.

"Sadie! Oh my gosh, I'm so glad you made it!" Calla rose from the booth in the corner, slipping out with grace and style and general magnificence to reach out for me like we were best friends.

But... *crap*. What did she want to do with that hand? Shake mine? Pat my shoulder? Hug me? Any would be fine with me—I wasn't averse to touch, though some might think otherwise based on the way I kept to myself.

I bit my tongue to focus my mind on anything but the runaway train it saw flashing by and wanted to dive onto. The one that said, *"Now you'll make it weird. You'll lean in for a hug like you know her. She'll end up punching you in the stomach with a hand outstretched for a handshake. Or she'll feel how cold your hands are even though it's seventy degrees and sunny outside and your hands should be warm. She'll know how nervous you are and—*

No. Not today. Not right now. No.

I breathed out while counting inwardly, then sucked in my stomach and came to a stop a few feet in front of her. "I can't stay long. I put in a to-go order but thought I'd sit with you guys while they get it together."

And God bless Warrick for that brilliant idea. It gave me an easy out, and despite the warm welcome, my heart had worked its way into my throat and was trying to strangle me.

Calla either didn't notice or didn't mind my awkward halt because she stepped close and leaned to kiss my cheek like we did that all the time. "So glad you made it, seriously. Even if it's ten minutes! I'm glad you could squeeze us in."

I smiled, then took the seat at the head of the table after she slid into the booth next to a beaming Sarah.

"So, *so* glad you came," Sarah said with a charming little wink.

Quinn and Dahlia both smiled and welcomed me while a waiter set down a new basket of chips and a little bowl of salsa just for me. After chatting about what we all ordered like it was some sort of test I needed to pass, which I evidently did, the talk shifted.

"Are you planning to come to *A Night in Bloom?*" Dahlia asked before shoving a chip dripping with salsa into her mouth.

"I'm not sure. I heard about it at the last CVB meeting I went to, but that's been a few months, and I don't think there were many details yet."

The Convention and Visitor's Bureau was a local organization that helped draw business and tourism to Silverton. I'd made it a point to attend their open meetings when I could—another step toward functioning like an actual member of society. But the last few had landed on bad days, and I hadn't made it.

"You *have* to come. It's going to be amazing. Aidan's a magician with landscaping and gardening. It's going to be awesome."

Dahlia's excitement for the event shimmered in her eyes. Or maybe that was exhaustion from helping to plan it. I wasn't sure exactly what her role was. Considering she owned the local flower shop? Probably significant.

I crunched on a chip, which saved me from responding, though I hadn't needed to worry since their conversation flowed easily without me.

"I'm singing, and you might sing, Calla?" Quinn asked her.

She finished chewing a bite.

"I wasn't sure if we'd be here, but Kristoffer"—she turned to me—"my assistant, a magical little elf man who keeps my life together, just made it happen."

Quinn clapped. "Yes! Are we singing together?"

"Up to you, my friend. But if I have my way, absolutely."

They beamed at each other. Sarah and Dahlia seemed equally pleased to enjoy their anticipation with them.

My heart ached.

Had I been like that with anyone ever? Had I been so purely delighted to do something with a friend I cared about that I had little sparkles in my eyes and a smile so wide it'd get stuck like that if I wasn't careful?

Quinn turned to me. "You should think about coming. It's perfect for a date night, but there'll be lots of people just milling around."

"They convinced me to go, and I don't have a date yet

either. Worst case, I'll go solo. So don't let the plus-one thing stop you," Sarah said.

I pressed my lips into a smile. "I'll think about it."

Calla set her hand on my wrist. "You should. But you've got some time. It's a little over a month away. Dahlia's just setting up her orders so she's steeped in it these days."

Dahlia nodded as she chewed and swallowed. "Totally. Lots of time. I think they'll keep selling tickets until the day of since it's the inaugural year."

"Wow. Do you think it'll become an annual event?" I asked.

She beamed. "I am a total new kid on the block here, relatively speaking, but I hope so! Aidan's got the whole founding-family connection going, and Julian's got his hands in it, plus Quinn..."

"Plus you're amazing, your flowers are amazing, and your idea is amazing. I cannot wait." Quinn was so firmly encouraging, it sounded like her words were law.

"It's going to be awesome, and I bet the whole state is going to be talking about it," Sarah chimed in.

"Thanks. I hope so. No, I know so."

Dahlia's response sounded like me when I needed to convince myself of something. Just that little twinge of doubt, and also determination. Maybe not everyone was as self-assured as Calla and Quinn.

"Sadie? Order's up."

Brodie, one of Guac's usual servers, waved a bag from behind the bar, and a mix of relief and disappointment hit me.

"That's me. Thanks for letting me sit with you for a few minutes." I set my salsa bowl into the chip basket to tidy up.

"Are you kidding? I've been waiting for a chance to sit down with you and gush over your bread and ask you a million questions! We're doing dinner next Thursday night. Will you think about joining us?"

Calla's genuinely hopeful tone sliced through whatever excuse I might've made.

"Of course. I'll need to see. And I don't tend to stay out late since I work so early, but yeah."

"Good. Okay, enjoy your enchiladas and we'll see you soon."

Calla sent me off, with nice goodbyes from her booth mates. I grabbed my food with a thanks to Brodie and shuffled out the door—again, with part regret and part relief.

Deciding against the walk all the way to the big kitchen, I slipped across the street, behind Rise and Shine, then inside and up the stairs to my loft apartment. The thirty-second commute definitely helped the three a.m. wakeups.

As I arranged the food on the table in front of me, I made a wish. Not a hopeless one like I'd sent to the heavens in the past, but a heart-deep desire to make friends. That I'd have people in my life like Calla and Quinn and Dahlia, and even Sarah, had each other. That someday, my worries over breaking my safe little routine and talking to people I didn't have planned out words for wouldn't make me feel so much like I sat in an observation room, watching life play out behind a two-way mirror.

I couldn't go back to that. And I'd had a taste of more— the very thing I'd wanted for so long. For whatever reason, the women I saw today wanted to spend time with me. And based on the last twenty minutes, I wanted to get to know them. I just needed a little help.

And I knew exactly who could provide it.

CHAPTER FIVE

Warrick

The checklist on my phone glared back at me, several easy items remaining unchecked thanks to my distracted mood. I should've been past dealing with invoices and phone calls by now, but no dice.

I'd been messed up since that conversation with Sadie yesterday, and then all morning, even through my early Sunday session. By the time I'd finished teaching, she'd been working away in her kitchen for hours, and I'd had to practically blindfold myself to keep from looking over at her and trying to read her through the clear but highly effective barrier between us.

Not that a glass window was the only barrier, obviously. There might as well have been a brick wall built up and over top of her since I'd known her. She'd *Cask of Amontillado*'d herself in there—shout out to Mrs. Wallace, my tenth grade English teacher, for that one.

But that right there—her seemingly self-imposed isolation from... everything—embodied the reason my mind had gripped on to the subject of her and wouldn't let go.

I couldn't shake the curiosity about what she'd wanted to say but wouldn't yesterday, so I'd barged in. And then, she'd been so sweet and complimentary, I hardly knew what to do with myself. Thankfully, in came Calla's text, and it gave me the perfect opportunity to encourage her to get out there.

I wasn't positive she'd gone to lunch, but she *had* left the kitchen. And she hadn't come back.

Normally when I returned for my Sunday evening session, she'd be here, prepping something for the next day or cleaning, even inventorying. She seemed to love her new kitchen as much as I loved my gym.

I sat down to work on invoices to finally check those off my list, and an hour after I'd started and gotten nowhere, a knock on the gym door pulled me out of any semblance of concentration I'd ginned up. And what did I find?

Sadie Miller. Apron free and standing in front of me.

"Sorry to bother you. I figured you'd still be here."

"Don't be sorry. Do you want to come in?"

She glanced around, then edged back a touch. *Okay, that's a no.*

"No, I just wanted to see if maybe I could buy you a coffee sometime? Maybe tomorrow afternoon, if you're off?"

Well, color me magenta and call me Mabel because *what is happening right now?!* I couldn't say that aloud, obviously, so I quickly got my crap together and said something.

"Uh, sure. Yeah. I'm done here at nine. Mondays, I'm pretty free." I closed the gym Monday afternoons to make my life easier, but something about her specific invitation for Monday afternoon made it seem like she knew that already.

"Good. Okay. I'll see you then."

"Here?"

Pink splashed over her cheeks. "Oh, I was thinking maybe Rise and Shine, if you're okay with that?"

"I do like supporting local businesses, so yes. I'm okay with that." I raised my brows, showing I knew I was a dork.

She smiled—small but genuinely, if I was reading her right. Which, I had to admit, I wasn't confident I could do.

"See you tomorrow," I said as she backed away, then turned to walk toward town.

Rather than watching her go the whole way, I shut the door and gave myself a minute to stare into the darkness of the space in front of me. My small office tacked onto the larger space, which was essentially a giant brick building divided up, was much different than the other mill building where Silver Ridge Brewing had settled in a few years back. Mine was the stubby neighbor and had needed hardly any major work before I was able to move in.

Flipping off the office light, I grabbed a stack of things to haul out to my current temporary house. I operated out of here to manage my other projects—property development, another StayBnB house like I had up next to the ranch house, things like that. The gym felt like my biggest venture because it required the most time, but I was only a few weeks out from feeling fully justified in hiring on some help. Just needed to find the right people.

Granted, the thought of not being here every day gave me a restless feeling I knew all too well. It cropped up between projects, whenever I hired out help for something or sold off a business. I'd done that a few times since leaving the NFL. I hated the in-between, not working toward a goal. Not knowing for sure that I had value in my days stemming from hard work.

Or worse, slowing down enough to have to deal with the nagging sensation I didn't have everything I needed like I told myself. Because that couldn't be true—I had a great family, Grit was growing faster than I'd imagined, and… well, I had this unexpected thing with Sadie, whatever that was. *If I don't slow down, the blur of things is exactly what I want. What I need.*

With those thoughts in my head, and resolutely no thoughts of Sadie, I made my way home.

"Where are you tonight?" Wyatt asked, shaking my shoulder.

I glanced at him to see worry on his face. "What? I'm fine."

He frowned and blinked slowly. "Sure. That's why you're living in your head and not responding to half of what anyone says?"

I swatted the tap off and slid the last plate into the dishwasher.

"I guess I've got some stuff on my mind. Shocking, I know." I widened my eyes and gave him a goofy look to take the edge off.

A five-foot-two thing with nervous energy and eyes that made me—*nope*. No. *You will not think about those puppy eyes of hers.*

"Like?" he asked, unafraid to prod and not derailed by my attempt to lighten things and deflect the question.

Laughter rose from the living room. Calla and my mom got along insanely well for only having known each other for five months. But I supposed the same could be said for her and Wyatt. Calla just fit with us, and it made me so happy.

Happy for them, I amended. I hadn't been truly happy in a long time. But I did my best to keep away from those thoughts, because what did that give me? Nothing but a mopey feeling in my gut and a mixed-up head. Not helpful, and it certainly didn't accomplish anything. Didn't change that there were some things some people didn't get to have —just plain and simple.

"Someone asked me out for coffee today."

Wyatt nodded, like this was a regular occurrence. And in truth, it was. What wasn't?

"I accepted."

Those same golden-brown brows jumped. "Really?"

I nodded.

"Who's the lucky girl?" He clicked on the lid of a glass container holding leftovers, then slid it into the fridge, never taking his eyes off me.

"War-baby? You've got a date?" Mom and Calla were both rounding the couch and hustling up to the kitchen bar to listen.

That made me curse inwardly, but I pasted a small, carefree smile on my face. "Just coffee, Mom."

"Still! This is exciting. You never go out with anyone anymore." She must've registered her wording and how it might've sounded, because she added, "Which is fine, you know. I'm just glad for you. You've only been out with friends, near as I can tell."

For a while, I'd tried. I'd gone out with lots of friends— girls who I squarely and immediately placed in the friendzone as soon as possible. It'd gone fine, all of them seeming to accept that, and in some cases, probably only wanting that in the first place anyway. But right around the new year, I just got tired of it. I'd been wearing thin on energy for anything other than work and the bit of family I had, and "friend dates" or even group hang outs hadn't been a priority. The desire to spend time with people who didn't know me past the friendly outward me, added to longing for someone I couldn't have, made it all feel like a waste of time.

Pair all my garbage feelings about dating and knowing I had no future with anyone with my new schedule at the gym, renovations, and other projects in the works, and I truly had no time.

Calla slipped into a seat at the high counter and studied me. "Who's it with? Do we know her?"

I slapped the towel I'd been using to dry my hands over the handle of the oven, then folded my arms and leaned against the wall in the corner of the kitchen. This way, I could see all three of them. *Surrounded.*

"First, it's definitely a friend thing." I think. I mean, she hadn't seemed like it was anything more. And our interactions the last few days had been odd, to say the least. "And, it's Sadie Miller."

"Oh!" Mom clapped her hands. "You know, I've been seeing her more often these days. Sarita told me she's popped into a few CVB meetings too."

Mom's blue eyes positively danced with this information. Like it was salacious gossip instead of a whisp of information that didn't help me one bit.

"She's pretty shy but seemed great. I was so glad she swung by our lunch today. I bet you'll have fun." Calla smiled when Wyatt cozied up behind her and kissed the side of her head.

Ignoring the ache in my chest, I pushed off the wall and grabbed a rag to wipe down the counters. "Again, it's not a date."

The edge to my voice cut through the space, and I immediately regretted the vehemence. It wasn't like I was upset. And I knew the second I mentioned it to Wyatt, I'd get some of this, especially with Mom here. But I wanted to dig this up like I wanted to drop a weight on my face.

"Uh…" Calla's surprise at my outburst leaked out of her.

"War and Sadie have a bit of history." Wyatt's tone sounded tight and concerned.

"Oh, that's right. I thought you told me she hates you?" Calla asked.

I forced a laugh. Maybe that was a simplification, but when a girl laughs in your face when you ask her out and then proceeds to run away from you for the rest of your lives? Yeah. Pretty good hint.

Except this whole coffee, friend thing. That had me tripping. "Thought she did."

Mom just frowned at me, and suddenly, I couldn't stand being there. "Listen, I've got to head back to town. I have a session at six tomorrow."

I tossed the rag over the faucet and rinsed my hands again.

Wyatt patted my back as I passed him with a nod, and I dutifully kissed Mom's and Calla's cheeks. By the time I got to my car, I was agitated. Full on crawling with emotions, a pinch between my shoulder blades. And the new addition to life after the NFL, a dull, pulsing ache in my left shoulder.

Having coffee with someone I worked next to every day and had grown up with in a small town shouldn't be sending me into what was rapidly becoming a tailspin. But I could practically hear the words that Wyatt would tell Calla to explain my behavior as soon as I left.

Something from Mom like *"He had a crush on her in high school."* Maybe with a side of *"She broke his heart and didn't even know it."* That would be dramatic and false, thanks very much, drama-Mom, but she'd probably say it.

And maybe Wyatt would kick in something like *"He hasn't been on a real date since his fiancée left him."* Some fun gem like that, which scraped far too close to the truth here.

At least none of them knew the lingering truth—that my feelings for Sadie, despite her rejection, had never died out completely. They'd muted when I was with Tracy, of course. I'd committed to Tracy and a life we could have together, and I was good with that. The rejection from her had been doubly painful—first, because she'd made it clear I wasn't worth a real relationship, especially if I didn't come with a pro baller's paycheck and access. And second, because it meant I had nowhere else to focus my attention on. I wouldn't date again. I wouldn't be looking for someone else to reject me.

And with that, I knew when I landed back in Silverton, I'd end up feeling that same damned heartache every time I even saw Sadie. My first heartbreak.

Of course she had to build a business on Main Street so she became downright unavoidable. Even though I didn't actually want anything from her anymore, I still just... felt it. It lingered there like ink spilled on wood—absorbed into the substance of the grain. I wished I could exorcise that soul-deep longing.

Didn't that sound pathetic? I'd tried to break myself of it. Sometimes, I lost the ability to pretend I didn't need to see her, and I showed up at the bakery and asked to talk to her. I'd caved to that impulse more than once. She'd always seemed completely uninterested if not bothered by my presence.

Until this week.

This coffee meet-up with Sadie wasn't a date, but apparently, it brought up all the feelings a date would've. Things that I didn't have to deal with when I kept to myself, kept everyone squarely situated in their friendly roles, made sure anyone asking me out knew what a great friend they were and how much I hoped we'd stay that way.

Sadie and I weren't a thing. We were oddly situated business owners with a past acquaintance thanks to small-town life. Sure, we'd interacted enough to sign the lease for her kitchen, and I couldn't resist talking to her sometimes, but there was nothing but proximity between us for the most part.

And maybe now, we'd be friends. This could be the situation that'd help me bury that niggling suspicion that she, for some reason, hated me. That her rejection had been a purposeful stomping on my teenage heart. That I wasn't good enough to be her friend back then or now.

Maybe this would be what changed all that. Maybe a real friendship would be the antidote to the seep of poison from memories of feelings I couldn't seem to get past.

CHAPTER SIX

Sadie

Warrick arrived two minutes before the agreed-upon time. I'd flipped the sign to Closed eleven minutes ago and happily nudged Garrett out the door before he'd done his usual close out on anything but the register.

Maybe all my changes in the last year or so had prepared him for that and the sight of me in the shop after noon, or maybe he was really that laid back. Either way, I was glad to see him go, flip that sign, and lock the door. We'd need privacy for this.

Warrick's brows hung heavy over his whole wheat eyes as I opened the door and let him in. Embarrassment flashed through me, but I resisted my former habit of wishing I didn't need this. I'd spent enough time wishing I was different, and I wouldn't do that today. My parents had enough wishes for me—it was their part-time job. Between the three of us, I think we'd used up all available wishes.

I'd planned this out after eating my takeout lunch upstairs the other day and realizing how great Warrick had been. I knew what I wanted, and for once, my anxiety wasn't going to be an excuse to not get it.

"Did you close?" He glanced around the small space, seeing chairs on top of all the tables save the one closest to the register.

"Yeah. Sorry. Guess I should've warned you. I thought we could use some privacy, and we close at three on Mondays." The hand on my watch ticked into place: 3:15.

"Okay. Sure."

He ran a hand through his hair and seemed to shrink up. His normally giant energy bounding off his big body filled spaces, large or small. But he'd arrived here in jeans and a T-shirt hanging off sculpted shoulders like he'd wrapped himself in pink insulation to muffle the heat and sensation just being near him normally caused.

I'd overheard someone talking about that once. About how Warrick walked into a room and the whole space shifted, everyone tilting just a bit so they could watch him move, hear him speak, see what charm he'd throw and wait for their turn with him.

I felt that way whenever I saw him and had always made an effort to ignore it. What good would it do me to be the weirdo eying him across the room when he wouldn't direct any of that charisma at me? He'd pour it out just before he got to my feet and offer me an empty vessel. And today, he seemed to arrive like that—already spent of his brilliance.

"Can I get you something to drink?" I asked as he sat in the seat with his back against the wall.

"Decaf Americano?"

I nodded and got to work. The crank and hiss of the

espresso machine filled the space. I shouldn't have turned off the music, but Garrett had done it before leaving, and I hadn't thought to turn it on again.

"Enjoy." I set the robin's egg blue mug and saucer in front of him. And though it was futile, since he didn't eat my food, I tacked on, "Any bread? We have half a sunflower whole wheat left."

"No, thank you." He placed a large hand on the table between us, a few inches from the mug, then gestured to the seat across from him and must've used a foot to nudge it out from underneath with a scrape.

I sat and folded my hands, my spine straight. Good posture was essential these days, both because it did infuse a little confidence in me, just like my therapist had always said, and I could get a little hunchy if I kneaded by hand, so I tried to compensate by paying attention when I sat.

Plus, being around Warrick made me particularly aware of my body. Maybe it was how large he was compared to how small I felt. Whatever the case, it felt markedly different than the awareness I felt when near other people. With anyone but Warrick, my head was a balloon on a string, and pins pricked the fingertips at the end of awkward arms that didn't know what to do.

With him, I was something else. Not a balloon threatening to float away or come undone, at least.

"No drink for you?" He hadn't smiled or leaned back in his seat like he usually did when he came in. He hadn't done anything but watch me, wary.

"No. I already exceeded my daily allotment of caffeine, and I need to concentrate." I pulled my phone out and set it on my lap, then navigated to my list.

"All right." He settled into his seat a bit, like my admission that I needed to focus calmed him. "Why am I here, Sadie?"

I ignored the little thrill that flitted through me. He'd said my name the other day, and I hadn't gotten to enjoy it. Hearing it now convinced me he should say it often, and I wondered how I could make that happen.

"So. Uh." I coughed into my elbow, cleared my throat, and pushed out the words. "I want to be your friend."

His brow furrowed. "Aren't we friends? We've known each other forever."

I studied him, wondering if he really believed we were friends. I didn't want to start this conversation by bringing up that how he dealt with me differed so starkly from how he talked to everyone else I'd ever seen him with, but if I had to, I would.

But no. His eyes were narrowed, and his shoulders had crept up a bit. He wasn't laid back Warrick, at ease with a friend. And that told me I was right.

"Are we?" I asked softly.

He blinked. "I guess not. Not really."

I dipped my head in agreement. "No. And so, I want to change that."

He took a sip of his coffee, then set it on the saucer with a clank and fiddled with the handle for a moment before saying, "Not to sound like a jerk, but why?"

"Because I've been making changes in my life the last few years, slowly but surely. And even if no one has noticed, that's fine—they're changes for me. But this is something I can't do on my own. I need your help."

"You need my help to be my friend?" He hooked a finger through the handle of the mug but didn't lift it. He just left it there, like the little curve of pottery would help him deal with my weirdness.

Because yeah. This was weird. I could admit it and had embraced that reality in the last few years, and especially the last day as I'd created this plan.

"I do. I need help to be your friend, and other people's."

He squinted. "So you want me to be your friend, and help you make friends."

I nodded.

His eyes flickered back and forth between mine, appearing truly baffled. Maybe not by the idea that I needed help making friends, but that I'd ask *him*. And as soon as that thought registered, I glanced at my phone to review my list of points and leaned forward as I organized my thoughts.

"You need to get that?" He nodded to my lap, where he must've seen my phone.

My cheeks heated. "Uh, no. I have a list on there."

"A list for..."

"This conversation?"

No idea why it came out as a question, small and unsure. I didn't have doubts about my lists. They kept me sane and helped me feel grounded when I faced something challenging.

Instead of judgment there, his face softened and his eyes crinkled at the edges. His mouth always sported a congenial upturn, a tilt like he was about to smile any second. They didn't spread into a larger expression, but the eyes told me they might any second.

"I'm a list maker too. I get it."

A breath whooshed out of me. "Good. I didn't mean to be rude checking my phone, but—"

He waved my explanation away. "Seriously, I get it."

"Okay. So, I guess I should stop and ask what you're

thinking about this. You haven't run shrieking from the room yet, but I know it's an odd situation."

He glanced to the side, probably looking out the window, where normal people bustled up and down Main Street, going about their lives making friends and doing things that didn't require a midconversation check-in.

"I'm not sure I get it, but I'm willing to hear you out. I'd be happy to be your friend, and I get why you said we aren't." He took a cautious sip of his drink, then set it gently down in the saucer. "I'm sorry. I feel like I need to say that before anything else happens. I haven't meant to treat you any differently, but I've been thinking about that since you mentioned it, and you're right."

"Thank you." But what I really wanted to know was why. Was it just because I was so different from him? He'd had no problem with Catherine, a woman I'd also identify as his near-polar opposite, or anyone else. Why me?

That wasn't the point here, though, so I focused on the rest of his statement. "I know this is coming out of nowhere for you. Not to sound like a creep, but I've been watching you run your classes. You're such a good coach, I can tell. And like you said, we've known each other forever. I know you could teach me how to do this."

"But that's what I don't get. *Do what?*"

"Make friends." A chagrined chuckle escaped before I continued. "I've had some really difficult years, and I've clawed my way out of them. I'm finally in a place where I'm ready to try doing something other than waking up every day and making bread."

My throat had dried out, so I hopped up and filled a glass with water. I'd convinced myself this would be the way to go for me. This would help me take that next-to-last step on my list of becoming a contributing member of society again.

My parents eagerly awaited another step—me marrying some strapping, wealthy man who could take care of me. Like that would solve all my problems, though they refused to actually understand my anxiety. But for me? That felt like a long way off. First up, a friend or two.

I could feel his eyes on me as I moved around the small space behind the counter, then met his gaze when I turned to rejoin him at the table.

"I'm not going to say no. You realize that, right?" He tilted his head and graced me with one of those easy, kind smiles. The one where his lips parted just a bit, hinting at his straight white teeth and teasing his dimple in the left cheek but not giving it away entirely.

The one that never failed to make my heart kick, and sure enough, it did again today. As delightful as it was to have it directed at me for once, I needed to focus on the matter at hand.

"You're not?" I asked, taking my seat again.

He shook his head slowly. "I've always wanted to be your friend, Sadie."

My heart turned over in my chest like a dog sunning its belly on a lakeside rock. The fragile little thing was downright basking in those words. "Oh."

His smile widened then, grew into one of those beaming, blinding events I usually looked away from when I saw it in the wild. Too beautiful and brilliant, it was hard to look at him when he did that. He was just so joyful, so very much like the sun.

He chuckled, which was probably the only thing more deadly than the smile. "Don't sound so shocked. I'm not the only one. I can name at least a handful of people, but probably more like a dozen, who I know would like to get to know you."

My heart flipped over from its place on the rock and dove into the ice-cold lake, paddling like a maniac. *A dozen?* "Maybe let's just… start small."

He beamed and smiled again. "Fair enough. When do we start?"

For some reason, I hadn't expected him to agree so readily. I'd had several additional points to convince him. I opened the list on my phone again and scrolled past all of those points.

His warm hand stopped me, the touch quick and casual. And yet, the contact was the first we'd had that I could remember, and it made my skin feel extra warm, which made zero sense.

"Wait. Wait. Can I see the list?"

Say no. Say no. Saynosaynosayno. But my mind was stuck on the feel of his skin against mine. A singular occurrence today, just like Calla's kiss to my cheek yesterday had been the only touch I'd had then. "Sure."

He plucked the phone from the table and squinted at it, sliding his finger along the screen. I knew right when he reached my bargaining chip section.

His brow dropped low as he read, then his lashes fluttered, and his head shot up. "Were you seriously going to offer to pay me?"

"Of course."

Disappointment, maybe even anger, flickered over his face before he wiped it clean and eyed me. "We'll have to talk about *that* at some point, but I'm glad you didn't."

Yikes. What did that mean? But part of me eased at knowing he wouldn't have accepted the money, and that he'd agreed to this without any coaxing beyond a very basic explanation.

"So the section on what to do if I agree only has one bullet point, and it just says *make plans*. I guess that's what we do now."

"I guess so."

He handed me the phone, took a sip of coffee, then folded his arms and swayed his head back and forth. He'd loosened up completely in the last few minutes, which made him both far more delightful and incredibly overwhelming.

"I'm thinking we grab lunch sometime this week. That's a very friendly thing to do. It works with both our schedules most days, from what I've observed, and it doesn't interfere with what I assume is a very early bedtime."

My turn to blink back at him. As much as I often felt like I observed him to a concerning degree, and then excused myself because we were near each other so often, he clearly knew a fair amount about me I wouldn't have guessed.

"Okay. Name the day."

He did. Wednesday—just two days away. We'd eat in the kitchen. He'd bring lunch.

And then, he stood and stretched out his hand. Instinctively, I grasped it. Warm, a little rough in places, and so large his fingers reached several inches up my wrist. We shook, two pumps up and down.

Then he let go, said something about seeing me soon, and left. And I sat, exhausted and relieved and excited, amazed at what I'd just done.

CHAPTER SEVEN

Warrick

I'd been expecting Wilder's call thanks to a heads-up from Wyatt, but I'd hoped it'd come after my lunch with Sadie. Instead, my second oldest brother called exactly as I walked into the gym with our lunches in hand. I could linger a few minutes and take this, but I didn't want to be late. I wouldn't do anything to make her feel like I didn't want to be there.

"To what do I owe this great honor?" I asked, trying to strike the cheery, joking tone and not mildly worried like I always felt when he reached out.

"You're my brother. We talk."

I glanced at my feet and shook my head. "Fair enough. What's up? How are you?"

"Heading out again soon, so just wanted to check in."

My stomach clutched. Wilder had been in the military since I turned twelve. I should've been used to him coming and going, but mostly? I didn't know him. Not well. I'd gone to visit him twice in my early twenties, and he came home maybe once a year, sometimes less than that. But hearing he was deploying, and knowing that for him, it wouldn't be a training deployment but something dangerous and intense thanks to being in Special Operations instead of the regular Army, never failed to set me on edge.

"Can't say where you're heading, I guess?"

"No, can't say."

"Okay. Can you tell me how long?"

"A bit."

"Okay. You…" I cleared my throat, wanting to sound normal and upbeat. "You doing okay?"

"Yep. Doing well."

"Good. I'm glad to hear that."

"You?"

I exhaled silently. "I'm good too. My gym's getting off the ground. I see Mom and Wyatt pretty regularly. Wy's girlfriend is great, by the way. I know I've mentioned that, but she continues to impress."

"Glad to hear it. Saw him in the news at some event on her arm—he makes good arm candy."

A chuckle snuck out at that, both from shock at the long sentence and the realization that he would look at pop culture news at all, and the joke. "That he does. I think he's finally found his calling."

"At least one of us has."

I laughed, though my chest stayed tight. "I thought the Army was your calling?"

"It was. No doubt. But I think my time's coming up. Retirement and all that."

Damn, but when he said stuff like *my time's coming up,* I never could tell if that meant time to be done or… something darker. Because there had been some years, after a series of rough deployments, when he'd talked like the Grim Reaper sat at his table every day.

Though it'd been so long since I'd visited, I didn't know if he even *had* a table these days. Maybe he just ate at work or restaurants all the time.

"Well, you're welcome back here, of course. There's even more built up since you were here a year ago. It's expanding and such, but not crazy or anything. Still feels like a small town, just more options."

He grunted, a sound I never quite knew how to take. "Not sure what my plan is just yet."

"Of course, yeah. You've got time." If I had the dates right, about a year and a half.

"Better get going now. Love you, Warrick. Take care of Mom for me."

Throat tight, I gritted out, "Love you too, Wilder. Be safe."

And then he hung up, and I stared at my phone and prayed he'd be safe—body, mind, and soul. I prayed he'd come back whole from wherever he had to go, and that someday, he'd be able to come all the way home again.

"Everything all right, Warrick?"

Sadie's voice came from a few feet behind me. I turned to find her standing, arms crossed over her aproned chest, head tilted in concern.

I scrubbed a hand down my face, shaking off the clay-like feelings coating my insides. Once they dried, they'd crumble to dust.

"Yeah, I'm good." I forced a bright smile. "Let's do this!"

Holding up the bag, I waited for her response. When none came, I lowered it down. "Or, you know, if you changed your mind about me, that's no problem."

"I didn't change my mind. But I don't want you to have to pretend everything is fine if you're upset."

Those piercing eyes of hers shot an arrow right into my gut.

"I'm okay. I probably just need to eat."

She took mercy on me and gave a quick smile before nodding and taking the bag of food. She then led us into her kitchen and to a tall bistro-style table to the left I hadn't noticed before.

Actually, no. I would've. Try as I might not to, I paid close attention to what went on in her side of the building. "Is this new?"

She pulled out the chair and hopped into the seat across from me. "I got it yesterday."

"Did you buy this table for today?" And did that run a hand over my shoulder, something soothing and calm?

She kept her head ducked, busily unloading the food I'd brought, but her cheeks pinked. "Yes. I thought we'd be more comfortable than on the stools. I had another delivery coming from the company and they tacked this on."

She glanced up and met my gaze as though she expected me to be critical of that idea. As though her being thoughtful would be problematic.

"This is *much* more comfortable than the stools. Plus, when you do your planning, or whatever it is you pour over in the late afternoons, you could sit here and take a load off."

"Recipe ideas, schedules, planning, checklists—I like working in here better than at Rise and Shine or back home. Maybe because it's so shiny."

She glanced around at the literally shiny stainless steel of the kitchen, but my mind had snagged on *checklists*.

How I'd even momentarily forgotten about the list on

her phone spoke to the power of the gut punch that had been this latest call with Wilder. Because that list, a list of reasons why she'd chosen me to help her make friends... Just the idea of this was insane, because like I'd said, plenty of people wanted to be her friend. Yet, her reasons for choosing me were a handful of unpolished gemstones, raw and brilliant, and they made my chest fill to the brim.

One—genuine.
Two—kind.
Three—humble.
Four—positive outlook.
Five—inspiring.

Did she really think all of that applied to me? Did she truly believe I was *inspiring?* I had a healthy ego—some might even say oversized in some areas; maybe her number three was a bit too generous. But reading that list on Sadie Miller's phone? A woman I'd been convinced hated me, and if not hated, very much disliked, until three days ago?

Or, the woman I'd had a not-so-deeply buried crush on. One that apparently rose from its shallow grave at even the slightest interaction with her.

Mind-blowing. And yeah, humbling, because apparently, I couldn't read her worth a damn. I had no idea how she truly felt about me, but I knew with certainty that this list reflected her own thoughts. There was no way she'd be blowing smoke just to get what she wanted—just no way. She hadn't expected me to ever see the list, only hear her version of it.

She pulled the tops off the aluminum takeout containers, and my awareness returned to the table in front of me. "Well, now you can do it here. That'll be great. And I'm happy to christen it with your first lunch date."

"Thanks for coming." She smiled and didn't seem fazed

by my use of the phrase *lunch date*. Fortunately, she didn't correct me, either, which would've been embarrassing. I knew this wasn't a date. Everyone used that language, and obviously, she had no problem with it.

So why did my saying it, and her not correcting it, make me feel a little antsy?

"How did you know this was my order?" she asked, and I glanced up to find her staring down at the salad in front of her. "I didn't even think about it."

Satisfaction snaked through me. "I've seen you order takeout more than once from the grill. I honestly didn't think about it until I put in the order and then realized I knew what you liked—at least one thing. I should've asked you, though."

"No, it's great. I am a creature of habit. I get the same thing from the same places every time." She grabbed a plastic fork and dove in but halted when the tines buckled. "Next time we do this, I'll make sure I have real silverware."

Her big eyes glanced up at me, nerves clear on her face, so I jumped in. "Good. Yeah, I hadn't thought of that. Better than using plastic every time too."

Wyatt would approve.

She nodded but seemed to shrink up a little. She'd been pretty open and lively, not quite so shy and mindful of her every step and action. I decided to forge ahead and fill the space rather than bring up the whole "let's learn to be friends" thing, why not just... be a friend?

"Sorry I was on the phone earlier. It was Wilder." And I didn't want to talk about it, but I did want her to know I felt bad for being a few minutes late.

"Is he okay? You seemed upset when you got off the call."

I chewed a large bite of grilled chicken, happy it bought

me a few seconds. "I guess I was. I only talk to him every few weeks, if that. He calls our mom weekly when he's Stateside, but I seem to only hear from him periodically. When I do, it's usually when he's deploying."

"That sounds difficult."

I paused before taking another bite. "I'm always glad to hear from him, but it also makes me so sad."

She blinked and reached out to set her hand on mine, then cleared her throat. "I don't know the situation, but I'm sorry. That sounds really hard. It also sounds like you're a great brother."

She squeezed and released me before I could turn my hand up and grasp hers like I wanted to.

My mom could be tender with me, and Wyatt always looked out for my best interests. He and I were close. But he'd been occupied with Calla right when I'd stumbled into this searching, unsatisfied phase I'd been in the last few months.

Having Sadie be the person to reach out and touch me gently, to want to offer me comfort, sent a heady mix of hope and dread through me. It felt so good—so right.

But I couldn't let it become too much, or I'd be a fool for breaking my own rules.

CHAPTER EIGHT

Sadie

Warrick's parting words bounced around in my head the rest of the day.

"Do something social with someone in the next week. It can be small, but it has to be in person and your idea."

Then he'd winked, told me to have a good afternoon, and left the kitchen without another word.

Our lunch had been good—maybe even great, based on the high of adrenaline that'd kicked in the rest of the meal and made me shuddery and anxious, but in the best way. Where my nerves might send my heart into my sandpaper throat and slow my brain so it felt like every thought had to break down walls to connect to my mouth, this had felt like a jolt of energy and anticipation for something delectable and sweet.

He'd shared about Wilder so willingly, even though I

could tell he hadn't wanted to. That openness was yet another thing I admired about him

I'd resolved to share about some of my more personal issues at our next meeting. Something about Warrick made me want to loosen the grip I tended to have on the details of my life—on everything.

But then he laid out that challenge. An assignment, he'd called it, right before he gave me the details. And while it'd sent my heart sprinting into overdrive at first, enough that after he'd gone, I'd taken a few minutes to talk myself down, the more I mulled it over, the more I wanted what he suggested.

I wanted to be able to ask a friend out for coffee. I'd initiated things with him, albeit messily, but I had. And I wouldn't pretend I'd hated the time with him.

Though I felt terrible he'd had the difficult phone call just before, it'd given me focus. I'd seen him pacing back and forth, head ducked with one hand fisting the phone to his ear and the other clenching the takeout bags, and I'd worried. Not about *me* and what I felt, how my fingers had gotten tingly like they did when the shop was especially busy or I attended a council meeting, but instead, I'd been worried for *him*.

It'd felt so good to guide him to a seat and unwrap that food. Never mind he'd brought it. I was able to help him in a small way, and it'd loosened the tightly wound knot in my chest I might not've rid myself of for the entire lunch otherwise.

It was official. Warrick Saint was my... whatever was opposite of kryptonite.

And now, four days after our lunch, I got stuck. I'd imagined scenarios where I wandered into Bloom and asked

Dahlia for coffee. Her hours were similar to Rise and Shine's so she'd be there. Or maybe Quinn's music shop when it opened back up on Tuesday.

"Hey, Sadie. You don't do a lot of cashier time normally, do you?" Sarah asked, her tone nothing but sweet.

No judgment or poking fun like I'd feared when I'd first started doing shifts out front.

All in all, the locals had only seemed happy to see me at the register. The tourists had no idea I'd just started taking small shifts in the front and interacting with customers. None of the scenarios I'd imagined had happened, just like I'd promised myself. Granted, I'd still had a plan in place in case someone did make a rude comment, but thus far, after more than six months of weekly forays out here, I hadn't heard anything negative.

"Just here and there, but not much, you're right. What can I get you?"

"Can I get a flat white and a slice?" She glanced at the chalkboard behind me where we listed the flavor of the day. "Ooh, yes. I'll take the blueberry lemon. I've wanted to try that since Calla and Dahlia were raving about it."

"Perfect. Give me just a sec."

I bustled around, prepping the espresso and steaming milk. I did love using this gorgeous machine. It'd been the most expensive thing I'd ever bought for myself, though as someone whose parents had given her a BMW for her sixteenth birthday, that probably didn't seem like a huge accomplishment.

But doing it on my own? Knowing this shop was all mine, not Randall and Arianna Miller's? Every serving of espresso brought me joy.

Despite their interest in my finding a man, they had no

real idea what I did day to day or what my business entailed. They had no idea I had employees, vendors, and suppliers I dealt with regularly, or that I had plans to expand. If they ever stopped to notice what my life actually looked like instead of what they thought it was, they'd probably still find a way to make me feel like I couldn't really succeed without a husband. They weren't all that old-fashioned, but after I left New York, they'd gotten hooked on that idea: that if I had a husband—someone contractually and legally obligated to care for me, in essence—then *they* wouldn't have to worry so much.

Lovely.

Pushing that fun reminiscence aside, I sliced the surprisingly fluffy loaf of bread. People always commented on the fluffiness because it sounded like it'd be denser with the blueberries, but it came out light and perfect for the warming weather. Next, I slid a little bowl with a soft pat of butter in it next to the bread and carried it to the table where Sarah had taken her seat. "Enjoy."

"Thank you," she said, genuine smile in full effect.

I returned it, then slipped behind the counter again. The rest of the place sat empty, the afternoon lull at work. I'd need coffee today if I was going to do anything worthwhile later, but Garrett had called in sick, and I'd happily taken his spot instead of bothering one of our part-timers on a Sunday afternoon.

As I stared out the windows at the front of the café, a thought elbowed in. *"It can be small."*

Warrick had said I could go small on this first assignment, and here before me sat the perfect opportunity. I'd enjoyed the time I'd spent with Sarah and the other women last week at lunch. I wished I hadn't been too chicken to stay.

Before I could talk myself out of it, I grabbed a carafe and dumped a small glug of decaf into a mug, spilling half into the saucer and ditching it in a bin before trying again, then hustled out the swing gate that walled off the area behind the counter.

"Sorry to intrude but... any chance I could join you?"

Sarah looked up from her phone where she had it set next to her cup and saucer.

"Of course! Please, sit." She gestured to the table with a flourish.

"Thanks. I won't stay long in case you have other things—"

"Don't be silly! I'm just scrolling social media and spacing out, trying to enjoy the calm before the week begins. I'd much prefer to sit with a friend and chat."

Sit with a friend. Her words injected me with a thrill I didn't have time to inspect but knew I'd relish later. "Well, good."

We smiled at each other, and I racked my brain for what to talk about. I couldn't pull out my phone and reference my list—that'd be too much. But I could recall a few things... *Work, mutual friends or acquaintances, local upcoming events, pop culture if that's an interest...*

Duh, Sarah had already given me a clue about something, and I just needed to follow it. "What's coming up this week that has you needing some calm pre-emptively?"

"I'm helping with the last week of school. They have field days and all kinds of things they can use a set of hands for. I don't actually expect them to hire me next year because I've helped out this year, but it can't hurt. Plus, it lets me get to know other teachers and some of the administration, and better yet, the kids."

"Is it hard to get a job at the school? I thought I'd heard

they were hurting for people last year." I didn't stay all that tuned in to things like that, but I could've sworn I'd heard the veteran's group chatting about it months ago. More than one of them had grandkids who were teachers.

She sighed and finished chewing a bite of the bread. Her eyes fluttered shut as she swallowed. "That is seriously divine. And schools are tough—it really depends on their needs. They wanted high school teachers and a middle school math teacher, but I'm primary education with certifications in reading, so my target grades are fifth and below, and ideally third and below."

"I hadn't thought that, but it makes sense. I hope something opens up for you soon."

Sarah's sweet personality seemed perfectly suited toward being an elementary teacher. I couldn't recall exactly when she'd moved back, but I remember she was always a nice older kid in school.

"Thanks." She toasted her coffee toward me and took a sip. "What about you? What's your plan for the new space over at the mill? Or did I miss the news?"

I smiled and my stomach flipped just thinking of my plans and saying them aloud. But Sarah sat there, so ready and seemingly eager for what I had in store, and it didn't even occur to me to curl into myself and not tell her. "I'm hoping to start distributing to a few more places. I've provided bread to Elk Street for their dinners on and off for years and a few other places, but the demand got so high I couldn't handle it in the kitchen here. I've been planning to expand, and now, once I get staff trained and all of that at some point, I'll be able to. Hopefully early fall."

Sarah's mouth dropped open and she grabbed my wrist. "I love it! Yes! That makes so much sense, and I can't wait to see how that develops. Do you have to go to culinary school to work in that space? Or... what training do people need?"

Culinary School sent the usual sour bolt of pain and reminder of failure through me, but she couldn't realize what the words would do. At the same time, seated with a new friend and not alone in my apartment on the phone with one of my parents while they stubbornly refused to acknowledge the crashing bonfire of failure that was my time in New York, I could breathe around the ache in my chest. It didn't swallow me whole like it had for years when I'd first dragged myself back to Silverton and hid under the veritable covers of my childhood small town.

"I won't require degrees. The two assistants I have now may just move over with me, but I'll need help here too, still. Food service experience is a bonus, and obviously bakery experience is great. But I'm not opposed to someone new to baking if they're hardworking." I liked the idea of having someone start with me and learn.

"I love that. I bet you're a great boss too."

"I don't know about that, but I'm trying, that's for sure."

In my gut, I knew the truth. I hadn't been a good boss for the first few years of this business. I'd foisted all communication and hiring onto Bel's shoulders, and I'd avoided everyone else. I'd blocked them out with huge headphones, and at that point, it was what I'd had to do to stay upright.

But you're changing. You've changed. And here you are, in the process yet again.

Those thoughts bolstered me.

"You've changed a lot, from what I remember. I'm so glad, because I desperately need friends, and it's been oddly difficult making them after moving back."

She'd stolen the thoughts from my mind. "It has? I

mean, it's always hard for me, but I'm not easy to get to know, and for years I basically had a sign on my forehead that read 'don't talk to me.'"

Sarah laughed and covered her mouth. A few seconds later, she said, "I nearly just spit out my coffee. I can't believe you said that."

I shrugged a shoulder. "It's true. And while not everything true should be said out loud, I've been trying to be honest about myself."

Her expression softened from delighted surprise to understanding. "I get that. Wow, do I get that."

The bell attached to the door jingled, and in came customers.

"Guess I better jump up and help them. Thanks for letting me join you."

"Let's do it again soon," Sarah said, her encouraging smile convincing me she meant it.

"I'd love it."

The rest of the day flew by, and though I'd only made it through half of my coffee, I seemed to have doubled my energy with just that little chat with Sarah. The more I thought about it, the more I registered how comfortable I'd felt with her. Almost like Warrick, but different, of course. Along with Warrick's openness and kindness, there was the very real challenge of him as a physical being. I could never *not* be acutely aware of him.

But Sarah? It almost felt like we'd been friends for longer than a week, if I was being generous. Maybe knowing each other or knowing *of* each other thanks to Silverton being *so* small when we grew up had something to do with it.

Whatever the case, I practically floated through the rest of the day. And though I reached for my phone to text

Warrick and tell him about ten times, I made myself stop. I didn't want to send the message and wait for a response. I wanted to tell him at our next lunch meet up and see for myself the look on his face.

Somehow, I knew it'd be worth the wait.

CHAPTER NINE

Warrick

Around eleven the following Wednesday, I slipped into Sadie's kitchen to find her pulling two loaves of something that smelled so delicious, I wanted to bathe in the scent from the oven.

"That smells so good."

She twirled around in surprise and pulled an earbud from her ear. *Whoops.* I hadn't meant to sneak up on her.

"Sorry? I was in my own world."

She swiped a hand over her forehead and left a smear of what had to be flour there. I tucked my hands behind my back so I wouldn't reach out and wipe it clean.

I hadn't realized how much I wanted to touch her until my arms practically shook with the effort not to. Though that could also be the upper body workout I'd led my eight a.m. class through. Probably that.

Yeah. Definitely that.

Of course she'd been in her own world. I was the dolt who hadn't anticipated that and barged in like I owned the place.

"I didn't mean to take you off guard. I said it smells amazing in here. What kind are those?" I nodded to the loaf pans she'd set on a wire rack.

"It's a spin on a white chocolate raspberry coffee cake. I'm not loving it. That combo is great for scones, and I've got those at the shop this week, but I thought bread might be fun." She surveyed the two loaves with a critical eye.

She was caught up in thinking about this recipe—focused on working out whatever problem she'd had with them. With her head turned toward the side, her jawline and delicate neck were on full display. She even had pretty ears. Everything about her was smooth and delicate and clean and polished.

Except that little bit of flour.

"That bread sounds amazing. I'm sure people will love it."

"You're welcome to have one of these once it cools. No guarantees it'll taste good." She offered a small smile like an apology.

"It will—I doubt anything that comes from your kitchen is less than delicious. But no, save it for someone else who's got that desperate 'I need Sadie Miller's bread or I'll die' look in their eye."

I didn't like rejecting the offer. This fledgling friendship needed encouragement, not me delving into the reasons I wouldn't eat her bread—not that it was some great mystery anyway. On the whole, I didn't eat much bread. I didn't feel good after I did, and after so long of being careful with what I ate, I'd figured out how to feed my body to make it function its best and feel satisfied.

Fortunately, she didn't seem upset. She just nodded. "Sure. So... did you need something?"

She took a tool from one of her apron pockets and flipped it up into her hands, almost like a beefy biker might twirl a butterfly knife. Then slipped the flat metal head of the thing around the edge of each loaf.

"Warrick?"

I startled, my eyes jerking away from her capable hands. "Sorry. Uh, yeah. I have to postpone our lunch for today."

Her face sank, giving away what looked like true disappointment. "Oh."

"But I was hoping maybe you could do an early dinner?"

Her brows jumped, and she bit her lip.

And I made the grave mistake of following that movement—of tracking the way her white teeth indented her full bottom lip with my eyes. My stomach dipped.

"What time were you thinking?"

I jerked my gaze away from her face and turned to look at the giant fridge on the wall opposite us. *I'm looking at this fascinating piece of machinery and not obsessing on the fantasy of your lips.* "Uh, what time works for you?"

"As early as possible, but I know not everyone keeps the hours I do. Could we do right at five?"

"Yep. No problem. I just had a meeting pop up at our normal lunch time, and I have some other stuff this afternoon, but by five I should be in the clear." I ran a hand over my head, through my too-long hair there. Time for a cut.

Time for anything to keep my mind off her mouth, her hands, the line of neck dipping into the collar of her shirt.

"Okay. I can do five."

It was the slight tremor in her voice that made me look back at her. The inner edge those perfectly arched brows nearly met in the middle. Obviously, my refusal to actually look at her had registered, and I'd confused her.

"Perfect. I'll see you then."

"Okay. Here?"

"Yes." We'd go out next, but not this time. Not yet.

"Okay. Sounds good."

That was the point at which I should've walked away, but the minute my mind decided it, my body stayed glued to the spot. My feet had cemented themselves into the floor of her kitchen, and it was just long enough to let my mind gray out the list of reasons why touching her was a terrible idea.

I reached up slowly, and those brows furrowed again, the teeth biting into the bottom lip.

"Sorry, you've just got…" I slipped my hand into the hair near her temple, and my thumb arced over the smear of flour.

Her hair was soft, her skin softer. Then I continued the crazy, out of body moment. I held up my thumb to show her the flour.

Her cheeks reddened, and she swallowed. "Hazard of the trade."

"Looked good on you, but I just…" *Had to touch you. Had to.* "Wasn't sure if you'd want it there all day." I added a wink to lighten the moment, or so I hoped.

She tucked her hands into her apron pockets. "Thanks."

"See you at five, flour girl," I said, turning for the door. Once outside it, I made a beeline for my office and slumped down into the chair at my desk.

What had I been doing? I didn't think I'd frightened her, but I'd definitely crossed a line. Hadn't I?

Or had I?

Maybe not. A friend wouldn't let another friend walk

around with flour on her forehead all day. That wouldn't be very neighborly.

But did neighbors feel their heart pound out of their chest from a simple touch? Did a friend's thumb feel like it glowed from the contact with his friend's skin?

Once I got my crap together, I practiced the art of compartmentalization the rest of the day. By five minutes to five, I'd managed to complete everything on my task list, had faithfully attended the board meeting for All Saints Ranch in Wyatt's place while he was in LA with Calla, and arranged to meet Aidan Wallace to talk about sprucing up the exterior around the mill building.

Nothing satisfied like destroying a to-do list. It was something I loved about working out—have a plan, execute that plan, see the progress from that execution. It was clear and without a lot of room for failure. Bad leg day? That's fine—we all have them. Shoulder driving me nuts so I can't push like I want? No problem—it's part of the process.

Running through my to-do list gave me the same feeling. I might hit snags—can't reach someone I needed to talk to, can't get a project approved by the zoning commission, whatever. But those were just steps along the way. If I got stuck, I tossed the item on another list and moved on to the next task.

There were some things in life that couldn't be helped. A few in my own heart of hearts, no to-do list would assist. Losing my father when I was a baby was one. I'd played football like he had as a way to be close to him, and when that was stripped away, I poured myself into accomplishing things he might be proud of me for. I wouldn't have made the connection without the therapist I'd seen for the year after my injury, but it helped me understand some of my grief over losing football, and some of the grief I still felt about a man I never really knew. He only existed based on other peoples' memories, but I liked to think that some of what I did each day was for him.

And no, I wasn't consciously that sappy, but today, I felt the triumph over my lists and my easily distracted brain like a pat on the back from my dad.

The second I walked through the kitchen door and found only half the lights on, my awareness of Sadie snapped back into place. She sat slumped at the tall table, pen in one hand hovering over a notepad, head resting in the other.

"Hey, you okay in here?" I stumbled into the chair opposite her, and the metal scraped along the floor just as the door swung shut with a bang.

She visibly winced, and her head seemed like it wanted to retract into her shell. "I'm okay. Headache hit about an hour ago. That's why the lights are so low. I'm sorry if it's dim."

"No, no, that's fine. Do you want to reschedule?"

"No. I mean, unless you're uncomfortable. But I can't let excuses get in the way."

Excuses? She seemed like she was about to keel over, or at least require time in a light vacuum to recover from this. Canceling on me wouldn't have fazed me, plus I'd already been the one to reschedule.

"Really, I don't want to change it. We can be quick, eat, and I'll head home and put myself to bed."

I gingerly pulled out the chair and took a seat. "Fine then. Let's eat."

"Would you mind grabbing the pizza? I popped it in the oven so it'd stay warm. There's a salad in the fridge too."

"Of course."

I squeezed her shoulder as I passed her to grab the salad, the touch so automatic I didn't have time to second-guess it. Touching her felt natural, so I'd need to lock that up before I did something that spoke to how much I wanted to do just that in all kinds of not-particularly-friendly ways.

She'd set out plates and real silverware and had obviously made the salad herself. But the pizza was from Basta, and when I peeked inside the box after taking it out of the warm oven, I must've made a sound.

"You like pizza? I was nervous since you don't eat bread, but I was also out of ideas, and you've been gone all day so I couldn't ask. We need to exchange phone numbers."

"Good idea. And yes. I love pizza. I would marry pizza, if I hadn't sworn off marriage entirely."

I danced over to the table and set two plates with large slices of Basta's margherita pizza with fresh mozzarella, basil, tomatoes, and chili flakes in front of her. After placing the bowls and some waters there too, I looked up to find her watching me with an odd expression.

"This isn't my business, but you said that so casually. You really don't think you'll get married?"

I'd folded the thin slice in half and shoved a third of it into my mouth like a beast, holding up one finger while I chewed. Her question shouldn't have been a surprise, but it was. For some reason, I'd assumed pretty much everyone in town knew I'd sworn off marriage since everyone definitely knew my history.

After wiping my mouth and taking a few glugs of water,

I took a breath. "My relationship history isn't exactly stellar."

"How so?"

That unguarded, free question told me two things in an instant, and my cheeks heated. First, she felt comfortable enough to pry into my personal life, and while this moment here sucked deflated footballs, more generally, it made me borderline giddy. But two, she didn't know my history. And answering this question required me to either tell her and make myself way more vulnerable in front of her than I'd planned for our second get-together, or look like a real jerk.

I didn't especially feel like doing either.

"You don't have to say, if you don't want. I'm sorry. I shouldn't have asked." She focused on her silverware, straightening them at the side of her plate.

"Hey, it's fine." She looked up and met my eyes. My stomach swooped low at the connection, and the feeling of slipping into a cool pool on a hot night came over me. "I don't like explaining it because it's not a great story. But since you're my friend, you should know."

"Okay." She folded her hands in her lap and nodded as if to signal that she was ready.

"Did you know I was engaged? I'd started dating this girl when I was at the U, and by the end of my senior year, we were exclusive. I got drafted and we got more serious, started talking about what came next, all that. She moved with me, and after my team won the Superbowl my second year, we got engaged. I was riding the high completely, right? But nailing down a time to get married was tricky, and she didn't seem in a rush, so I got through my third season, things going well still, and then halfway through my fourth season, bam."

"Your injury."

I nodded. "Destroyed my shoulder, which doesn't work out so well when your job is literally crashing into people and catching footballs. After the repair and PT, I was still in rough shape, and the team released me."

"I'm so sorry. I can't imagine how difficult that would be."

Her face practically glowed with compassion, and the texture in her voice told me maybe she could. I'd never figured out why she'd landed back here when she should've been in New York, but I wondered if maybe she knew exactly what it was like. I didn't even really know why she'd gone except that the Silverton gossip mill had learned she'd gone to culinary school, then come back even more with-drawn than she'd been before she left.

"Anyway, after I explained to Tracy I wasn't going to try to get picked up by another team, she got distant. I wasn't in the best place, for sure, but she backed away. About a week after I told her I was pretty sure I wanted to move back here to Silverton, be around family, figure myself out, she told me she was with my former teammate."

Sadie's mouth dropped open. "What?"

"Yeah, it was brutal. It wasn't even a breakup. Or an 'I can't be your fiancée anymore.' It was just 'I'm with Gordon now. Best of luck.'"

"That's horrible."

It'd been five years now. Not quite, but almost, and it still made me feel like I'd chugged bad milk. Everything in me shuddered with the urge to vomit up my guts and erase the memory of the choice that'd led me there. Not that self-loathing and utter roadkill feeling I used to get, but I couldn't think of her hopping right into Gord's bed without wanting to puke a little.

"It brought me pretty low—not just her, but losing

myself there for a while. I don't know what I would've done without Wyatt." And Mom and Grandma to a lesser extent.

The combination of losing my career and what I thought was my future wife in a matter of months had shoved me out into a wasteland. I'd never thought of myself as a superficial man. I valued family and community. The money from going pro was great but never the goal.

But it'd taken me a long time and a heap of hours in therapy to recognize that losing my job hadn't simply been losing a source of income. It'd been losing something that I'd loved, and something that connected me to my dad. And I'd known him for such a short time—the first six months of my life—that football had felt like a kind of tether through time.

To be honest, lately that connection between me and the secondhand memory of my father still felt like a rapidly fraying rope or something slipping between my fingers at times. I'd accepted it wasn't lost with the change in my career trajectory, but I had no way to braid it back together. Some days, I felt the connection in the lists of things. Other days, I felt a little lost.

Then, the woman I'd loved and trusted had abandoned me when she saw my future didn't hold more playoff bonuses and endorsement paychecks. The cruel clarity when she'd announced she was with Gordon had hit like a slap—she'd never actually loved me. She'd hitched her wagon to my little football-running horse with the lifestyle of a pro baller's wife in mind, and when that disappeared, she'd tapped out.

I'd recovered from both train wrecks, but I hated thinking about Tracy. Anytime I did, the list of signs I should've seen way before she left filtered through my mind, and I felt more angry at myself for staying in a one-sided relationship and existing off her scraps than I did anything else.

"You were like a really long practice for the real thing, Warrick." Damn, but I could still hear her.

So? I wouldn't have the chance to play ball again professionally and risk truly destroying myself physically. I also didn't have to delve into a relationship and offer up my heart on a platter just for the next woman to decide it didn't meet whatever elusive barometer of worth she decided. I didn't have to, and I wouldn't.

Sadie hopped off her chair and grabbed my hand. She tugged and I stood up, curious. Then she stepped forward and wrapped her arms around me. She pulled me close, pressing against me, her head against my chest, and when I glanced down, her eyes were closed, brow furrowed. Like she wanted to do something more than console me. Like she wanted to erase it all.

I rested my hands on her shoulder blades, no pressure in case she wanted to back away. But her arms didn't move for a solid thirty seconds, which was a surprisingly long hug considering we'd hardly touched *ever*. By the end, my throat was tight, and that spoiled feeling had eased.

By the end, I realized I was done for.

CHAPTER TEN

Sadie

Hugging had never been my favorite thing.

It wasn't that I didn't like physical contact. I'd realized lately that I was practically starved for it, and nestling into Warrick's chest for a hug felt like coming home.

Says the emotionally and physically starved woman. Fine, fine, it just felt good. Just like he looked, he was warm and solid. Firm, but gentle. His hands covered my shoulder blades and warmed me through completely.

I'd taken him off guard, for sure. It'd been a few seconds before he'd reciprocated, and even then, he touched me like I might break if he put any weight on me at all.

How would it be to be hugged by this man—to be fully enveloped in his arms, all concern for my frailty or his size erased from our minds completely?

"Thank you," he said, his voice low and rough.

I pulled away—very reluctantly, I noted for my internal record books—and smiled up at him. "Thank you for telling me what happened."

He nodded, almost shy in the aftermath. Wasn't that my job? To be the shy, awkward one? But sliding into the bouquet of confusing feelings for the day came a stem of affection for him for not handling this moment perfectly.

I mean, it was perfect. But it wasn't smooth. It wasn't charming or polished or organized. It wasn't solving someone else's problem. And as much as Warrick gave off an impression like he was just a super nice guy doing his thing, I'd observed him enough to know he worked his gorgeous, sculpted butt off and had a plan for almost everything he did.

This was another reason I'd asked him to meet with me —aside from basic personality traits and ways of interacting with the world, we were remarkably similar.

"So what about you? Are you on the hunt for a Mr. Miller?"

I folded my slice of pizza, ignoring how it'd cooled during our hug, and working even harder to ignore the squishy feeling having him ask me this question created. Why did that happen? No idea. But I pushed past it.

"Friendship first, I think."

He didn't need to know that my parents wanted a Mr. Miller, or at least for me to be a Mrs. *stat*. And while no, they didn't actually control my life at this age, I'd unfortunately fallen from a tree that meant I cared way too much what they thought. I wasn't about to get married, but their position, repeated at any point we had a conversation lasting longer than five minutes, chafed.

Warrick nodded, thoughtful. Then, "But... and I mean, not to sound rude, have you ever dated?"

A laugh tumbled out of me. "Shocking as it may be, as a nearly thirty-year-old woman, yes, I have."

He held up those giant hands. "I didn't mean it to sound —dang it, Sadie, I didn't mean to sound like an ass."

His cheeks burned red, like he found his question utterly humiliating in the wake of my answer.

I shook my head, pleasure at his blush and joking coursing through me. "I'm messing with you. I know what you meant. I haven't had a relationship since I left New York."

And there it was, dropped between us.

"Can I ask about that?"

"You can ask me whatever you want."

And saying it aloud helped me realize I meant it. Like the words floating out of my mouth stitched them into the fabric of my reality and made them so.

"Okay then. Will you tell me about New York?"

I nodded but took another bite of pizza, knowing I needed fuel. Then it hit me—my headache was gone. Maybe I'd just needed food.

After another minute, I took a drink of water and centered myself with a deep breath. All the calm and ease I'd felt with him since he'd arrived vanished, and my pulse pounded in my neck. He hadn't exactly relished telling me about losing his career and his fiancée, so I could do this.

I can do this.

And Sharon's—my therapist's—voice slipped in and reminded me, "*Telling your story aloud takes away its power over you.*" I'd tried to tell my older sister Marguerite. I'd tried to tell my parents, though I'd gotten no farther than the first sentence before they waved it away as "an adventure gone wrong" and not what amounted to a nervous breakdown that changed the course of my life irrevocably.

Close on the heels of that invalidation? *"Maybe it's time to settle down." Blergh.*

I took another steadying inhale. "I've always had trouble with anxiety, as I'm sure you've figured out. I finished all but the last semester of culinary school with a specialty in baking and pastry arts, and I just... lost it. Had I lived a hundred and twenty years ago, I probably would've been committed for mania or something, but I essentially had a mental breakdown."

My heart tripped and scraped along in my chest, taking up too much space while it churned through telling this story.

"What—" He cleared his throat, then tried again. "What does that mean?"

One more deep breath, and I launched in again.

"It means I wasn't sleeping, or eating well enough, or even drinking enough water. It means I kept weird hours during my internship and missed my anxiety medication enough that it became a problem. I was dragging myself to class, to the internship, and one day as I stared down at this gorgeous millefeuille I was making—that's this layered dessert with crème and sheets of pastry between—it was like I couldn't see it. I felt so underwater, I couldn't even breathe right. I couldn't speak, so I just left. Right in the middle of my shift. I'd deteriorated enough that I couldn't get out of bed once I got home. Everything felt too big—too much, too huge. I couldn't manage to do anything but text Marguerite and tell her I needed help."

Half his torso leaned over the table between us, and he'd stopped eating almost as soon as I started talking. "Did she come? Did she help you?"

Gratitude, regret, love, and grief braided into a cord and wrapped around my chest.

"She did. Two days later, we were on a flight back to Salt Lake, and then she got me home to Silverton. She stayed with me a week after that but finally had to get back to work, and by then I'd come out of the worst of it, mostly thanks to my therapist and correcting my meds. But she did help."

When I'd tried to talk to my parents about it weeks later, they'd pretended it hadn't happened. They'd asked how my stay at the house had been—they'd been on Safari in Africa. They'd refused to discuss anything serious while gone, and by the time they got back, I'd moved to my tiny apartment above what eventually became Rise and Shine.

When I asked Marguerite about it, she'd refused to say much more than that she was glad I was okay. I suspected her response came more from being upset upon remembering how rough I was, but it still hurt.

"I had no idea," he said, jarring me from those still-painful memories.

"I haven't exactly advertised it. And for a long time after, I wasn't ready to talk about it. I poured every bit of energy I had into getting Rise and Shine up and running, and after that, I burrowed into my routine."

"Why, do you think?"

The question came out gentle, not demanding. Not expecting to dig deeper into a scabbed-over wound, but almost a balm. Something that promoted healing instead of aggravating it.

This was something I'd spent a lot of time mining in therapy, and on my own. Pounding out loaves in the Rise and Shine kitchen, thoughts of how I'd lost control so completely at the end of culinary school occupied me almost exclusively about that first year of the business.

"I was struggling but felt I shouldn't be. I was already

medicated, and I was doing something I loved, in theory. It felt like I shouldn't need *more* help. Acknowledging that my dream degree and work was tearing me down, not building me up, was too painful to accept."

I took a slow sip of water, but Warrick didn't speak. He gave me the space to continue, so I did.

"I went for the polar opposite. And while becoming a small business owner might seem insanely risky, I'd actually thought about something like it a lot. I think I'd been daydreaming of Rise and Shine for years before I let it become my dream and take the place of working in a fancy restaurant crafting dainty pastries for wealthy customers."

"It's amazing that you did that on the heels of so much hardship."

His brown eyes conveyed his sincerity and respect so clearly, and it filled me up in a way I couldn't have imagined.

And because of that, I continued spilling my guts. "When Bel moved to LA a few years ago, it woke me up. Made me realize that staying in the back of the shop, hiding away from people who I couldn't control, interacting with the world I couldn't control, wasn't really healing. And so I started working on inching my way back into being a person in the community, not just a person who existed inside its borders but never engaged with it."

Had I done enough? Saying it now and wondering what it looked like through Warrick's eyes—someone who was so completely a part of this city and so many of its citizens' lives—made me tuck my hands under my legs.

"You're amazing. You know that? To overcome that and take these steps just because you decided you wanted to? You weren't forced—"

"I kind of was. I didn't have Bel here to deal with all the personnel and everything."

He waved that away with one giant hand which then dove in to grab his slice of pizza. "Nah. She could've done all that remotely if needed. You chose to do it, and I respect the crap out of that."

I had imagined a handful of scenarios involving Warrick Saint over the years, but never had I imagined something like this—a moment of him saying something like that to *me*. Again, his openness spurred my own.

"Well, I have to tell you that your handling of your injury has always inspired me. I don't know the ins and outs of it, but seeing you come back and try new things, do what you wanted even if it didn't quite work out the way you planned—watching all of that, even at a distance, has encouraged me to try."

He swallowed hard and looked at me like I'd shocked him. Eventually, he scraped out, "I'm glad."

"Me too."

The mood had become heavy, and though everything we'd talked about had been amazing, I felt myself shutting down. Not purposefully, but I didn't recall speaking that many words, and especially not on the subject of my spectacular failure in New York and the ensuing years, in... ever. Maybe not even to my therapist, since it'd taken so long for me to find words for it all.

"So you said you hadn't had a relationship with someone since New York. Were you with someone when you left?" He speared lettuce on his fork but fiddled with it rather than bring it to his mouth.

I finished my salad with one last bite and summoned the words. "I was with another chef. My, uh, my boss, actually."

He straightened.

"In retrospect, that was another unhealthy area of my life. I dated someone early in college, but not anyone until Georges, and when I left... I honestly didn't talk to him again. I think Marguerite sent him a text or something, but I don't know."

His eyes widened. "Wow."

"Yeah. I felt more relief to be done with him than I felt sad. Same for the program and New York, in truth. Certainly not heartbroken." Not like Warrick had been when his fiancée left him and betrayed him with his own teammate.

What kind of person did that? And what kind of man just... recovered? Continued functioning and being so generous and kind? He'd declared he had no plans to marry, but he wasn't grouchy or cruel. He wasn't some wounded hero. He was basically Hercules.

"Well, good riddance to *Georges,* then." He used a gross French accent for the name.

I chuckled. "Yeah, my parents loved that part. Loved the idea that their Mercedes would marry a Frenchman."

He did a double take. "Wait. *Waaaaaiiiit.* Your full name is *Mercedes?*"

I pressed my lips together to hide my smile. "Yep."

"Seriously?"

"It's not *that* unusual of a name."

He ran a hand through his hair like this news both delighted and troubled him. "Yeah, but all this time, I've been thinking of you as Sadie Miller. And now I find out you're actually *Mercedes Miller.*"

I piled my bowl, utensils, and napkin on top of the plate where only my crust sat uneaten and abandoned. I forcefully ignored the fizzy feeling in my belly thanks to his saying my full name, so I hid my smile. "Sorry to turn things upside down for you, Saint."

The troubled twinge to his expression fled, and a gleeful fire lit behind his eyes. "Oh, that's just fine, Miller."

We smiled at each other for a beat, and I knew I needed to leave. That face and the playfulness made me feel downright muddled after all our talking. I needed to get out of here before I said something embarrassing. "Well, I'm about a half hour from all systems shut down, so... what's my homework this week? Wait!"

His brow dipped, and he held up his hands. "Okay..."

"I just remembered I did last week's homework, and I've been dying to tell you. I sat down with Sarah and we talked and it was—" I let out a sigh. "It was great."

The Warrick Saint sunrise special hit me then, a full beaming grin that made my stomach and my heart flip-flop. "I'm so glad."

I nodded. "Me too. So, this week?"

He clapped his hands and rubbed them together. "Two things. One, plan a lunch with more than one friend."

I nodded and inhaled, elbowing the *no way that's happening* right in the face. "Okay. And two?"

"Find a date to *A Night in Bloom* event and buy tickets."

I swallowed hard, and my heartbeat took off. "Uh."

"Doesn't have to be a romantic date. Just has to be a date —interpret as you will."

Heart thundering, I forced a slow exhale and nodded. "Fine. Okay. As long as you do the same."

CHAPTER ELEVEN

Warrick

By the next week's meeting, I'd secured a date for _A Night in Bloom_ and bought tickets and spent approximately a hundred hours berating myself for not just telling Sadie I was taking her.

Because despite all my rules and plans about not getting close to someone, the thought of _her_ getting close to someone was downright troublesome.

Irksome.

Problematic.

Complicating, at least. Because, what if she got together with this Joe Schmoe date and ended up having to cancel our friendship lessons? That just wouldn't do. I wasn't about to step back into the crowd of people she held at arm's length now that I'd gotten even an inch closer.

Or worse, what if she ended up with someone like _Georges,_ who clearly didn't take care of her and was a total snobbish jerk? Okay, fine. I didn't know the guy or all the details. But Georges could suck it. Any man who let go of Sadie clearly hadn't appreciated her. Nor had he realized something was wrong or tried very hard to check on her before she left New York, from the sounds of it. The fact that she wasn't torn up about it made me happy, for sure, but how did a man let go of her like that? He had to be an idiot, and I wouldn't be convinced otherwise.

Alas, I had no hope of changing course now, and we still hadn't exchanged numbers. Granted, I knew where she was at pretty much any given time on any given day—not in a stalkery way, but just in a *we live in a small town and work at least half our days next door to each other* kind of way.

I spent the morning using a sledgehammer on a tire, burning off what'd rapidly become the closest thing I had to identifiable angst, and screwed my head on straight. Then I got caught up in reviewing a few reservations for my various StayBnB properties for the end of June and fourth of July weekends. I'd snatched up a few little places in the spring before the market got hot right along with the weather, so paired with the cottage up at the ranch, I had a nice little line-up that would keep growing if my contractors ever finished my current house. I set up meetings with the zoning commission for a project I hoped to make headway on and started brainstorming ideas for new ways to expand the gym without spreading myself too thin.

Sadie's knock startled me from the daze I'd slumped into sometime in the last half hour.

"Am I interrupting? Thought we could go ahead and eat, if you're hungry."

I turned to see her leaning in the doorway to my office. She'd removed her apron, as she seemed to be in the habit of doing for our time together. Today, she wore jeans that fit her well and accentuated the curve of her hips, bright yellow kicks on her small feet, and a white shirt that looked silky and had little lemons on it. It wasn't tight, but it flattered her, nipping in at her waist and showing the pleasing expanse of her collarbone and firm arms.

My stomach flipped when my gaze reached her face, both because she stood watching me with a small, amused smile, and because I realized I'd taken a rather lazy perusal of her that she very clearly hadn't missed.

I cleared my throat and shot to my feet. "Sorry. I think my brain quit about half an hour ago. Let's go eat."

I followed as she led us outside, and we both sank down to sit on the curb of the small parking lot.

"We should get a picnic table out here," she said, setting a canvas Rise and Shine bag between us.

"I'll ask Aidan if he can work one in. I hadn't thought about it with the original request, but I like it."

I took the container she gave me, ditched the lid, and shoved half a grilled chicken breast into my mouth. My eyes shut in relief as I chewed and swallowed bite after bite before finally breaking to chug from my water bottle.

When I came up for air, I could feel her eyes on me. That same subtle smile graced what I'd always thought were delicious-looking lips when I met her gaze. *All right, hungry boy. Bring it down.*

"I feel like I should've gotten you two." She glanced at the small bite of chicken I held pinched between my thumb and index finger, the only remnants of the original, full-sized thing. And yes, I was an animal who'd just eaten with my fingers instead of bothering with the fork she'd supplied. *Whoops.* I grabbed it now and speared a few pieces of grilled vegetables I hadn't even seen when I first opened the container. The chicken had sat on a bed of quinoa and veggies—delicious.

My eyes snagged on the soft skin at the collar of her shirt under the neat whirl of hair that was her bun. Obviously, I wasn't quite firing on all cylinders yet, and it was darn near making me a starving man staring at her like steak.

"Yeah. Sorry. I didn't realize I forgot my snack this morning, but I did. I should've realized when I spaced out like that a while ago. My body gave up until it found sustenance. Thank you for providing that."

My big dumb hand came up and patted her back over her shirt, all but two fingers that accidentally on purpose pressed against the skin at the slope of her neck.

I hadn't planned on it, but as my body remembered what planet it was on, I wasn't fully thinking yet. The food hadn't hit bottom, and I still felt disconnected from myself as I watched my hand connect with her body, as the pads of those two blessed fingers felt her skin. Only when I mentally wrenched my hand from her with an internally shouted, *She's your friend, you idiot!* did I come fully into myself.

"I'm glad we ate early, then." She took a bite of her chicken from the end of her fork, and I pointedly averted my eyes.

"So, how was your week?"

"Actually, really good. I was dreading both assignments, but I did them." She beamed over at me, all gorgeous teeth and radiating joy.

I exhaled sharply to clear out the weird twist in my chest. "That's great. Tell me about them."

"I had lunch with Sarah and Quinn, and then I also found a date to *A Night in Bloom*."

Her cheeks pinked, and I immediately wanted to snarl. Probably a clue that I needed a bit more to eat, because I did not usually snarl.

"And who's the lucky fella?" I managed my breezy *Warrick is so laid-back* tone. I'd had enough practice using that when I didn't feel it to make it thoroughly convincing despite my off-kilter start to this interaction.

"Uh, well..."

"Oh, wow. You really like this—"

"It's Sarah."

I blinked. "Wait. Sarah James? You like her?"

That changed things. Quite a bit. I hadn't even considered—

"No. I mean, I do like her, very much, but not romantically. But I don't know any other men, and as I racked my brain for who to ask, you were the only man I could think of. So instead, I decided it could be a friend date." She took another bite of chicken.

I could've smacked myself right there. *You were the only man I could think of.* Why hadn't I just asked her to go with me and saved myself the grief? But her statement seemed so matter-of-fact—*I thought of you, and you weren't a good option.*

Well, damn.

The news that she'd asked Sarah unromantically should've made me happy, but that she thought she couldn't ask me proved to be problematic. I sat squarely in the friendzone, right where I'd convinced myself I wanted to be from day one, and in a matter of a week, I'd realized just how little I actually wanted that to be the way things stood between us.

So, I decided to push a bit. "You could've asked me."

Her brows shot up.

"Oh. Uh... yeah. Good point, I guess. If I'm taking Sarah as a friend, I could take you just as easily. I guess it felt like since you were the one assigning the homework, it'd be cheating." She pointedly avoided my eyes.

Well, she had me there. Guess I had shot myself in the foot. Cool.

"On a more serious note, you know you can tell me to shove it at any time. I'm trying to come up with stuff that seems helpful, but it's not like I know what I'm doing." I ran a hand through my hair, realizing just how presumptuous I'd been with the assignments.

"Of course I know that. I kind of did with this one." She eyed me more closely. "Are you really worried I don't know that?"

"I don't know. But I don't want to do anything detrimental. I only want to help you, and only as much as you want me to."

Her expression softened. "I appreciate that. I've still got a professional therapist, and I do have a backbone, too."

"I didn't mean to imply—"

Her laugh cut me off. "Seriously, Warrick, I know you're a good guy. That's why I asked you—why my therapist encouraged this whole thing. And when I mentioned feeling unprepared for a date, she pushed me to figure out why. Once I realized it was more because I don't know any men well enough to feel comfortable than I was *scared* to date, that was a great revelation. Not that I thought I was scared, but it was just good to sort of say it out loud to myself."

"That's awesome. And also... should I be concerned your therapist knows about me? Am I about to get a referral to deal with my many issues?"

I meant it as a joke, but I wondered if they'd discussed

my shortcomings. Because I had them. Unavailable for commitment. Compulsively busy to distract from... whatever made me feel restless and wrong when I slowed down. The youngest brother to Wyatt, an insanely successful, prematurely semiretired rancher, and Wilder, an actual freaking American hero, not that he'd ever tolerate anyone saying such a thing—definitely some fodder for therapy there. Oh, and of course, probably a handful of daddy issues.

She grabbed my wrist and squeezed, her grip surprisingly strong but not painful. "I told you I admire how you've handled everything these last few years. I've talked to her about that—about wishing I'd been more like that. But as time has gone on, it's less about wishing and more about doing. So here we are."

Damn. Who just laid it all out there—weaknesses, failures, hopes? Who admitted to struggling so hard and then being determined to change like that? I never would've imagined her being so vulnerable. In high school, she'd seemed like this tiny fortress walking around with high walls surrounded by a moat.

My heart kicked as my mind skated by the memory of her rejection. I couldn't exactly forget it. I'd spent weeks observing her, figuring out when I might snag a moment without a crowd and just talk to her. I figured if it went well, I'd ask her out. We had like four classes together, so I saw her all the time, but she managed to disappear in between.

When I finally approached her, I'd been nervous. You know the kind—hands clammy, voice weird and froggy, and I'd said, "Hey, Sadie. Would you want to hang out some time? Grab a shake?" It'd been back when the original diner was still around, and they'd had these ridiculously good shakes. Perfect casual date, right?

Her brows had furrowed, and then she'd laughed. Like full-on laugh—two sharp *ha has*—and then turned on her heel and practically ran away.

And my heart had never recovered. Sitting here next to her, I still felt that wary, hopeful interest in her. All the more so because time had passed, and she'd already proven to be different than I'd thought she was.

I'd changed immensely since then, so why wouldn't she have? She'd already described the things that'd forced her into action to change her social habits. Still, it shook me. I'd been honest with her about how things had gone with Tracy, but that felt fairly distant. I'd made my peace there. I hadn't told her much about me *now* other than that I didn't plan to get married.

"Well, I'm impressed. You should be proud," I finally said, hoping she wouldn't notice how she'd scrambled my brain with her words and general splendor.

She wiped a hand from high on her quad to her knee once, twice, then leaned her elbows on her knees. "That's what Marguerite says. She never focuses on the mess I was in when she came to get me, but..."

Her soft exhale had me studying her. "But?"

She sat up and her gaze shifted out to the mountains in the distance. It didn't matter the season, having this view of Silver Ridge Peak was unbeatable.

"She also won't really talk to me about it. It's more than my parents will do, which is absolutely not even begin to acknowledge that I have anxiety, but at the same time, her 'you should be proud' always feels like a period on the sentence. Like she doesn't want the details, and I can be happy that I'm not still curled up in the fetal position under my covers in my apartment, refusing to leave or dress or eat or sleep."

Her words punched into my gut. The thought of her in such pain, hurting so much that she couldn't eat, made me ache like I'd just done a hundred sit-ups. Worse.

"Siblings are tough. I just have my mom, and we're close, but even me and Wyatt are pretty different. We get along, but there are those friction points you can't escape. And I'll admit I sometimes struggle with being a bit of a dud compared to him and Wilder."

How I got along with Wilder? I had no idea, because I didn't know him. But that was its own problem, and I only hoped we'd get to deal with it someday soon.

"There is no scenario in which *you* are a dud." Her words were fervent.

I chuckled, brushing it off. "Well, littlest brother syndrome, I guess. You and Marguerite are pretty different, right?"

She nodded. "I do need to remember that we're very different people. She's in this professional, high-speed world, and I'm... just not. Nor do I want to be. Never have. My parents have only acknowledged how I'm different from her in their expectations that I not follow in Marguerite's footsteps." She made a face.

I laughed, and delight slipped through me. I'd never imagined she was funny—how shortsighted. "How kind of them."

"Again. They're different people. Grew up in a generation when anxiety wasn't a thing anyone talked about. They have no clue how to deal with it, so they just ignore it." She shrugged.

I wanted to hug her. As a tactile person, someone who liked to touch and be touched, I *desperately* wanted to hug her. She'd hugged me just the other day, right? But that had come in the wake of my confessions about Tracy and losing my career. It had been a truly sad moment. And me hugging her now might seem like pity.

I jumped to my feet and reached a hand down to her. "Well, screw 'em. You know you're doing what you need to do, and you're an amazing person."

The corner of her mouth quirked up, and she took my outstretched hand. When she gripped me at my wrist, waves of heat swept up my arm. Eyes on our clasped hands, my mind chased itself in circles, enjoying the contact. Enjoying her closeness.

Enjoying a bunch of crap we don't enjoy anymore, right?

"Everything okay?"

Damn, she must've seen my expression, and now I had to think of something more to say than, "*I like your hand on my hand.*" Gah.

Couldn't say *that*, but feeling a little scrambled, all I got out was, "Oh, uh, I was just thinking your hands are really strong."

CHAPTER TWELVE

Sadie

The thing was, I did have strong hands. Maybe freakishly strong for someone my size—technically on the small side, for sure. Next to Warrick, I looked downright miniature. But then, he was unusually large so...

"Did you expect me to have a weak grip?"

"No, of course not. I just—you're so—uh, I don't know. I guess it never occurred to me."

His cheeks brightened, and the sight of it shouldn't have charmed me, but it completely did.

"I work with my hands. All the time. If I'm not kneading for a test recipe, I'm stirring or scraping batter or lifting giant pans from ovens. A strong grip, lopsided arm strength, and wrists striped with burns are kind of a baker's signature."

He hadn't released my hand yet, and at this, he turned

us so he could see the aforementioned wrists. "Holy crap, this is brutal."

I jerked my hand back. "Hey. I wasn't saying it so you could gawp at them. Don't guys dig scars or something like that?"

I sounded like a raving idiot, but if he'd swept his thumb over the inside of my wrist again, I'd probably make a face or moan, which would not be helpful.

He let out a belly laugh that cued my turn to blush. "I think the phrase you're looking for is *chicks dig scars*, but sure. I dig *your* scars because they're part of you. How about that?"

He eyed me, that Warrick twinkle in full force, his smile a bright, unbearable thing in the moment.

Ha. *How about that?* Like it wasn't the most perfect thing someone had ever said to me. Even if he didn't mean the emotional scars, he was the first friend I'd ever told about them. And it made me wonder if eventually, someone could appreciate the wounds from my past, ugly and unexpected as they sometimes were.

"I'll take it." I folded my hands behind me. "So any homework this week?"

He blew out a low breath. "I think another friend thing. Maybe make a point to, uh, talk to a guy? Any guy would do. Just so you have someone besides me since I'm—well, you know, it's good to work on it."

"Sure, of course. All right then. See you next week."

After last week's homework sending me into a mild panic and requiring some serious calming down before I talked to Sharon and realized I could do what I wanted and didn't have to do what he said, this suggestion didn't make my stomach clench or my throat dry out. I didn't look forward to it exactly, but the idea of making friends with more than just him seemed nice. Plus, I'd talked to Jamie Morris over the years, and he was great. His brothers Liam and Danny, and strangely, even Jonas Bauer, had all been nice. I wouldn't call them *friends*, but I'd never been as nervous around Jamie after he and Bel finally worked out their issues.

And then of course Wyatt Saint was the consummate gentleman, always polite and courteous and kind of dreamy in an untouchable way—all the more so now that he was glued to Calla's hip.

So, I could do this. I *would* do this. And I'd report back to Warrick next Wednesday. Then, a few short days later, I'd attend *A Night in Bloom* with Sarah.

Six days later, I'd completed the assignment *and then some*. I'd talked to no fewer than ten men. Granted, eight of them were part of the Vet's coffee group that came in twice a week, but still. They counted.

The other two were Aidan Wallace and his cousin John. They were from one of the founding families around here, and just like the Morrisons, everyone knew them. John and his older brothers were sweeties. Aidan was... intimidating. Talented, honestly kind of gorgeous, and had the intensity of a widowed single dad who didn't have time for much more than work and his son. The fact that he'd sat at the table with John for more than fifteen minutes seemed like a momentous occasion.

But by the time I dragged myself upstairs, I wanted nothing more than silence. I'd talked to John and Aidan today, and that output, plus my two hours of customer service interaction, made me feel like a face sucker had come and stolen every word out of my brain.

I tossed my mail onto the small wooden table and sank into the couch just as my phone rang. *Marguerite.* Sigh. I couldn't skip this or she'd charter a plane and show up in the morning, banging down my door ready to rescue me again.

Her voice came through, light and crisp, sending a pang of homesickness through me. It didn't make much sense considering we hadn't lived in the same house since before she went to boarding school when I turned ten. We were three years apart, and yet it felt like we'd grown up in entirely different families and lives. Despite everything, I missed her.

"How's my lemon squeezy?"

I chuckled, amazed to hear the ancient nickname rooted in my forever love of bright yellow and all things lemon coming out of that prim, fancy mouth after so long. "I am actually great. How are you?"

"Oh, you know. Working like a dog and very curious if you've received your mail yet today."

The excitement in her voice had me sitting up, and my heart lurched forward, pattering away in an instant. "Uh, I have. Let me go check, though—I didn't even look through it."

Most of the time, it was junk mail that'd followed me across the country to New York, doubled in quantity, and then tailed me back here.

"Let me know when you find the one from me."

I swallowed, or attempted to, my throat a desert. "Payday loan ad, discounted printable stamps, ooh, a pamphlet with a schedule of events for the library."

I'd peruse that later—maybe Sarah would go with me. I didn't want to monopolize her, but she'd mentioned enjoying reading too.

"Oh, Silverton. Your small-town ways never cease to amaze," she said, like she lived in a bustling metropolis and not an hour away in Salt Lake. Like she hadn't spent her first thirteen years here too.

And then I came to it. Though I'd known immediately what she wanted me to find in the mail, holding the textured cream letter pressed paper in my hand, my chest seized.

"Okay, open it! Your breathing just changed, so I'm guessing you found it."

That she could read my breathing so well was something I'd need to think about later. Right now, I needed to open this letter. It was just a letter—an invitation.

"Are you freaking out? This isn't a wedding invitation, if that's what you're concerned about. I gave you a heads-up this was coming, and I really want—"

"I'm fine," I all but wheezed, then ripped into the envelope and pulled out a single printed card inviting me to *A Fantasy Under the Stars* Engagement Party for Marguerite Alaine Miller and Douglas Allen Wilson.

And that tripped me from tight, anxious dread to an ill-timed giggle. "Doug's middle name is *Allen*? You guys have the same middle name?"

"You get my engagement party invitation, and the thing you want to talk about is my fiancé's middle name?"

Another giggle tripped out. "I guess so. I mean, it needs

addressing, doesn't it? Will all your children have the same middle name too?"

She groaned. "No and no. And fine, be like this. Avoid the main thing. I'll get right to it. I want you at this party, and I want you at my wedding. We've got a date, but I won't burden you with maid of honor stuff. You can just show up and power through. But please consider coming. You have a solid month to find a date and figure out how to cope."

Her sharp words whipped across my ear, slapping as they went. "I'm sorry. I've had a stressful day. I didn't mean to—"

"It's fine. I get it. I just want you there, okay?"

A vise clamped down on my chest, and my voice came out small and sad. The same way it'd sounded at different times in my life, and the way that made me hate myself. "I'll be there. I'm sorry, Marguerite."

"It's fine."

The silence hung between us, ballooning into the airspace between our cities.

"Okay," I finally scratched out.

"Don't worry about it. I'll talk to you soon."

The phone went dead in my ear.

Regret tunneled through me, a feeling so claustrophobic, I gasped for breath. I was an awful sister. I should've been happy—rejoicing with her instead of laughing at middle names to distract from the white-hot dread searing my gut. My apology was genuine, but not enough. From her clipped response and hang up, I knew it was far from enough.

My heart raced, and my hands curled into fists—tight, inescapable little knots. Crap. *Craaap.* My hands were always a clue things were about to get bad. My breathing too, the heavy weight pressing in on my chest, causing my ribcage to collapse and crush my lungs.

I should've known this was coming. I'd felt off all day, despite the goodness. I hadn't eaten in six hours, missing my afternoon snack thanks to work. I hadn't slept well the night before—I'd been too excited for the day.

My mind struggled against the closing walls of the beginning of a panic attack. But I'd learned over many, many years to combat this. Eyes open, I focused on the thread of the pillow where my head rested. Bright yellow—happy, cheery, summery, a tick brighter than the color of good butter. Soft against my face, though the shell of my ear was smashed and starting to feel it. Once my hands relaxed enough, I pressed them together, stretching the tight muscles in my wrists, then wiggling my fingers.

The pressure in my chest eased by degrees, slowly but steadily. Shutting my eyes, I mentally stepped into my kitchen and kneaded a double batch of baguettes—simple, specific, familiar. By the time I'd slipped the loaves into their imaginary forms, a half hour had passed, and I'd recovered almost completely.

The exhaustion that accompanied something like this threatened to drag me into sleep, but I pushed off the couch and made my way to the kitchen. After slicing a few pieces of sharp cheddar cheese, I grabbed the box of Ritz crackers and sat at my table. I ate the cheese quickly, this time forgoing the cheese-cracker combo, then finally took a bite of one of the blessed little crackers.

Salty, buttery, and the perfect, toothsome crunch made me sigh audibly, and with that familiar, soothing taste on my tongue, the gates of my mind opened wide.

I couldn't change my initial reaction to Marguerite's news, but I could apologize for it. I could tell her how happy

I was, confirm I'd be there for her, and then find a date. I scratched out these items on a to-do list—paper this time, since staying as tactile as possible after being so far in my head always helped me feel tethered to real life.

I could repair things between us, and I'd figure out the date thing, and it'd all be fine.

CHAPTER THIRTEEN

Warrick

A note taped to my office door knocked my day all out of whack.

It should've been a lunch day with Sadie, but the note had changed that plan. No explanation as to why, either. Simply, *"Can't do lunch today. See you Saturday. Sadie."* I tried not to let it, but it felt like rejection. Was I so fragile that a change in plans affected me so deeply?

Apparently so. At least when it came to this woman.

And maybe some of that had roots in our history—the overarching memories of our early high school interactions feelings like I wasn't good enough to even talk to her, and then of course the resulting laugh at my attempt to ask her out. But hadn't she effectively explained that by talking about her anxiety?

Yes. Yes, she had. Logically, it made sense that her

anxiety might've had something to do with who she was back then, and like I'd tried to convince myself, I was different more than a decade ago too. But concern dripped into my mental bucket all day until it ran over—she hadn't come into her kitchen this afternoon either.

Then it hit me. Maybe something was wrong—really wrong. Not to flatter myself, but she seemed to enjoy our time together. The last friend assignment hadn't been too pushy, and she'd explained how she'd only do what she was comfortable with. So her missing had to mean something was wrong.

Didn't she know friends told each other these things?

Or, wait. *Did* she know that?

An idea wormed its way inside my mind, and by the end of the day, I couldn't shake it. I decided to hold off another twenty-four hours and see if she came to the big kitchen tomorrow, but by the end of the day Thursday, more than twenty-four hours after we should've met and an unusual length of time to go without seeing her even from a distance, I'd convinced myself checking in on her was simply the right thing. The job any friend would do when concerned about his friend.

She lived above the bakery. I knew this. Everyone knew this. But would it be too much of an invasion to just show up?

Shaking out my hands and rolling my neck, I warmed up for the interaction. I'd had dinner with Pete and hadn't heard a word he'd said. When he finally just rolled his eyes and left, I knew I had to go see her.

Rise and Shine's building had the front store entrance, then a back door to the kitchen, but if I remembered right, there was additional rear access to the building that led directly into a stairway to the second floor rather than through the coffee shop. At least, that was how the space above Odds, just next door, was. I'd looked into buying that building but had ultimately opted for a larger, more updated space on Silver Street.

After finding my way to the back side of the building, I knocked on the outer door. No answer. Then I tried the handle, and to my delight and dismay, it opened. Didn't she lock this to keep strangers out? Yes, this was a small town, but even in summer, we had tourists all over the place. Especially leading up to a big event and into a holiday weekend—I'd talk to her about that, for sure.

I climbed the stairs and saw there were two doors. Apartment 2A and 2B. *Huh.* The Odds building hadn't had a hallway, but rather a single door that led to quite a large space. This had a small hallway splitting the space, and on each side sat a door.

I went with A, but no one answered, so I sucked in a breath and said a prayer as I knocked on unit B. Clicking and sliding sounds scraped against the frame, and a second later, a bewildered Sadie peered out a crack in the opening.

"Warrick?"

"Hey. Sorry to freak you out by knocking on your door, but I was worried about you."

She blinked. "Worried?"

I shoved my hands into the back pockets of my jeans to keep from attempting to press the door further open and get a look at her to appease this now wild need to see she was okay.

"Yeah. I realize canceling our lunch date doesn't necessarily mean something's wrong, but paired with not seeing you in the kitchen the last few days and talking to Garrett who said you'd been keeping minimal hours, I just wanted to check in. Make sure you were okay."

She widened the crack in the door so her whole body filled it. She wore sweats and slouchy socks, which made my eye twitch, because who could stand that? And a baggy T-shirt. Her hair, instead of a neat bun at the base of her neck, plumed out on the top of her head in some kind of mess secured by invisible hair ties and witchcraft.

"I'm okay. I had a rough couple of days. Sometimes when that happens, I just need to take a step back and hunker down. Invest back into my routines and focus on what I can control instead of..."

"Everything you can't?"

A thin smile spread her lips. "Yeah. I'm sorry if I worried you."

"You don't need to be sorry. And I don't mean to be nosy. But if you wouldn't mind, I'd like to exchange numbers. If you'd be up for that."

Her smile widened into something still small but far more genuine. "Sure. That'd be great."

We quickly swapped numbers, and determined not to overstay, I stepped back. "Okay then. Still good for Saturday? Will I see you there?"

"Yes. I'll be there."

She ducked her head again, all that hair bobbling with the move. I'd never seen it disorderly, and this glimpse made me itch to see her even more undone. But before that thought carried me away, I had to say something else.

"Hey, one quick thing."

She gave me her eyes.

"If you don't mind me putting on my friendly, teachery hat? Friends talk about stuff. Maybe you're not used to that, and you don't have to be. But if you ever *want* to talk to me, about anything, you can. You don't have to shoulder it all on your own."

Her lashes fluttered, and she frowned just slightly before saying, "Okay. Thanks."

"See you soon."

The next two days flew by. I caught sight of Sadie, and we swapped smiles but were always moving in different directions. At least she hadn't locked herself away. And once I understood that'd been a method of self-care, I'd felt much better about it. The crazy scenarios jumping through my mind about why she'd canceled and what she might be going through had put me too close to the edge of grabbing her and holding her to me the second I saw her. Luckily, she hadn't looked bad, just... relaxed. At home and decompressing and more than a little adorable.

Had I daydreamed more than once about sitting on the couch with her, talking to her and getting more doses of that wry humor? Yes. Yes, I had.

Had I let those daydreams veer off into the territory they repeatedly kept pulling me? *No. No, I had not.* I had to chant that to myself, reminding me of all the reasons I didn't get involved romantically with anyone, much less someone who so clearly didn't have an interest in me. Even if I couldn't help but feel things for her.

Just like before. Just like always, really.

I didn't want a relationship. I didn't want to feel beholden to someone else. I definitely didn't want to deal with the awful need to trust someone else with myself. I didn't want to fill someone's space and help them mark time until a better offer came along.

See? There. Back on track.

Tucking my crisp white shirt into my pants, I inspected that thought. I'd been over it a hundred times by now—the fact that she hadn't been stuck up when we were younger. And she certainly wasn't now. Nothing about our interactions spoke to her being haughty or thinking she was better than me. If anything, she didn't think *enough* of herself.

Was part of all of this some kind of retroactive friend-making thing in my head? Or some way to prove that I was good enough for her? Maybe not romantically anymore, but simply as a person. And if it was, was that so bad?

My phone buzzing on the nightstand kicked me into action. I tightened my belt and inspected myself as best I could. I'd stayed in town the last few nights to give Calla and Wyatt privacy. They'd made it back from LA this week, and while they didn't ever make me feel unwelcomed, I felt more like a little snot-nosed brother when I came around them than other times.

So my current setup? Not great. I'd purchased this small home as an investment, and the contractors were making great progress. It'd be ready to rent by next ski season. They'd left me one of the bedrooms in the upstairs, and they'd been able to turn the water on for me this week while they worked on other things. Fortunately, the pipes were in decent shape. But I didn't have a mirror, so my date would have to fix me.

And speaking of, she messaged. *"Are you ready? I just pulled up."*

"Be right out," I shot back and grabbed my jacket, keys, and wallet. I shuffled down the stairs, glad I hadn't put my jacket on when I scraped against the bottom of the staircase.

I trotted to the front door and locked it behind me, then knocked on the driver's side window. "Am I driving?"

Mom frowned and gestured to the passenger seat, so I loped around and slid in.

"I'm picking you up. Why would you drive?" She shot me a glare and shifted to drive while I buckled.

"I thought I'd at least offer."

Did it make me pathetic that my mom was my date tonight?

No. It made me awesome. Because Jane Saint was an actual saint, a generally awesome person, and I didn't see her nearly enough. Add to it that most of my actual girl*friends* were busy or working the event itself, it made taking someone else more of a hassle.

"And tell me again why I'm going with you and not some hot guy I met on RuralMatch?"

I groaned. "Are you still meeting people? How is this possible? How many dates have you found through that app?"

She'd become a serial dater in the last few months since starting on the app.

"Oh, one or two a week. No love connections yet, but it's been fun. So?" That Jane Saint brow rose in a perfect arch.

"I'm honestly all for you dating, but I'm not sure how I feel about this whole *my mom talking about hot guys* thing." I shuddered.

Without looking away from the road, she shoved my shoulder. I winced, just as she gasped. "Oh, I'm so sorry. I didn't think—"

"No, it's fine. It's been years." It shouldn't have hurt as much as it did for my mom to playfully nudge me, but it'd been testy this week after I pushed a little too hard. I'd paid my penance with ice strapped around me for much of the week.

"I'm sorry it's still bothering you. I should've remembered."

"Really, it's fine. Normally, that wouldn't have bothered it at all. Don't feel bad." She'd sit over there and punish herself for having a moment of teasing. I loved that about her and didn't want her to stop because I had a sissy shoulder. "I don't want you treating me with kid gloves, or going easy on me."

She chuckled. "Fine. You got the shove because you are more mature than to say I can't be attracted to men."

I groaned again. "I know. Good for you. But I need as few details as possible."

"How funny! That's the exact opposite of me, because I want every single detail of the time you've spent with Sadie Miller. Ready, go."

I glared at her and she rolled to a stop in the parking spot, then winked obnoxiously.

"There's nothing to tell."

She pursed her lips, unamused.

"Seriously. We're friends."

Brows raised.

"We are. We get along well. She's different than I thought she was, but in a good way."

She pressed her hands together and the tips of her fingers to her lips in a hopeful, almost prayerful, pose.

"I'm not dating her. You know I'm not getting married, and I'm sorry to disappoint you, bu—"

"That's not what this is, young man. I know what you've said. I know your reasons, and while I disagree with them, I'm not going to pretend I think you're going to change all your convictions over one girl you crushed on in high school. It's been over a decade! But I also know you."

My heart sank. That look and tone told me she *did* know me. Better than I thought she did. I cleared my throat. "I'm fine."

The look she gave me then was so close to the *I'm not mad, I'm just disappointed* look, I withered all the same.

"You're struggling. I want you happy, and I want you honest with yourself about that. I don't know if Sadie Miller will have a part in that, but I can see how you'd be good for her. She might do the same for you." She exited the car and shut the door before I'd unbuckled.

I moved slowly, my thoughts swirling. My mom saw I wasn't happy. She could tell. But did she know why? I scrubbed a hand down my face and slipped out of the car. I wasn't so sure I knew, so how could she?

But maybe she was right—maybe this thing with Sadie had a purpose beyond just me helping her make friends and practicing personal control over my attraction to my new friend. Maybe I could learn from her too—something about determination or... baking bread.

Mom had walked ahead toward the city's new gardens, which had opened last week but were officially debuting tonight. She crossed under a high ivy archway a hundred feet ahead of me—how long had I taken to get out of her car? The sky was still fairly bright since we'd just passed the solstice, but since the gardens were lined with trees, it gave whatever lay on the other side of that arch an unearthly glow.

I tromped down the cobbled pathway from the parking lot. Technically, this was the library's lot. Most people in town would walk to the event, but my current house and

Mom's were both a bit too far to be comfortable trekking back and forth in dress clothes.

I blew out a big breath and stretched my arms out, adjusting the cuff of a sleeve under my jacket. I was warm, but the night would cool off quickly and it'd be fine. My bouncy ball thoughts joggled around in my head as I neared the arch, and just then, Sadie stepped into the space inside the garden, framed by the arch.

What did I say about maintaining my self-control over myself when faced with my attractive friend? Had I thought that was going to be easy?

She wore a yellow silk dress with tiny, barely there straps connecting over her shoulders. She held a glass of champagne and smiled at someone just out of sight. Then she twisted away from me and revealed the back—swoopy, soft material dipping at her shoulder blades.

Oh, crap. *Crap, crap, crap.*

She'd twisted her hair back, but instead of her usual bun, it sat higher on her head, leaving the beautiful slope of her neck uncovered and highlighted by a few wisps of hair that'd fallen from the twist.

She turned toward me just as I stepped through the arch, and she might as well have been a double team from the defense because she tackled me so hard with that soft smile. Like she was really glad to see me. Like she'd been looking forward to it.

Before I spoke, I reviewed all the reasons I didn't date. I even let that crapheap Gord's face shoot through my head, right after Tracy's barely regretful frown when she told me her big news. I renewed my policy to never be in that situation again. I reviewed my opportunity to learn from Sadie, which would only happen as her friend. I reminded myself how essential it would be to keep my hands to myself, so I slipped one into my pocket.

But that other disobedient hand reached out and set a palm on her shoulder. The stupid head that'd just made itself all kinds of promises leaned down, and those idiot lips kissed her soft, warm cheek like it was inevitable.

The truth? It was absolutely inevitable.

CHAPTER FOURTEEN

Sadie

Glasses clinked together behind me as someone toasted their champagne flutes while the band played classical renditions of popular songs like they'd snatched our event out of the warm Utah summer night and lopped us in the middle of a Bridgerton ball scene. Everyone wore cocktail dresses and suits, and we all looked fabulous.

Aidan Wallace's redesign of the park was gorgeous, and to put the whole thing over the top, Dahlia had created sprays of flowers that looked like something straight out of a fairytale. Paired with the bubbly champagne in my glass and the plan I had for the night, the whole event had a surreal feel to it.

And then, there was Warrick.

I'd felt him coming, an awareness between my shoulder blades and my stomach tightening the first clues, but I'd refused to let myself look directly at him. Seeing him dressed up in a suit and tie would be far too deadly, and seeing him with a date? Quite possibly fatal, but in a very different way.

And then he walked right up to me. Sarah and I had been talking, and she'd said hi to him with a slight widening of her eyes. Just after, the tips of his fingers brushed the bare skin at my shoulder, and he leaned down and pressed a kiss to my cheek.

"Evening."

"Evening," Sarah said, a laugh in her tone, while I managed, "Hi."

I'd have to do better than that if I wanted to convince him of my plan—the one I'd hatched after he'd so sweetly checked on me a few days ago. I hadn't imagined something like this, but Marguerite's call had me panicking, and Warrick had showed up days later like the answer to a problem. It only made sense to ask my new friend. But for now, I could take a moment to recover from the nerves of being here, seeing him, everything.

"You look fantastic," he said, his eyes still on mine.

I let my gaze slip and take him in, and sure enough, the sight of Warrick in a well-fitting suit proved just as hazardous as I'd imagined it'd be. It looked like a dark navy-blue color, almost black, and his pristine white shirt popped in crisp contrast. He had on wingtip black shoes, which reminded me he'd always had a little quirk to his style when we were younger, too.

"You do too," I finally said, my gaze stopping at his chin to avoid taxing my heart. It'd already been on high alert just getting ready for tonight, then actually showing up. Just when I'd started to relax and enjoy the gorgeous floral arrangements and the beauty of this little park, Warrick walked in and sent it for the hills.

"I'm just going to... go over there. I'll check back in a bit." Sarah slipped away, and though part of me registered I should feel awkward that she'd left us alone so obviously, another thought had occurred to me, and I knew I wouldn't be able to shake it. I had to ask.

"So, where's your date?" I asked, then quickly sipped my champagne. It was cool and refreshing, and a relief to have something to do with my hands and mouth.

His answering smile made my heart flip. "My lucky lady? Ah, she's over there."

He ducked his head and nodded to a group across the garden.

I braced inwardly and looked over, wondering who he'd chosen to bring. I hadn't thought about the jealousy factor until seconds ago when I realized he might not have a date who would want him chatting with me for much longer. But now that he'd arrived, he was the only person I wanted to talk to.

"Which one is she?" I asked, squinting to see better. Jane Saint, Nan Darling, Carol Wallace, and a few others stood in a small circle, laughing and toasting. I didn't see anyone young enough to be Warrick's date.

"You know my mom, right?" he asked, then tucked his hands into his pockets.

"Of course I know her, I—wait, you brought your mom?" I checked his face, and sure enough, he was smiling, but not joking. "Why?"

His gaze cast around the garden before settling back on me. His eyes gleamed that pure brown color again today. I'd never thought about one eye color being more appealing than another, but looking at his made me wonder if I could like someone without brown eyes. They lent a dashing kind of darkness to his kind, handsome face.

"Something like this would probably create expectations of a real date. More than friendship. I don't want to mess with anyone like that. I try to make sure I'm always clear, so... Mom it is."

I nodded, mind racing. Would my suggestion, that I hoped I'd work up to in the next hour, be problematic in the same way? Would he dislike the idea of dating, even as a fake relationship, because it'd leave him open to others thinking he would date? Because that was the big plan I'd come up with after Marguerite's call. I wanted to run my hand over my face, but my makeup looked perfect and I'd hate to smear it all around.

"Cocktail?" A waiter held up a tray of highball glasses, some rimmed with salt, others rimmed with what looked like red sugar.

I held up my champagne. "No, thank you."

Warrick smiled politely. "No thanks, Brodie, but great work tonight."

The waiter, apparently Brodie who I hadn't even recognized, and now that I looked at him, he was indeed the waiter at Guac the last time I'd been in. My cheeks flushed as I took the hit of not realizing who he was and that it came back to my tendency to live in my own world. Or more accurately, to block out anything not immediate and necessary.

"Do you know everyone in town?" I asked.

"Not *everyone*, I wouldn't say." His brow dipped into a little v.

"But most people."

He tilted his head to one side, then the other, and flashed a bright smile. "Probably."

My choice to stay locked away in the kitchen since I'd come back from New York had definitely created a challenge. Even if I recognized people from living here before college, unless I directly interacted with them for work, I didn't know them anymore. Add to that the influx of more people during the tourist seasons and Silverton's growth overall, I really didn't know everyone in my small town anymore.

But looking around tonight, I took solace that I did recognize quite a few faces. In fact, most of them if I let myself look closely. John and Aidan Wallace had stopped by to say hello earlier. Of course I knew Sarah and Dahlia, and Quinn would be around here somewhere. I'd heard the general hubbub when Calla and Wyatt had entered the garden from the East entrance a few minutes ago—two more people I'd consider myself on speaking terms with.

I knew people! Enough for them to greet me and not be entirely put off by my historical hermitude. It helped make the large group of people less overwhelming, and paired with the outdoor setting, allowed me to feel as close to normal in a public gathering as I'd probably ever felt.

And then, of course, I knew Warrick. He tugged at the lapel of his suit jacket and stretched his neck to one side. He looked ridiculously good in this suit.

"Ms. Miller."

A voice behind me drew my attention, and I turned to see—*Oh.*

The man thrust out a hand. "Julian Grenier."

"I remember you, of course. Nice to see you, Mr. Grenier." I took his hand, and the instant our skin touched, he briskly shook it with a firm grip, then dropped it.

"Grenier," Warrick said, stepping closer to my side.

What a severely good-looking man. Julian Grenier had

an almost hawkish way about him, like he might be able to see at night and catch his prey just as well as he could sit in a boardroom and make billion-dollar deals. Or whatever he did.

In all the ways Warrick was warm and big and welcoming, Grenier's energy was closed and tight and almost foreboding. Except that handshake, which had been direct, just like the man.

"Saint," Grenier said, his eyes narrowing ever so slightly when his eyes flicked up to Warrick, then back to me. "Ms. Miller, I—"

"Please, just call me Sadie."

He nodded. "Sadie, I have a proposition for you."

Warrick's warm, giant hand pressed into the silk over my lower back, then slid around and anchored at my hip. Zips of energy cartwheeled out from his touch. I glanced down at his hand, which only made my heart rate triple. His hand on me felt good, but *seeing* his hand on me made synapses skip.

"You're propositioning her? I thought your business tended to be above board, but I should've known you were an evil genius," Warrick said, his voice low and tinged with humor.

Grenier straightened, if such a thing were possible. He'd seen Warrick's hand slide into place around me, and he couldn't miss the way I was now pressed in against the large man's side.

"Of course not. I have something I need to discuss with her." He blinked at me, like he wanted to know what I thought and had no interest in Warrick.

"I—"

"Sorry, Grenier. My date's off the clock, and she's not available for meetings with other men tonight."

The man's face didn't change other than another blink, then a nearly imperceptible nod. "Of course. We'll talk another time."

"Okay," I said, trying not to vibrate out of my skin. I could tell I was shaking from the pure adrenaline jolting through my veins. Even so, I didn't twist around to stare at Warrick until Grenier had walked away, body language just as stiff as ever.

"I'm not available for meetings with other men tonight?" My voice rose a little, got that high, thin quality when I was wound up.

Warrick's hand dropped away.

"Sorry." He held up those big hands. "Sorry."

"What just happened?"

He glanced after Grenier, then back to me. "I don't like that guy."

"So you have to shut him down, and shut me out of what was probably a pretty good business opportunity?"

I didn't actually care. I wasn't mentally prepared to talk business, and I didn't want to be in a conversation with Julian Grenier when I could be in one with Warrick, but he didn't need to know that. We were talking principles here.

"I did have to shut him down, yes. And I highly doubt he wanted to talk to you about *business*." His tone cut the word into finely diced cubes.

"What else would it have been?" This man made no sense.

I searched his face, but the look he wore now was something fully incredulous, like I was missing something insanely obvious. Fed up, I threw up one hand. "What?"

"I know you're used to being in your own little world, but even you can see every untaken man with a pair of eyes has been watching you. Waiting for their turn with you.

Grenier's not the type to wait in line, so he's going to come take his turn when he wants it."

Take his turn? Wait in line...? The idea that more than one person was looking at me right now made my stomach hollow out and my throat dry up. I took a large gulp of champagne, then immediately regretted it as the bubbles burned my throat on the way down.

"Hey, whoa, I'm sorry." His hand came to my upper arm, and he dipped his head so our gazes connected. "I'm a jealous jerk and I shouldn't have said that. No one's staring at you. That was my idiot way of saying you're beautiful, and I think Grenier wanted to ask you out. I shouldn't have shut him down, and if you want me to go eat my words and tell him we're not here together, say the word. Just... forgive me. Please."

Concern stitched his brows together, and all his easy humor had fled. His words swirled through my mind, warmth and disbelief lapping at the banks of my frazzled brain. But through all of it, I saw the window and I wasn't about to lose it. So instead of telling him to go eat crow with Grenier, I turned into that big, warm body.

His hand still rested on my arm. I grabbed the material of his jacket on either side of his waist and looked up at him. His bewildered face gazed back at me.

"Don't tell Grenier we're not dating. In fact, don't tell anyone. Keep pretending we're together, and I'll forgive you."

CHAPTER FIFTEEN

Warrick

"Pretend we're together?"

My question came out far calmer than my insides were. I'd gotten all kinds of worked up, a two-liter of soda shaken mercilessly, when Grenier spoke to her.

He might pretend he had actual conversation to make, but what he wanted was Sadie's attention on him so he had an excuse to look at her and talk to her. It's what anyone with a beating, unattached heart would want.

"It's odd, I know. I just thought it might help me ease back in. I'm comfortable with you—I trust you." Her eyes flickered over my face.

What could she read there?

What was I even thinking? I'd hit the odd precipice of a ledge I hadn't seen coming. Seeing Grenier try to get her attention had shoved me dangerously close to the edge. Now she wanted... what?

"Sorry, what are you saying? I guess I'm thick—you know, good old footballer's helmet up here. I'm not getting it." I reached up to run a hand through my hair, then shook that off. I wished I had a drink—if I did, I'd slug it back and feel the burn down my throat just for the distraction.

"I'm suggesting we date. But like fake-date, just for practice. For *me* to practice."

Someone hit the mute button and my brain quit processing sound. It reminded me of standing up after being hit by the defense and knocked down hard enough you hit your head. There's a faraway ringing when you rise, a surreal quality to the air and a coppery taste in your mouth.

Practice.

I understood the purpose of practice. I'd done it in football all my life, and I did it now. But being someone's practice boyfriend knowingly? As though the whole idea of playing that role for Tracy hadn't gutted me?

A waiter passed by, and Sadie slipped her unfinished glass of champagne on his empty tray. Then she stepped closer to me, and I realized I hadn't answered her.

"You want to practice dating... with me?"

Damn, my mind was stuck in mud. It wasn't just that loathsome word either. Some primordial ooze got dumped in my head by her nearness and the thought of her walking away with Grenier. *Who even am I right now?*

I didn't get jealous. It wasn't my thing. If I did, I would've lost my ever-loving mind over Tracy's cheating with Gord. But I didn't. Yes, it'd pissed me off. But how could I be jealous when she'd chosen freely? Hurt, yes. Damn near destroyed for a while, if I was honest, but that came down to the whole idea of being a practice run. A practice run for years. But *jealous* hadn't been a part of it. If

I let myself get jealous of things I didn't have, I would've spent my life with a hulking green monster on my back. First target would've been Wyatt, for getting to spend time with our dad and actually knowing him. And that wasn't me.

I'd had to make the choice repeatedly, some times harder than others, but I always came back to this. I didn't want the kind of life where I spent it whining. No amount of complaining would bring my dad back, my career back, or change what'd happened with my cheating ex and former friend.

I didn't stand around wondering how to change my circumstances. When I was miserable after Tracy left and I lost what I thought would be my career, as soon as I was physically healed, I got to work. I started testing out what I might want to spend my time on. There'd been a lot of failed ventures—I'm looking at you, smoothie restaurant franchise. But eventually, I figured out some solid options.

Ultimately, I wanted a life of *doing*, not wishing.

So I wouldn't sit here and mentally whine about not understanding what the heck was happening with Sadie. Nope. And I wouldn't secretly complain that she'd said *practice*, like the thought of actually dating me was somehow ludicrous.

That did bother me. Way more than it should. Even so, I whipped out my Warrick Saint, Charming TM smile and dipped my head. "You want to date me, Miller?"

She blinked once, slowly. "I want to *fake*-date you. But only if it doesn't mess things up for you."

Ah, crap. This couldn't be a good idea. But this woman was too sincere and thoughtful to refuse, not that I was about to. I'd just been thinking about how much I wanted to spend time with her, then she stood framed by the archway looking like a dream. I might not have plans to marry, but I could fake-date Sadie Miller.

Based on several other dudes eying her occasionally, even now, she'd easily find a replacement. And probably not of the fake variety. My only chance of making sure our friendship lessons continued was this.

Yes, because those friendship lessons are the thing you really care about.

Curse the snarky internal monologue!

If I wanted a life of doing, then here it was. I could do this, instead of just wishing for an alternate reality where I got to be with Sadie and didn't have all the crap baggage of my history with Tracy *and* her. I could have her for a time, in some way a little more than friends, and I could escape unscathed because it would end, but I could see it coming. No need to rethink my position on marriage or be at risk of wanting too much because the lines were drawn from the beginning.

Fake. *Practice.*

"Why would it mess things up for me?" I finally asked.

"You brought your mom tonight to avoid people thinking you're available. I don't want to do something that'll make all the single women of Silverton flock to your door." One eyebrow raised and her lips turned up, just barely, at one side of her mouth.

Something in me wound tight at that move, that slight uptick of her lips and the brow arching in challenge.

"It's nothing. I don't care what—it's fine." Now I did run a hand through my hair. I swear I could feel my mom's eyes on me, likely shaking her head at my bad habit of messing up my hair while I wore a suit. "The single women of Silverton will survive somehow."

"Okay. Good." Her smile widened.

My stomach dipped. "Good."

I had no idea what any of this meant, but based on how things had been with Sadie so far, they meant exactly what she said they did. She wanted to practice dating, and she wanted to practice with me.

My chest got all twisty. *Maybe she'll want to practice holding hands. Kissing. More—*

"So how are we doing over here?" Calla asked, sliding up between us in a black dress and looking glamorous as usual and nudging my shoulder with hers. "Sadie, you look gorgeous."

"That she does. We're doing well. And you two? You ever get sick of dressing up in suits, Wy?" I asked my brother, who stood quietly at his girlfriend's side.

"I'll wear a suit any day if it means I get to be her date."

His eyes flickered over Calla with so much heat and adoration that I felt my own cheeks burn even after I looked away.

"I never imagined you'd be so sweet," Calla said, turning to my brother and stepping into his space just as he reached out and gripped her waist.

And that was it for me—I couldn't do the whole *stand by and watch them be in love* thing. I didn't begrudge them their feelings or fire, but I didn't have to get smoke inhalation either.

"Sadie, need another—anything? Anything at all?"

She laughed. "Yes. I've been needing one of those."

Calla and Wyatt didn't protest, and they likely didn't notice. I kept my eyes on the prize—a bar in the corner.

"I don't actually need anything," she said quietly, hands clasped in front of her.

And maybe it was the weird crush of longing that hit me after seeing Wyatt and Calla, or the leftovers from Grenier trying to get Sadie alone. Maybe it was her asking I fake-date her. Whatever the case, I reached down and plucked one of those hands twisted in her purse strap and laced our fingers together.

I did it casually, and the connection was instant and right. Her small, strong hand in mine felt like it should always be there. I briefly wondered how I'd been standing around without holding it all night.

Her hand squeezed mine, so I squeezed back. My pulse started drumming in my neck again, just like it had before Calla had interrupted. That change of topic had come at a good moment because I felt downright crazy tonight. On the verge of something—maybe that cliff again.

Sadie's hand tugged a little, then her second one joined in a move both thrilling and comforting. I stopped on one side of the pathway.

She took a big breath. "You can stop. I don't need anything."

Her eyes flicked over toward the bar, and it clicked that there were a lot more people over there. She hadn't seemed all that nervous tonight, but maybe she'd drawn to the edges of the party to keep away from the most stressful space.

I couldn't read the look on her face—concern? Amusement? Both with a healthy dose of confusion and anxiety? I needed to spend more time looking at her face, to learn every version of her.

"I just wanted to give them space."

"I figured."

I nodded, suddenly nervous about leaving Wyatt and Calla. Nervous to hold her hand. Nervous to stand by her. "Actually, I could use some water."

"Let's get some, then."

"I can get some and bring it back to you, if you want." I

didn't want her to feel pressured to join the crowd. She'd done an amazing thing just by showing up tonight.

"I can go too. Just… don't let go."

Something was *wrong* with me tonight. Like I'd gone out into the sun to find the ozone missing and just burned right up. Because that soft request to keep hold of her felt like an arrow right to my heart. No need to pierce any armor there, or skirt around the usual padding I put in place to keep possible pain out. Around Sadie, it seemed to be missing, and so did my ability to not be charmed by every damn thing she said.

"I won't," I said, and then into the fray we went.

I wondered if she regretted telling me not to let go of her hand, because our public display of togetherness drew eyes. Nothing crazy, just eyebrows raised or nods, and satisfyingly, Julian Grenier's scowl. Though he was always sort of scowling, so that likely wasn't related to our handholding. Impossible to know, really.

"You sure you want to do this?" I asked quietly, not sure if I meant the handholding or pretending to be together, or just coming closer to the crowd.

Her eyes met mine after we each took fresh glasses of iced water from the bartender.

"I'm rarely sure about anything dealing with other people, but yes. I mean, we're already doing it, so…"

"Fair enough, Miller. Table?" I gestured to a lone high-top bistro table decorated with a tall vase full of tiny wild roses in every shade of pink.

Regretfully, we broke the connection between us. It'd be weird to stand at a table and hold hands, right? Yeah, no, it would be. Instead, we stood close but not touching, each drinking down our waters like we'd gone a full day without hydration.

"If we were actually dating, what would you call me? Not *Miller*, I hope." She leaned an elbow on the table and stood facing me, a light in her eye I had only seen once or twice before.

My heart kicked at the expression, the joking tone in her voice, and from simply looking at her. Now that she was facing me, talking directly to me again, I couldn't keep my eyes from slipping over her and admiring the fit of the dress.

"Uh, no. Probably wouldn't call you Miller."

"I could see me calling you Saint. You are pretty saintly," she said, tipping her head up like she was thinking of something better.

"I am? How so?" Call me a beggar, I didn't care. I wanted to hear what she thought of me. She'd fed the beast with that little list on her phone, and if I could get more words from her, more of her good opinion spelled out, I would.

"You're friends with everyone. You give back to the community—don't pretend you don't. And you take on charity cases." Her lashes fluttered before she met my eyes again.

It was the little drop in her brow after she said it that made me realize this was... something. Maybe not her outright asking if I was viewing her as a project, but just checking in, especially in the wake of our recent conversations, which I still didn't understand.

I faced her and stepped into her space like I would if—well, if we were anything more than friends. If I had a right to be this close to her. Our bodies only about eight inches apart, I stroked her bare arm from shoulder to elbow, then held her gently but firmly just above the joint.

"First, I'm not friends with everyone—just ask Julian Grenier. Second, I deny your accusation. And third... you are not a charity case, Sadie. You're my new friend, who I'm very glad to have. You're beautiful. And I don't totally know what you're wanting with all this, but we'll figure it out. And for the rest of the night, I'll do whatever I can so you have a good time."

She swallowed, then cleared her throat. "Okay."

So we did. We stayed on the fringes most of the time, but different groups wandered by, chatting easily with me and happily acknowledging Sadie, who often moved closer to me at certain times. I couldn't tell for sure, but I thought maybe those moments were the times she got overwhelmed.

Mostly, everyone moved through the time in their own surreal worlds just like we did. The live auction featured outrageous offerings from all over the state—a weekend stay at the fancy spa east of the ranch that'd grown more popular and drawn celebrity interest, fine dining tours of the state by helicopter, a songwriting workshop from Jamie Morris.

I didn't have anything that extravagant up for offer, but I did have a few memberships and personal training packages in the silent auction. I even noticed Sadie had a package of a loaf per month that had bids in the thousands. Apparently, everyone wanted to support the local ecology and the park, and they wanted to do it by eating their choice of Sadie's bread.

When the evening started to drag into night and my shoulder started aching, I noticed Sadie droop a bit before she straightened her spine like she'd shoved a steel rod into it.

"Ready to go?" I asked, unsure what might happen now. Mom had abandoned me for her girlfriends, and one of them had driven her home. She'd told me to drop her car at her house in the morning.

"Yes. But you don't have to leave if you don't want to.

Let me find Sarah and see if she's ready." She moved toward Sarah, who chatted with Dahlia, Calla, Quinn, and Quinn's mom, but I caught her hand with mine before she got more than a step or two away.

"Tell her I'll walk you home."

CHAPTER SIXTEEN

Sadie

The June sky sparkled with giant stars so close, it felt like I could reach up and grab one. It fit with the surreal glow of the whole evening.

Warrick walked beside me, his hands in his pockets. We'd left holding hands, back out the ivy and flower archway, and into the surprisingly brisk night. The heat had burned away as the June sun inched down, and no more than fifty feet down the path back toward Main Street, I shivered. In seconds, Warrick dropped my hand, shucked his jacket, and tucked it around my shoulders.

His radiant heat engulfed me, as did the crisp scent of his cologne and soap. The material was surprisingly light, but considering he was genuinely a giant person, it utterly swamped me.

"Tad big, but I figure your little dress isn't going to insulate you very well." He tugged at the sides of the jacket until they met at my neck.

"Thank you," I said, and gripped the lining from the inside, trying not to inhale too obviously.

We walked along together quietly. I missed holding his hand, but now that we weren't at the party, were no longer pretending, it didn't make sense. He'd agreed to pretend, but I knew he wanted to understand what I meant. *I* needed to understand. More than anything, I needed to feel like I could go to Marguerite's engagement and act like a human. Keep my anxiety under control.

I'd done that tonight, and it'd gone so much better than I ever dreamed. I'd thought I'd stay an hour and walk myself home in time to binge Netflix and turn in early. But now, hours later than I'd imagined, I walked side by side with Warrick. We crossed over to Main Street and I realized how long it'd been since I'd been out this late at night. I couldn't remember the last time I'd seen the darkness of night in summer as opposed to the dawn.

"This is so strange. I'm never up this late. Feels like a different world."

Twinkle lights twisted up the light poles and branched into trees. I knew they did this in winter, but it'd never occurred to me they turned them on in summer too.

I really need to get out more.

"That's probably a sign you need to get out more."

I laughed. "I had that exact thought."

"Glad we agree."

We followed the small footpath around the back of the row of buildings on my side, the only sounds our footsteps on the cement, then the light *pat* of my toes and the *thunk* of his feet on the stairs leading to my apartment door. I didn't say anything, nor did he. My stomach tightened, like something might happen at this doorstep. Like him walking me to this point meant something it didn't.

It couldn't.

Key in hand, I turned to him right at the door. "Thanks for walking me. And for being a good pseudo-date tonight. I hope your mom wasn't bothered I stole you away."

"She would've abandoned me either way. I'm glad you kept me company."

His smile seemed genuine but tired. I had no doubt I looked similarly haggard. More of my hair had escaped the fancy twist I'd coaxed it into hours ago, and I probably had raccoon eyes from the mascara I'd layered on a little thicker than usual.

"Well, here," I said, shrugging out of his jacket. "Thanks."

He took it and draped it over his forearm. "Of course. You working tomorrow morning?"

Some of the nerves I'd kept wrapped tight burst through their restraints, and my pulse raced. "Actually, no. Well, not officially. My two assistants are taking over—doing it without me for the first time. I figured it'd be a slow morning since ninety percent of the town is out late. Plus, Sunday mornings are slow anyway."

"That's great. Good for you."

His broad smile soothed a little of those ruffled edges in me.

"Thanks. I feel like I might cry or throw up if I think about it too much, so I'm hoping I'll just go inside and pass out."

His expression softened and without warning, he leaned over and wrapped those muscular arms around me. My body knew what to do even if my brain had stuttered at the feeling of his hands on the skin of my back, partly over the dress and partly connecting with me. My actual skin. It felt so, so good.

"They'll do great. You trained them, and I know you wouldn't let them do it if they weren't ready. Let yourself relax. Sleep in. Rest."

My palms pressed flat against his back, and because there was nowhere else for it to go, my head rested on his chest. The pressure of his hug felt like a weighted blanket after a long day—after a day like this. But better, because he was deliciously warm and firm and again, he smelled so dang good.

"I'll try," I said, and pulled back enough to look up at his face. "But what about you?"

"Me?" he asked and dipped his face down toward mine.

"Will you rest, too?"

He swallowed and exhaled a slow breath through his nose, his face so serious. At this range, just inches apart, I saw the lines around his eyes, the darkness underneath them more clear than ever. His hands flexed on my back but didn't move, and I resisted the urge to arch closer to him, to bring our bodies near enough to touch. *That is not an option here, lady.*

"I'll try," he said, his voice low and rough.

An achy sweetness poured into my belly, like someone had dumped pure cane sugar out to measure on a scale hidden there. I rose to my toes and pressed a kiss to his bearded cheek. "Good. Then I'll see you Monday."

He released me, and I slipped inside my door. We hadn't talked about the fake-dating or really anything. We'd gone from friends who'd hugged once to people who'd kind of sort of pretended they were dating by holding hands in public and standing near each other.

We'd need to talk about all of it—that I wanted to go out

with him, to practice how to behave in a crowd at a restaurant where I couldn't stand at the edge and avoid some of the things that sent my heart racing. And eventually, I'd need to get up the guts to tell him the full truth—that I wanted him to be the one I took to the engagement party.

Warrick slipped into the booth across from me at the diner three days later. His hair stood up in short spikes like he'd just run his hand through it after a shower, and he had one of those mind-numbing smiles on his face. The kind I never used to get. But he gave them to me these days, now that we were friends.

"How has the day gone? How did Sunday go?" He snatched a menu from where they'd been slotted between the ketchup and salt and pepper shakers but flattened it on the table and gave me the full weight of his attention instead of reading it.

"Today has been good. And Sunday went well, overall. A few hiccups, but they're doing it again next weekend, and if that goes well, they're going to try for a weekday the following week."

A trill of anxious anticipation shot through me. Though I'd tossed and turned Saturday night, when I did fall asleep, I didn't wake up until six. I'd made myself stay in my apartment and not go downstairs to check until nine. Overall, a triumph.

"That's awesome. Congrats."

Huge smile on his face all for me, he held up one of those big hands. My stomach flipped and I couldn't hold in the odd little chuckle that snuck out as I clapped my hand to his for the high five. "Thanks."

My palm tingled with the sting of the contact, but we hadn't hit hands that hard. More than anything, it felt like an accomplishment to receive one of those high fives. Like it signaled that we were truly friends now, and I'd summited a small mountain.

"Did you take Sunday off?" I asked, wondering how long it would take until my hand stopped buzzing from the small accomplishment.

A sheepish look crossed his face. "Uh, kind of?"

"Is that a question?"

He dropped his chin. "I stayed in bed until seven. But after that I had nothing to do, so I went in to my office, and then did my afternoon class. I don't have anyone else to teach the classes yet, and I hate the thought of my people missing out because I was lazy."

His bear paw of a hand splayed across the table, and I reached for it, laying mine over his. "You know you don't have to apologize for working hard, right?"

His brow dipped like he didn't believe me.

"I fully understand working too much. I also understand having your own business and not enough bandwidth to even find appropriate help. But let me encourage you, as someone who has had one entire morning off, that it's worth it."

He flipped his hand over so our palms touched, this time in that stomach-twisting, intimate way they had on and off Saturday night. What was it about our palms touching? Maybe because I worked with my hands, the contact felt particularly important. Or maybe the fact that I hadn't touched someone regularly in any capacity—friendly or romantic—in years.

Whatever the case, this odd hand hold we shared felt like a connection far beyond two people sitting at a candy apple red booth chatting about work. It felt important.

"Thanks. I guess you definitely do understand."

I nodded. "I do. But I'd also strongly suggest you not take notes from me."

He scowled then, an expression so foreign to his face, my own smile dropped.

"Don't say that. You've done amazing things with Rise and Shine. I'd be lucky to have the kind of success you do with anything I do. Did you see what your items at the auction went for?"

I flushed with pleasure. "I did. People were really generous."

He squeezed my hand, then released it to sit back and pick up his menu. "And you make great bread."

I caught his eye. "I do. I'm not saying I don't. But anyone could walk in and buy a loaf of bread for less than ten dollars a month—way less. People bidding thousands of dollars for twelve loaves?"

His gaze sharpened. "You should do a subscription thing. You could run it out of the big kitchen. Everyone gets a certain loaf each month and they pick it up on a certain day. That'd be awesome. The subscription thing is huge right now."

I gripped the sides of my own menu. "I love that."

Catherine swung by and took our orders while we talked through some of the logistics of the idea. Time flew, and soon, she delivered our food—a giant grilled chicken salad for Warrick and a turkey club with avocado for me. We both attacked our meals with gusto, though he seemed to downright inhale his in between asking questions or tossing out ideas for the currently titled Loaf a Month Club.

It was nearly the end of our meal when I realized I hadn't broached the subject of dating, but in true Warrick form, as he held the door for me, he snuck in that directness I'd grown to appreciate.

"So are we going to talk about the dating thing? Can you clue me in here?"

My cheeks warmed, even though I'd convinced myself there was nothing to be embarrassed about. He didn't need to know I had a crush on him—dating was all in the same zone we'd been in with the friendship project, just a different level. I stepped to the side of the walkway into the diner so we wouldn't be blocking anyone, though Tuesday at twenty after five wasn't exactly prime dinner time for most people.

"Yes. Sorry. I'm not trying to avoid it—okay, maybe I have been a little. Basically, I need to practice dating."

He blinked and a beat passed. "Why?"

A laugh tumbled out. "Well, eventually I'd like to get married, maybe have kids, so there's one reason. But more immediately, I need a date for my sister's engagement party, and I need it to feel comfortable. I figure that's not going to happen without some effort, so I want to start now."

He folded his arms and settled into a wide-legged stance. "So you want me to pretend to date you so that you can then find someone else to take to your sister's engagement party?"

The warm evening seemed suddenly stifling, and my response came out as a question. "Yes?"

He glanced up to watch a red-tailed hawk sail by, that iconic screech making me feel the height of summer all the more.

"Why don't I take you to your sister's thing?" he said

after a moment, his gaze only dropping to mine at the very end.

My heart kicked. *Yes.* Obviously, I wanted that. But I'd planned to ease him into the idea. "Um…"

He stepped toward me, that towering frame casting a shadow over me. "Seriously. When is it?"

"Third week of July." My voice sounded weird. Could he hear it? Probably. *Ugh.*

"I'm probably free—generally am. *Where* is it?"

My heart was a springing mess. Was he serious? "Are you serious? You'd agree to that?"

"Take you to some fancy party and pretend to be your date? Yeah. Or am I missing some big piece of this puzzle?" He dropped his hands and waited.

I pulled in a deep breath and exhaled slowly. Thinking about the engagement party made my anxiety hike up its pants and wade into the puddle of my brain with nothing to stop it. Having Warrick drop his willingness to go with me should've been a welcomed thing, but he didn't understand the problem. And though we'd been honest in our new friendship thus far, I didn't know if this might be *too* much.

Saying something like, "*I'll be using you to shut my parents up about finding someone to marry*" just didn't feel right. Not *yet*, anyway.

"Lay it on me, Miller." He slipped a hand into a pocket.

"There's nothing big. It's—I'm just—I'm really nervous about it. And I'll probably be kind of a mess, but also, I'm going to try to keep it together because I know it'll stress my family if I'm not *normal*. So if you're up for that—for me being… just me, I guess, then yes. I would absolutely love for you to be the person with me."

Just saying it out loud made ten layers of dread slough off.

His dark eyes bore into me for probably thirty seconds, though that was long enough to leave a mark. By the time he nodded quickly and repeatedly, like he was agreeing with something someone had said aloud, I'd broken out in a full-on sweat. Only half of that had to do with the summer temps.

Then he grabbed my hand, laced my fingers with his, and pulled me into walking next to him as he said, "I'm definitely doing it. And we're definitely going to practice first."

CHAPTER SEVENTEEN

Warrick

Three days later, I knocked on Sadie's door for our first unofficial date.

I couldn't explain why I kept mentally qualifying it as *unofficial,* but I did. Because we weren't actually dating. We were preparing for a bigger event—the engagement party. And though I didn't particularly look forward to hobnobbing with a bunch of snobs, I knew not all rich people were jerks.

The Millers? Yeah, what I remembered of them the few times I'd seen them in Silverton back in the day was mostly that. They kept themselves apart from the city, and their home was actually quite far—but not because they farmed or had cattle like we and many others did. Simply because they needed the space for their mansion.

By the time high school rolled around for Sadie, they typically resided at their house in Salt Lake. Her sister had opted for boarding school, while she had begged to stay at Silverton High.

Her grandmother's boyfriend had been at Silverton Springs, and she was close to him. So, they let her stay there at their giant house forty-five minutes from school. She had a driver deliver and pick her up every day. It created a mystique around her that didn't make much sense considering everyone knew all too well who she was.

Yet the knowledge of that history told me one thing—I was unlikely to get along with the Millers. So there was that—that knowledge that meeting her parents would be awkward and I'd have to go full-on *Warrick Saint, charmer* mode, but I could do it. I could do it for Sadie.

Damn, the way her voice had quaked when she'd explained she'd be nervous for it, like she didn't want to have to say it to me, but she needed me to know. And I appreciated understanding it was a big deal to her—it helped put in perspective why she'd want to practice. I'd balked at the word because for me, it had thorns. But for her, it simply meant she needed my help. And help, I could offer.

If that help happened to offer *me* the chance to be around her, touch her, maybe eventually be closer to her, well? I am but a flawed, selfish man.

So here I was, knocking on her door for our first of two practice dates we'd put on the calendar leading up to the actual event.

We'd keep it simple—just dinner at Basta and maybe walk along the Riverwalk if we felt like it. Because the other thing we'd need to nail down was why she needed her parents to believe she had a boyfriend. I mean, practicing going on a date when we'd already hung out a handful of times and were comfortable was completely unnecessary. Her need to practice told me one thing: she needed them to believe it was real. Not just a one-time thing, but something enduring.

And while I didn't mind playing any part she wanted me to, I wondered if buried under all this, that was the puzzle piece I was missing. Not pretending with Sadie, but being with her. Someone to care for and look after. Someone who was mine and I was hers—who I had the right to check on and be concerned for.

Whether I had the right or not, here I was. I knocked again, impatient to see her after a few days of only glimpsing her through the glass that separated us each afternoon. When the door swept open, I inhaled at the sight of her.

Crap. Why was I doing this to myself again?

Because you're her friend and you're helping her.

Oh, but *damn*, she looked good. So good, just like at the bloom thing the other night. Just like anytime I saw her, but tonight, she'd dressed up for *me*. Specifically for me, and that made my stomach curve in on itself, all the muscles tightening.

"Hey, sorry. I was wrestling with my—you know what? Never mind. Hi. Thanks for coming." She said all this as she locked her door, then turned around and walked right into me.

Just pressed in, arms coming around me so fast, she nearly pinned mine at my sides until my brain jolted to life and I reached for her and wrapped my arms around her back. She had on a white swishy skirt and a silky tank-toppy light blue shirt... I had no names for these things, but she looked good. The fabric, not unlike everything else she'd worn that I'd ever touched, was soft, and I fought the urge to drag my hands down her back to feel it under the pads of my fingertips.

"Hi. You look great," I said belatedly, relishing her newfound tendency to hug me. Ever since the night of the garden thing, she'd done this when we said goodbye. I didn't know why, and I wasn't about to ask on the off chance that made it stop.

"You do too," she said as she pulled away.

Her eyes slipped over me, and *guh*. That might've been more affecting than the hug. Actually no, her hugs had become the best part of my day whenever I got them. She wasn't limp or little in a hug. Despite her tiny stature, she gave big hugs—full hold, good pressure, and she always did this thing where she held on to the material of my shirt at my back.

I may have become mildly obsessed with the hugs. This was number four in the history of our relationship, and I didn't think I'd ever stop counting.

I cleared my throat and knocked my head toward the stairs. "Shall we?"

She smiled, looking completely relaxed and happy to be with me. That alone pulled a gauzy scrim over the evening.

I followed her down the stairs, catching her light lemon scent and feeling like I'd just won a playoff game. We walked side by side, two of her steps to every one of mine, and in just a minute, arrived at Basta's door.

I loved living in Silverton, but the commute to the restaurant tonight hadn't given me time to put myself in order. Seeing her in that outfit, her seeming *lack* of nerves, all of it twisted me up, made me feel like I'd fallen through a hammock and couldn't extricate my limbs.

Another minute or two and Lizzie had us seated at a window seat overlooking the outdoor patio. They'd closed it for a private event later tonight, or I would've requested we sit back there.

I did my best to focus on the menu, but my eyes kept inching their way back to her—a face so lovely it made my stomach clutch. Her hair was pulled halfway up tonight, out of her face but hanging down in the back. It softened her appearance somehow, or maybe made it seem unique in that I only ever saw her hair out of a bun in social situations. It was almost like we were in some kind of period piece that made her taking her hair down particularly intimate.

And sure, yeah, that was all a little dramatic. We weren't in a movie and we weren't intimate.

You wish, sucker.

I inhaled a deep breath and let it out, skimming the entrees.

"What's going on over there?"

I flattened the menu on the table and wondered whether she could read every thought on my face. She always seemed to ask me what I was thinking when I'd just had an incriminating thought.

"Just thinking how good you look," I said, abandoning the initial plan to pretend I couldn't decide what I wanted or crack a joke to distract like I might normally do with someone else.

Thing was, I could always decide what I wanted. I was a decisive guy, for one, and I also generally found several options in any given scenario acceptable. I could be satisfied with any number of outcomes, whether it be selecting from a menu or something more involved like business negotiations.

So pretending I couldn't decide what to eat would be a flat-out lie. While I didn't plan to be completely honest about just how attractive I thought Sadie was, how long I'd wanted to get close to her, how much she'd flattened me back in high school, I could be that honest. Because she was beautiful, and I wanted her to know it.

"Thank you. You look good too." The apples of her cheeks brightened as a ridiculously pretty flush swept over her.

"Thank you. Didn't want to show up and have you wish you'd asked someone else to be your fake date," I said, eyebrows pinched in exaggerated worry.

She shook her head, but a smile tugged at lips that— *nope, don't look at her lips*. Yeah, but they were this berry color or something that I just knew would be downright edible.

"I would never think that."

I glanced at her again, blurring my eyes just slightly so I wouldn't snag on any of the glorious details of her face that'd apparently become so alluring to me I couldn't think straight tonight. And what I saw there? Complete truth. She wouldn't think that, whether I dragged up to her doorstep in sweatpants and a torn T-shirt or in my current jeans and collared shirt.

How had I thought she was arrogant and classist before? She was warm and kind, and I couldn't imagine that'd all come in the last ten years. That'd been there, buried under all her anxieties and *I'd* been the problem. I'd been the fool who'd taken her refusal to speak to me as her judging me or thinking herself better than me. I had never accounted for the fact that she might've been tongue-tied or scared. It didn't explain the laugh in my face when I'd asked her out, and I didn't want to hope it'd just been nerves, though I'd wondered plenty since we'd started up this little friendship. Right now wasn't the time to drag up that old sleeping dog, but I did need to address it.

And in this quiet moment, sitting across from her, a candle flickering low on the table between us and menus in our hands, I *had* to talk to her about that. Initially, I'd decided to ignore the past. Look at *now* and enjoy the process. That line of thinking kept me from a lot of heartache and regret, so why not employ it here?

The more time we spent, the more I realized that I'd wronged her. She'd never done anything to me, not really, and that realization made my shirt feel too small.

"Sadie, I—"

"Okay folks, have we decided?" Josh, the waiter, arrived at that moment, of course.

Her eyes found mine, and I nodded for her to go first. She ordered, and then I did, and Josh left us again.

"Were you saying something? Before he came?" she asked.

Anxious energy shot through me, and I shifted in my seat. "Yeah. Uh, so I need to apologize to you."

One brow raised in question, but the rest of her stayed still. Not stiff, exactly, but braced in her seat. And that posture had me realizing I'd missed that she was nervous. Her easy smile had fooled me. She wasn't anxious like she had been at the garden the other night, but she wasn't completely calm.

Of course she's not, idiot!

I sighed inwardly. "Well, first I need to say I'm sorry for not finding us a more tucked-away table. I didn't even think about how being at this table would be a little much."

"Don't apologize for that. That's part of what we're doing here."

A flicker of something I couldn't identify crossed her face, but I believed her. That calmed some of the worry in me, but that wasn't the crux of my concern.

"Okay, good. But the other thing is, we need to talk about high school."

The face she made said just how much she didn't agree. "Why would we do that?"

Embarrassment crawled up my neck. "I, uh... I had a one-sided thing for you back then, and I thought you kind of just ignored me, or even rejected me. But getting to know you lately has made me realize that more than you hurting my feelings and not returning my interest was my failure to see you. To really understand that you were hurting and dealing with anxiety, and I didn't do anything to make things *better* for you."

Her mouth had opened by degrees. "You—you couldn't have known that. I didn't walk around publicizing it, and I probably would've been too sensitive to tolerate being asked about it."

I let out a breath, not absolved, but she'd thrown water on the embers in my chest. "Still. I was thinking about myself and... that probably shaded things for the last few years."

Not that I'd treated her in a less friendly way because I still had a crush on her, current hungry eyes notwithstanding, but I'd just gotten the bad taste of what I thought was her superior attitude in my mouth and never even attempted to get it out.

And yeah. Some of it may have been a little bit of self-protection. Like if I believed it was all her being a jerk, I could shove away how much I'd liked her. I could pretend the person I'd thought I'd liked wasn't even real, and that it had nothing to do with me not being enough for her.

"I appreciate you saying that. Still, though. I'm sorry." And I couldn't help but wonder what might've happened if

I'd gotten over myself. Not gotten so upset when she wouldn't talk to me.

"You're forgiven, not that you need to be."

Bright golden warmth washed over me. "Thank you."

The waiter arrived with bread and butter, and when he disappeared, her blue gaze hit me with purpose. My stomach dropped low and my pulse ticked higher because I could feel it coming, even before she said the words.

She tipped her head to the side, a soft look on her face, and said, "Now, can we talk about the one-sided thing you mentioned?"

CHAPTER EIGHTEEN

Sadie

Warrick shifted in his chair, obviously uncomfortable. That was novel since he always seemed so at home. In his body, in a room, on the street—he seemed settled down into who he was so sturdily, it was hard to believe he could be made to feel anything else.

And yet, here he was, dusky slashes of blush across his cheeks, squirming.

"Sure."

I pressed my lips together to hold off a giant smile. It didn't matter if I was thirty or nearing eighty, hearing Warrick Saint had a crush on me in high school would give me no small amount of pleasure. It felt like he'd turned the key on a butterfly exhibit in my chest, and now they all fluttered loose.

"You said I hurt your feelings. Rejected you."

We'd need to start there. My memories of Warrick were

so particular and so vivid, I couldn't imagine what I'd done. I remembered him talking to me once or twice, and I didn't remember ever managing to respond.

He'd had that easy, larger-than-life air about him. I could hardly conjure a scenario where gregarious, popular, friends-with-everyone Warrick Saint had his feelings hurt by awkward, painfully shy, alienated Sadie Miller.

He cleared his throat. "I mean, I—yeah. I thought you did. I guess the reality is, I let my feelings get hurt."

"Can you tell me when?"

He shifted in his seat. "One day after school, I saw you hanging out waiting for your ride. Everyone else had cleared out, so I thought it'd be a good chance. I said hey, and you acknowledged me, and then I asked you out."

I blinked. "There's no way that happened and I didn't remember it."

He chuckled, but it wasn't the sweet, happy sound I was used to from him, and his cheeks turned red. "I definitely thought you did. You stared at me, then laughed, and then bolted past me and slid into your ride which had pulled up without my realizing it. I totally thought—"

"I'm not sure what happened on my end, but I'm sorry. I'm guessing I was thrown by David running late and all twisted up about that—I used to get anxious about not having any way to get home. And then you even talking to me probably sent me into a mind blank or something because you were so popular and way out of my league. I hope you know I thought you were amazing, even back then. I wouldn't have wanted to hurt you. But I wasn't in a healthy place at that age—I hadn't figured out what I could bring to a friendship." I laughed at that. "Honestly, I'm still working that out now. Slow learner."

His brow dipped low. "My point is, I shouldn't have

been thinking about myself. I should've been wondering about you."

Gah, this man. He was too sweet. And evidently determined to punish himself for being human. I knew for a fact I hadn't heard him ask me out because, while I likely wouldn't have been able to speak, I wouldn't have laughed or run away. If I'd truly registered it, I would've been more likely to faint in a fit of disbelief and glee. "You were a kid. So was I."

He frowned, and though I shouldn't have, I let a laugh escape. I shouldn't have felt so completely pleased knowing he'd asked me out, but I did. I hated I'd hurt him, but I hoped he believed I hadn't meant to.

His frown deepened. I leaned across the table and pressed a hand over his, where it rested by his empty bread plate.

"Please stop feeling bad. I'm sorry I hurt you, even if I didn't know I'd done it. I had no idea you were thinking about this, and I'm glad you mentioned it. It's in the past. And I'm so glad we're friends now. Truly."

His face relaxed, and I retreated to my side of the table. Josh refilled our water glasses and assured us the food would be out momentarily. Quiet settled between us, and I marveled at how comfortable it felt. Though I was keenly aware of the fact that we were sitting at a small table in what was essentially the center of the Basta dining room except for its being near the window, I didn't feel that itchy, anxious energy I sometimes did when I had to be out in the midst of people.

That didn't shock me, since I'd been to the diner with him days ago, and the celebration the other evening, but still. It was like a sticky dough had developed enough to knead—no longer a mess, but a smooth, pleasing texture instead of that mucky, finger-coating problem that came from jumping in before the rise completed.

Dinner arrived, and we both happily set into our meals: his a large vegetable and meat thing, and mine a heaping pile of penne arrabbiata—spicy enough to make my tongue burn for a while after I ate each bite, which I loved.

"So, can we talk about this, all cards on the table?"

His question came after light conversation, a check in about the Loaf of the Month Club planning—the name was still up for debate—and his update on his current StayBnB project. Despite the seemingly random question, I instinctively knew what he meant.

"I guess we should, huh?" My heart pattered away in my chest, but this was good. This needed to happen.

"So I get practicing all this—just the ritual of the thing. Especially where you haven't felt super comfortable with being out and about in the past. But it feels like there's more to it. Like there's a lot of weight on this engagement party and showing up with a date isn't all you need to do. I don't know, I might be wrong. And I know I'm a highly eligible bachelor, so I am not saying you haven't chosen well, I just..." He added a crooked smile that softened what would've been a bit arrogant, even if accurate. But typical Warrick, he didn't bluster. He flashed those pretty teeth and made my heart flip.

"You're not wrong." I took a fortifying sip of water and wished it was wine. Something stronger to give me courage, though I never drank more than a few sips, so that didn't make much sense. *Just tell him. Just tell him!* I steadied myself with a slow exhale, then launched in.

"I think I've mentioned that my parents don't really like to acknowledge my anxiety."

He nodded, face solemn and strikingly handsome.

"As I've gotten older, they seem to have become comfortable with admitting I have something going on, at least in some sense, because they often make comments about me just needing to find the right person. I think to them, they see all my problems being solved if I meet a sturdy, rich man who can support me. And that'll work out well for them, because they'll gain a son and won't have to worry, even the little that they maybe do, about me."

His face clouded over, and if Warrick Saint had ever looked thunderous, it was now. "That is utter bull. You don't need anyone else—you've proven that in spades!"

His defense of me felt like a hug, which I wanted to savor, but I had to clarify this too. "I do need people, though. That's part of what this whole thing is about—everyone is built for community. I believe that, and I'm trying to change the way I live to embrace that more openly. It doesn't mean I want to be you and have everyone say hi to me anytime I step out on the street, but I don't want to lock myself away. I want friends to call when I'm sick. I want a partner to share my life with."

I'd said all this before, to my therapist and myself, but sharing it with him left me feeling like the shower door had swung open midrinse. I was fully exposed, and the draft felt downright skin-prickingly chilly.

"I love that you're doing that. But their thinking is antiquated, at best."

"Oh, trust me. I know this. *Logically*, I know this. But with Marguerite getting married, they seem to be concerned I'll be left in the dust to fend for my sad little self. Though they refuse to admit it, they know what happened in New York—at least that she came to get me. If she's married—in their minds, I guess—then her focus is elsewhere. And that's probably going to be true—should be true."

He grabbed his water, shot it down his throat, then nearly slammed the glass on the table. Warrick was an incredibly deft person when it came to his exercises, and even the orderliness of the spaces he occupied that I'd seen, but it was almost like once he left the gym, all that athleticism needed an outlet and it came out in clunky movements and a kind of endearing indelicacy.

When he didn't speak, I pressed on. "At some point, I need to sit them down and try to get through. Or, try again. But last time was so exhausting, and honestly, it set me back. So I thought that if I go to this thing with someone who's sturdy and admirable, who I seem safe with, maybe they'll stop pressing on those bruises and start accepting me."

And speaking of those aching places, they doubled inside and seemed to burn, begging for attention like an open wound. But they weren't open anymore. They weren't still hurting so brutally, and I wouldn't allow myself to sink into the drowning feeling that came with thoughts of how little my parents thought of me.

Warrick leaned both forearms on the table and clasped his hands. This didn't look natural at all, but based on the tightness in his shoulders and around his eyes, he was containing himself in some way.

When he spoke, his voice was low and just a little gruff, which made it all the more gripping. "I'll do whatever you want. *Whatever* you want, Sadie. Take me to the party, use me to make your point—however you want it to play out. If that's something I can do for you, then consider me your boyfriend until this thing is over."

Oh. *Wow*. The vehemence in that voice made me want to crawl under a blanket and shut my eyes so I could more fully absorb it. That, or climb into his lap and press close against him. Breathe in the scent where his neck joined to his shoulder, just inside the collar of his shirt.

Josh came by and brought the check, slicing through the intensity that had snapped between us with Warrick's words and my spiral into longing to be closer to him. To physically absorb those words.

He walked me home, all the way to my door. He let me hug him again and returned the gesture with what felt like feeling. And then I went inside, and after about twenty seconds, I heard his footsteps as he plodded down the stairs.

Pulling a heavy blanket over me, I lay curled on my couch and waited for my heart to slow its beat. Who needed cardio when you had Warrick Saint's surprising intensity staring you in the face? And his smiles? And his giant hands that felt so good whenever he touched mine?

I crushed my eyes closed and asked myself the question I'd been avoiding. Was his agreement to this—the full extent of it—the best thing that'd happened to me lately? Or had I just set myself up for even bigger problems?

CHAPTER NINETEEN

Warrick

S adie looked rough. Like, rough enough that I couldn't stop worrying about her since I'd seen her walking over to the big kitchen earlier today and almost let a guy drop a barbell on his chest kind of rough.

The second my training sessions were finished and I ushered everyone out, I hustled to her door. After a quick knock, I pulled the handle and found it open. She sat on a stool at her worktable, a giant blob of dough in front of her. The alarm bells sounded.

First, she never sat to knead dough—not enough leverage, she'd said. Second, she had curled in on herself like a pencil shaving—she looked dangerously fragile and hollow.

"Hey, what's wrong?"

She raised her head enough to see me, and so I could confirm my suspicions. I grabbed her shoulders to allay at least one of my fears, which was that she was about to keel over backward off the stool and crack her head open.

"My head is killing me. I took some pain reliever, but it's just putting me to sleep." She flopped a hand out and it dropped back lifelessly.

"What kind of pain reliever? Horse tranquilizers?" Even her words seemed lazy and slow. Not quite slurred, but enough to make me genuinely concerned she'd taken something accidentally.

"I used to get migraines a lot. I don't anymore, and this isn't one, but I thought it might be and got scared, and now I just am all just…" Her eyes drooped and her head lolled forward.

Gripping her shoulders firmly, I moved around to face her. "I'm taking you home."

I cast around, eying her purse on its hook and making my plan to get her over there. I'd carry her if needed, but something told me she wouldn't accept that unless we were truly out of options.

"I need to finish this loaf. I'm trying a new technique on one of my boules and I have to shape it." That useless little lump flopped around again, a fish on dry land hours out of the water.

"Okay. How long will that take?"

"Three minutes. More? I can't remember what I had planned to do." Her spine bowed further and her head dropped forward so her forehead and temple rested on my forearm.

I clucked, the Jane Saint, Mother Hen part of me coming out. "Nope. I'm taking you home now. Can you stand? Can you walk?"

"I'm fine. I just need to finish this." But she didn't move. She stayed slumped on her stool, head resting against my arm, for a few more seconds before she sniffed. "Okay, I'm ready."

I stifled a laugh. "You tracking that you didn't actually do anything to the dough? You're amazing, but I don't think you can knead dough with your mind just yet."

"Hmm? Mmmhmm. Lesgo." Her desire to speak had deteriorated, apparently. If she was as exhausted and in pain as she seemed, it made sense.

"Can I carry you?"

Her head pulled back, not quite sharply, but what I imagined must be about as fast as she could move right now. "No. No."

"Okay, no pressure. Let's get you up, though."

I slipped one arm around her and pulled her up off the stool to standing. She immediately sagged, but I pinned her against my side and walked us to grab her purse. Should've done that before I got her, but I hadn't wanted to let go of her because she seemed like she would've oozed off the stool onto the ground if I hadn't busted in there.

I wasn't getting a hero complex here or anything. She was practically boneless even now, all except a little life in her legs keeping her standing.

"All right, Miller. Let's get you home." I'd come back and trash the dough later. For now, I cut the lights and pulled the kitchen door closed as we exited.

After a few more steps, she put her arm around my waist, which made this set-up easier. Her shoulder and arm had been smashed against me, so this improved things. We walked the path toward Silver Street, then slipped through to Elk Street between buildings—a lesser-known shortcut, but it saved us a few minutes. Finally, we hit the backside of her building, made it through her door and up the stairs, and finally to her apartment.

"Thank you. I'm sorry. Thank you." She'd kept up this chant amidst my encouragements that she could do this, we'd get her home and taken care of, she'd be able to rest, whatever dumb thing that came into my mind.

I coaxed her door open and eased us inside. The reality of being home must've given her a little burst of will because she lurched away from me, stumbled forward ten paces, and flopped over the side of her couch onto her face.

Shutting the apartment door, several things hit me at once. First, this place was tiny—a one-bedroom, and I could see the doorway and the postage stamp room that barely fit what had to be no more than a full-sized bed, which made absolutely no sense. She came from crazy money, and her business was doing well. Why the crap was she living in this little spot?

But the second thing? It smelled like her. It was like walking into one of her hugs, being surrounded by it—the lemony freshness that somehow always stuck to her, paired with something earthy and vital. Probably from all the bread baking. It was the single most intoxicating scent I'd ever experienced.

Right now, though, I needed to help the woman. She hadn't moved since she hit the couch, and part of me wondered if she'd passed out. I rounded the couch and knelt by her head. "Sadie, can I get you medicine or something?"

She groaned.

I chuckled and set a hand gently on her head. "Should we take your hair out? If it's a headache, that might help."

She rolled to her side and curled into a ball, and my hand fell from her head to the edge of the cushion next to it. Those blue eyes were rimmed with red and broadcasted her misery enough to make my heart twist.

Her voice came out soft. "You should go. I'm sorry."

"I'm not leaving, and you don't need to be sorry. Just tell me what I can do to help." I reached up and smoothed a few errant strands of hair behind her head. Her eyes fluttered shut and she inhaled slowly.

"What can I do?" I asked, in almost a whisper.

"I think I just need to sleep. I can't take anything else right now anyway." She pressed her eyes closed, shutting out me and the world.

I took the note. "Got it. I'll leave you to sleep, but I'm coming back later to check on you. I'm taking your key, so don't get freaked out if you hear someone coming in."

She mumbled something that sounded like *'kay* and stayed completely still. I pulled a neatly folded blanket from the back of the couch down to cover her up to her chin, and her contented sigh reassured me that had been the right move.

And then, I left to go take care of business.

Hours later, I returned to Sadie's house, letting myself in as quietly as I could in case she was still sacked out on the couch asleep. Sure enough, I found her exactly where I'd left her. It was eight o'clock now, and I'd left her a little after five. She needed to eat, especially if she wanted to take more meds.

In her little ball on the couch, she looked even smaller than usual. I'd felt anxious every minute since I'd left her, even though more than half of what I'd been running around doing was taking care of stuff for her. Kitchen was cleaned up the best I knew how, and I'd called Garrett, who got ahold of her weekend bakers and had them scheduled for the next few days.

I'd also collected a small bag for myself and gotten some soup and other food from the diner. Though it styled itself in a 1950s throwback feel, their food was fresh and very good. Gerry's chicken noodle soup was the kind of stuff that did a body good.

Was soup the thing to bring to someone who was exhausted and had a headache? I had no idea. But it seemed like a comforting meal, and most of the stuff in soup could be easily chewed, so... hopefully, it'd help her.

After arranging the bag of food on the counter, I tiptoed to the couch.

"Why are you here?" she asked without moving or opening her eyes.

I froze midstep, a cat burglar caught in the act. Except I was no such thing. And she didn't sound upset by my return, just truly confused.

"I brought you something to eat." I took a knee so I could take a closer look at her. Her cheeks were a healthy-looking pink and her overall color had returned. She'd seemed pale and definitely *looked* sick hours ago, so the nap must've done her some good.

"I'm not really hungry."

She was kind of a grump, and it made my insides do stupid things like try to liquefy. "I might not take no for an answer here. Can you open your eyes?"

At first, she scrunched them up, then slowly blinked them wide.

Oof. Less red after some rest, those gorgeous eyes hit me like a linebacker.

"You okay?" I pushed out.

She nodded. "A bit better, I think."

"Good. Can I help you sit up?"

She nodded again. I reached out and pulled the blanket down to her waist, then took her hand and helped her angle up so she sat upright. She shut her eyes again, brow furrowed, and I could see that no, the headache wasn't gone, and she wasn't all better.

"Stay right there. I'm bringing you food."

"I have to get up—"

"No. Just chill. I'll get whatever you need. What do you need?"

She pressed up to her feet and steadied herself on the arm of the couch. "I *need* to use the bathroom and however Prince Charming-ish you're being, you're *not* about to help me do that."

I laughed because I couldn't help but agree. "Fair enough."

Minutes later, she'd returned to the couch in a tailor sit on one end, and I'd doled out soup, some bread for her, and waters for both of us. She nestled the bowl in her lap, and we ate in silence. Not quite companionable, because knowing she felt bad unsettled me. But not awkward, for sure. Considering I'd never stepped foot inside her apartment until I'd hauled her in earlier, things were going well.

And now that I took it in with a closer look, it was nice. Comfortable and lived in, but genuinely nice. I could see why she'd stayed. There was a little built-in window seat facing Main Street—in fact, it had a perfect view of Guac. The living room held her quite comfortable couch, a coffee table, and a TV. She had a four-person table and then the kitchen, which was small, but opened to the living room and helped both spaces feel larger.

I hadn't peeked into her bedroom, but I wanted to—I wouldn't pretend I didn't.

"That was good, thank you."

Her words interrupted my meandering thoughts. And sure enough, she'd eaten every bit of soup and bread. Seeing the evidence that I'd provided something she needed gave me a small shot of satisfaction.

"I'm glad. I've been impressed with the diner's quality. I guess I thought it might be bad, but they're top notch so far."

I barely remembered the old diner. It'd gone out of business sometime while I'd been away and had only reopened earlier this year. I didn't eat out all that much—or at least I hadn't before I started meeting Sadie every week. But the discovery that the diner had such fresh, good food made me glad for myself and the town. We needed more variety, especially during ski season when the restaurants were packed to the gills with tourists looking for a hot meal before their next day of adventure.

"Yeah, they're good. They want my bread."

I chuckled. "Everyone wants your bread."

"You don't."

I turned in time to see her brows shoot up in question, then drop low as she shook her head. "Never mind."

I stuttered over my next words. "It's not—it's not that I don't, uh, think it's good. I've had some over the years. It's all excellent."

Every bite I'd allowed myself had been better than the last.

That was only part of the problem.

"I get it. You don't eat a lot of bread stuff. You're like, carved from stone or something, and I know that's your brand. Can't go diluting that with love handles like the rest of us, even if it is for the sake of the bread." She set her bowl on the coffee table and sipped from the water glass waiting there.

I cleared my throat, working to find the right response to that. "I eat bread sometimes. Not a lot, though, you're right. I generally feel better when I don't do a lot of grains. But it's not because I don't like what you do, or—"

Her arm swung out, and she pressed her hand to my chest. My *chest*. We both looked at that hand, pressed over my heart. She blinked at it, then up at me, then snatched it back like touching me had been a mistake that had singed her.

"You don't have to explain," she said, her voice low and almost somber.

The place where her hand had been felt different—like it'd been an iron she'd touched me with, and the material had melted to my skin. The small moment of contact had shaken all my thoughts and excuses loose.

"Okay," was all I said, then stood to gather up our used bowls. Once I'd cleaned the kitchen, I returned to the couch, dropping down into it with enough force to make her whole body bounce. "Whoops, sorry."

"You can go. Thank you for dinner, and everything, but I don't want you staying up late because of me. Plus, I need to try to get some sleep before work."

"Ah, but you don't have work tomorrow. Your backup team is on it, and Garrett is opening, and you're off. So let's watch TV or something, if that won't hurt your head, and just relax. It's been a long week."

She stared at me like I had two heads, blinked a few times, and then slumped back against the couch, a growing smile on her lips.

That smile, the way her body deflated of stress and

concern as she absorbed my words, made me want to straight up chest-bump somebody. I needed to call up Jacob Whistler, my best friend from ball and still one of the top quarterbacks in the NFL, and do our lame handshake like we used to.

Her relaxing into the cushions and reaching for the remote felt like triumph, and damn, did I love to win. After flicking on the TV, she handed me the remote. "I'll probably just fall asleep again. Please just leave whenever you want. And thank you."

"Of course. I'm glad I could help." I meant that to my core, and I hoped she could tell I did.

She shifted around, trying to find a comfortable spot, so I grabbed a pillow, then her hand, and tugged her my way. "Lay your head down and stretch out."

And she did. She let her head press into the bright yellow pillow I'd set against my hip and upper thigh and stretched her small body out on the length of the couch. I rested my arm along the back of the couch, trying not to touch her too much, though the plane of her back was there just asking to be rubbed. I wanted to bring her comfort, but at this point, I couldn't tell if touching her would work toward that end or away from it.

Clicking the remote on the first thing I saw, I stared at the screen, not seeing it. Her body relaxed more and more by degrees, and eventually, she tucked one hand under my thigh. Oddest little move, but it made my chest light up like she'd strung twinkle lights along my ribs.

I took that as a sign she was okay with some touch and spent the next few minutes gently tickling her back.

"You're really good at this," she said in a whisper, just before her breathing deepened and she was asleep.

It was the same thing that had me tiptoeing out ten minutes later.

Because yeah, I was actually a damn good partner. I knew I was a good friend. But I had too many friends these days. And what Sadie'd made me want today was someone for that energy—that mother hen, taking care of someone energy.

Someone to cuddle. Someone to hold when they needed it, to care for, to *love*.

I slipped out, no note. I'd text her tomorrow. Because I couldn't be here when she woke up. I couldn't be the one to carry her to bed. I couldn't be that for her.

I was good at this, but not good enough.

So I left.

CHAPTER TWENTY

At ten after six on Saturday morning, I woke with a start. The buzzing phone against the coffee table noise had invaded my dream and had finally poked through the deep sleep to jar me into consciousness.

I knew immediately I was alone and Warrick had left. I also knew, without having to work too hard to convince myself, that he had actually been there. I hadn't hallucinated his concern for me in the kitchen, his gentle guiding me home, or his waking me to feed me soup and bread.

If I had a love language, it was being fed soup and bread. Specific, I know, but one reason I'd always loved baking was rooted in the comfort and pleasure a good slice of warm bread could bring. Certainly, my expression of love came through baked goods. Which would make it tricky if I ever wanted to properly show Warrick my gratitude, considering I had yet to see him eat anything I'd made.

"Stop being gloomy," I said, pushing myself to sitting upright and waiting for the headache to crash back down on me. Mercifully, after gingerly opening one eye, then the other, I sighed my relief.

The phone buzzed again. I eyed it, curious to see who would be messaging this early on a Saturday before my heart rate skyrocketed when I realized it might be someone from downstairs and picked up.

"Hey! You answered! I wasn't sure if you'd be up." Sarah's voice sounded chipper and clear as a bell in my ear.

"Hey, yeah. I just woke up."

"Oh, shoot. Did I wake you? Go back to sleep! I'll check on you later," she said, her voice lower, like my saying I'd woken up necessitated her to be quiet.

"No, it's fine. I just slept eight hours."

Eight blissful hours of sleep on top of napping almost three hours before Warrick had come back and insisted I eat something for dinner last night. I probably would've woken from the dead sleep around midnight and had to scrounge up sustenance from a block of cheese and Ritz.

"Are you feeling any better?" she asked, pure sympathy in her voice.

It might've been the disorienting experience of falling asleep with my head fairly close to Warrick's lap and his fingers tickling my back, or the memory of sending Sarah a text telling her I was feeling bad and couldn't make dinner, which she'd invited me to the day before.

I'd planned to go. I'd wanted to go. But the headache and exhaustion had dragged me down so fast. I hadn't slept for days, and then I'd taken a pill I hadn't realized was so strong. Almost any other time I'd taken one, I'd immediately gone to sleep... I should've known. *Stupid!*

"I am. I needed sleep, and as long as the bakery doesn't burn down around me, I think it's all going to be fine."

The words sounded... right. It would be fine. I had planned on opening tomorrow since I'd be taking next weekend off to shop for a dress in the city and the following weekend for the engagement party. I didn't want my assistants to burn out. But I had never been more thankful to have them in place.

How had I gone so long without them?

And how had I gone so long without this—a person on the end of the line, wondering how I was. Not because they felt obligated, but because they genuinely wanted me to be okay.

My mind slipped back into the hazy, almost dream-like night before. Warrick's fingers gently sliding over my back, his warmth and scent surrounding me. He'd hit such a helpful mix of stubbornly insisting and deferring to my opinion. He didn't just take over and boss me around—he asked me what I needed, and he listened.

Without my permission, my stomach flipped right as Sarah said, "Hello? Seriously, where did you go, friend?"

A new warmth flooded me. *Friend.* We were genuinely friends. "Sorry, I was just remembering everything Warrick did for me."

"Warrick? He helped you?"

I heaved myself off the couch and peeked in the kitchen to see he'd set the dishes in the sink. If he'd actually washed them, I don't know what I would've done. "Yes. He saw me at the kitchen and basically carried me home—"

"He carried you! You couldn't even walk? Sadie—"

"No, not really, just kind of helped me along, and upstairs, and then he tucked me into my couch and left for a few hours. When he came back, he force-fed me soup and bread, and then…" I swallowed, the sweetness of the memory catching in my throat. "And then he tickled my back while we watched a movie and I fell asleep. He left sometime after that."

"Oh. Wow."

Her voice came out soft, but I heard the questions hiding behind those simple words.

"He's a good friend," I said, hoping that would suffice.

"Just a friend? You held hands at *A Night in Bloom*. You looked…"

My stomach clutched. We looked, what? Silly together? Mismatched? "We looked…?"

"Honestly, you looked great. I mean, Warrick's like a brother to me, even still, so I've never looked at him like *that*, but you two are gorgeous together. He's got that giant, bear-man thing going on and you're this tiny little prim package. Plus, you seem to enjoy each other."

"I—" I stopped, frantic little sparklers shooting off in my chest.

"At least from an outside view. I mean, I know you work next to each other and so, if it's all friendship, that's awesome. But if you're heading for more, that's great. I don't know him all that well anymore, but Warrick has always been the sweetest."

A sad little chuckle bumped out of me. "Yeah. He is. Honestly, I like him a lot, but we're just friends."

I liked him too much to be fake-dating him. That said, people here didn't need to know about our little deal. I mean, yes, they'd see us together, but the engagement party was coming up, and the time would come and go. After that, he'd be off the hook and I'd…

Well, I'd be friends with an incredible man. And I'd continue to develop that relationship and the ones that were blooming with Sarah and several others. I'd always be thankful to Warrick for his role in that—for pushing me to go to lunch before he even knew I needed the push. Or at least before I'd ever asked.

"Well, I think it'd be great if you wanted to see how that went. You haven't dated much, have you?"

"No. Not for a long time. I haven't been in the place for it or anything." I'd told her the gist—a surface-level review of things I'd told Warrick in greater detail. She knew I struggled with anxiety, and that'd hampered my social life, if one could call it that, for years.

"Well, I'm glad you're friends. And if it works out that it becomes more, I'll be cheering you on."

I smiled at that, her genuine support so refreshing. So unlike all the recent conversations I'd had about my love life. Whispers of the last conversation I'd had with my parents banged on the door of my mind, but I pushed them away.

"Are you still up for shopping with me next weekend?" She and Dahlia had offered to take me next week. Quinn was hoping to join too but was having some kind of scheduling issue with work or something like that, so we weren't sure.

"Absolutely. I cannot wait. And hey, let me know if I can drop you some more soup or anything at all."

I promised I would and hung up clinging to the good feelings our conversation had brought. Unfortunately, halfway through my shower, the cold water of my chat with my parents soaked through.

"Mercedes, you need to show up for your sister in a profound way. She's had a rough time these last few years—working tirelessly and you know how she's always dreamed of her wedding."

My mother's voice had come crisp and certain I *wouldn't* show up for Marguerite, though I had no idea why other than their expectations of me always being so ridiculously low, like I was half a person.

"I'll be there. I'm looking forward to it."

"Yes, but can you try to... just *try* to seem happy for her? I know you haven't got much going on right now, so I don't want her to feel like she needs to downplay her happiness to protect your feelings."

I'd sucked in a silent breath, then slowly breathed through the pain cinching tight around my heart. "I—of course. I'm bringing my boyfriend, too. She won't need to downplay."

The words had come out, strangled and small, but she'd gasped in a delighted expression of approval and peppered me with questions about my new beau. And yes, she referred to him as *beau* like it was some old-timey courtship.

And I'd leaned into the lie. Because I'd already told Warrick I needed him to be my date, not just casually, for the event. So it shouldn't have been that much worse to go full out and call him *boyfriend*. He'd wanted to help me— he'd promised he'd do anything I asked.

I just hoped he meant it, and this wasn't asking too much.

CHAPTER TWENTY-ONE

Warrick

S adie's intensity practically rippled off her in waves. She'd been hunched over one of the metal prep tables in her kitchen since before my last session of the day. She also hadn't done more than say hey and chat in passing since I'd left her house last week—five days since we'd had a real conversation. And she might not even remember much of that, considering how out of it she'd been.

I'd texted her the next day. She'd said thank you, I'd said no need, and then we sort of fizzled out. I'd wanted to press her for more—how was she feeling? Could I bring her anything? But she'd said Sarah had checked on her, and then she'd gotten a huge bouquet of flowers from Dahlia. More than a little happy that she had friends caring for her, I'd said, *"Your friends have your back."*

She'd sent a little smiley, and that was it.

How could I say thank you to *her* for that night? For

letting me help her? It'd come out too weird, so I hadn't. But I'd been insanely busy thanks to some issues with the house I was contracting, plus what felt like a million other little things that sucked the life out of me. These little problems cropping up—delay in parts for the main bathroom redo at the house, missing delivery for the gym, and so on—would've been challenges to solve. Not anymore, though. They drained my energy and reminded me, like so many things had lately, that there was more to life and I was missing it.

By the end of the week, I'd promised to show up at a dinner with Mom, Wyatt, and Calla, and then I was supposed to see Pete tomorrow for a workout slash catch up.

But all I wanted to do tonight was talk to Sadie. Just like I'd wanted every day this past week. And we hadn't had our Wednesday lunch thanks to scheduling conflicts, so I'd decided to check in and see if I could talk her into leaving with me.

By the time I stood right next to her, literally inches away, she still hadn't looked up. The apron strings were tied up tight around her waist, a little loop at the back just calling to me.

"Sadie," I said, and despite the point-blank range, she didn't stir. I could see the earbuds in the ear facing me, but dang, she was in the zone.

"Sadie," I said again, a little louder. No dice.

And then that desire to mess with her, to get her attention and touch her all at once, took over. I pulled on her apron string slowly, and when the knot unraveled, she jolted. Her wild eyes met mine, and after about a second, she relaxed.

"I thought you were a creeper!" She practically boomed

this before removing her earbuds. "Sorry, I thought you were—"

"A creeper. Yeah, I got that. Sorry. You've been so focused in here, I had to make sure you were still alive since saying your name didn't do the trick."

She made a face, then ducked her chin and shook her head. "Sorry. I've been in my own world planning and making lists. I used to do that at home, but I'm just anxious to have everything up and running in the fall."

My hand itched to run over the smooth skin of her arm or grab her hand. *Anything.* I shook that off. "No apologies. I love that you're so focused. I'm just glad I'm not an actual creeper."

She squinted. "TBD."

"Oh! Miller with the burn!" I laughed, genuinely pleased with her playfulness. Not what I'd expected after such a hit-or-miss week.

"So, um, how are you? I feel like I haven't seen you," she said, smoothing a strand of hair behind her ear.

"I'm glad it's Friday. I've missed seeing you. How are *you?*" I leaned one foot on the first rung of her stool.

After a big sigh, she said, "I did something bad. And a part of me has been avoiding you because of it, but now that you're here, I just have to tell you."

Not great news, but a relief considering it'd felt like she'd been avoiding me, but I also knew we had a different kind of friendship than I'd had with any other woman.

"All right. Let me have it."

She exhaled slowly, eyes on her lap, then inhaled and met my gaze. "I told my parents you're my boyfriend. Like, serious boyfriend."

She paused like she expected me to lose my temper or

react dramatically, but hadn't that been what we'd already talked about? "I thought that was the plan?"

"I mean, sort of. But not."

Wow, she was worried. I couldn't stop myself from pressing my thumb to her wrinkled brow and smoothing it along the lines there. "That's what I was expecting. I thought I was rolling into the Miller mansion as Mercedes Miller's man. Envy of everyone in attendance. It'll be great for my sad little bruised ego, and I'm looking forward to it."

She huffed. "I appreciate the humor, but I feel like this might be more than you signed up for."

She wasn't listening. She'd gotten caught in a loop, telling herself I'd be angry or upset about this, and it just wasn't the case. If anything, I'd been looking forward to the engagement party. I wanted to show up and show her off, make sure her parents could see how awesome she was. They clearly had no idea about her expansion plans, or likely even the success of Rise and Shine itself.

I set my hands gently on her shoulders and ducked my head. "I told you I'd do whatever would help. I meant it. Can you tell me what you're worried about specifically? Or is it just that, generally, you're worried you're asking too much?"

She swallowed, and the movement of her throat made my thumb reflexively arc over the delicate skin of her neck.

"Uh, um—" She cleared her throat lightly. "I hate that it matters so much to me. So I think there's some self-loathing there, which then makes me mad. I hate that I said it, that I lied, and yet I'm also so relieved you'll be going with me, even if it is weird that we'll be pretending."

Warm, bright goodness poured over my chest at those words. "I'm glad I'm going too. So let's just leave it at that. Trust me to tell you when it's too much, okay?"

She swallowed again and nodded. Unbidden, a flash of an image hit me. My hands slipping from her shoulders to cradle her head, then dipping down and taking her lips with mine.

I dropped my hands and stepped back. "Okay, so now that you know I'm not going to be upset, whatever you told your parents, I want you to come to dinner with me and my family."

Just toss it right out there, just... get it out. Get away from the weird, close feeling that'd risen between us and the tightening in my gut at the image of us kissing.

"Tonight?"

"Yes. In like twenty minutes. It's just Calla and Wyatt, and my mom." Her eyes got big, and I chuckled. "Seriously, Jane Saint already loves you. You know Calla and Wyatt. Please come with me? We'll practice the boyfriend-girlfriend stuff. I feel like we probably should test-run it a few times before next weekend, or we might seem awkward together."

Yeah. That's it. Purely for the purpose of practice.

Even though touching her, being near her, never felt anything but good. In fact, it felt far too good, and my stupid little brain ran right away with the idea whenever I gave it an inch.

"Uh..." She fiddled with the pen resting on a pad of paper, then her eyes snapped to mine. "Okay, yes. Yeah, let's do it." She hopped up from the stool. "Where is it? Should I change?"

"It's at Elk Ridge, nothing too—"

"I'll change. I can't meet your mother with a fine coating of flour on me."

I laughed, delighted by her frazzled gathering of things. She slid a handful of spiral-bound notebooks and pads of paper into a canvas Rise and Shine bag and hoisted it over her shoulder, then scuttled to the hook where she kept her purse. "Okay. I'm going to go. And I'll meet you there at—"

I reached for the bag and plucked it from her, then ushered her to the door with a hand on her lower back. "No. I'll meet you at your place in twenty minutes and we'll walk over together. We're going to practice being together, and if you were my girlfriend, I'd absolutely pick you up."

She double-blinked. "Okay."

So that was what we did. She left in a hasty blur, power-walking down the street with the bag I'd given back once she'd locked the door outside, and I jumped in my car and took the fastest shower ever to get back to her in time.

My heart raced as I climbed her steps. I sucked in a breath when she opened the door and smiled at me, such a sweet, pleased-to-see-me smile it felt like a sucker punch. Like a pre-emptive tackle before I ever had the ball.

Like I was playing a completely different game than I'd realized until right this moment.

CHAPTER TWENTY-TWO

Sadie

Calla's hug set me at ease and Wyatt's subtle nod with his kind eyes reinforced it. I was welcome here.

But it was Jane Saint's greeting that made my heart squeeze in my chest so tight, I lost my breath for a few seconds.

Warrick had arrived looking downright delicious in a button-down dark gray shirt and jeans. He'd kissed my cheek, grabbed my hand, and we'd left my building in a way that felt very much like he was my boyfriend. Certainly, my insides felt that way, twisted pleasurably in the wake of his kiss and attention.

On the walk, he'd reiterated his plan that we practice. When I'd asked if he felt bad lying to his family, he'd said simply, "They'll live."

I wasn't sure whether that answered my question or not, but it'd shut down the questions, and my mind quickly switched back to worrying over what I'd talk about. I'd made a mental list of questions to ask each person who'd be there.

But, now here was Jane, taking both my hands in hers, gripping them with enough pressure to tell me she meant it. Then she pulled me close and hugged me. "So glad you're joining us, Sadie."

And there went the heart clutch. Her easy acceptance of me, her excitement at me coming with Warrick, felt both like a triumph and the worst kind of failure. I wanted that approval—on some level, I suspected I needed it. And yet, it wasn't actually mine. It didn't belong to me, because I wasn't actually Warrick's.

"Thank you for having me," I said, the words echoing back in a taunt.

Thank you for having me? Are they having *you here, purposefully, or did Warrick just bring you along?*

As I scooted my chair in, Warrick's big hand providing the thrust of the movement, I exhaled a controlled breath and worked to find something to banish the doubt. I'd called Sarah earlier and spilled the whole situation in one long burst. Something like *I'm going to dinner with Warrick as his girlfriend, but we're fake-dating because of my parents and I'm in trouble.* Her ears had pricked at *trouble,* and she'd demanded all the details.

What it came down to was embarrassingly simple. I'd asked Warrick to help me with the engagement party, but it was also a way to get close to him. She'd kept pity from her voice, but I wondered if she felt it. If this whole mess was as pathetic as it felt.

Still, telling her had calmed the raging adrenaline and nerves. Just knowing someone else besides me and Warrick knew the truth helped. And for the hundredth time since our first little coffee chat, I said a prayer of thanks for Sarah and all my new friends.

Warrick took his seat next to me, close enough his leg bumped mine. Calla was saying something, but I couldn't hear it, because Warrick's hand closed over my thigh an inch or so above my knee. The warmth there pressed through the silk of my skirt, and my heart bolted. But instead of being something suggestive, he squeezed, then flipped his hand over and rested the back of it there on my leg.

Waiting.

I grabbed it, lacing our fingers together and relishing the little burst of flutters that came with the contact right along with the break in the pace of my galloping heart. When I glanced at him, he looked so serious, I wondered if I'd done something wrong. Then he squeezed my hand and shook his head with a quiet smile like he could tell right where my mind had gone.

I shot him a sheepish look, then released his hand so I could open the menu and study it. Maybe in honor of sitting here in the wintergarden at Elk Ridge, actually sitting *in* the restaurant for the first time in over a decade, I'd get something new. I'd get a special of the day, something I'd never order in.

"So Sadie, how are things coming along for your expansion?" Calla asked, leaning forward in her seat like she genuinely couldn't wait to hear.

"Really well, I think. I've got two solid bakers I'm working with right now, and they'll end up taking over a fair amount of the work at Rise and Shine so I can supervise at the big kitchen. But I've still got to hire at least two more assistants so we have some flexibility. I'll start distributing here, actually, and a few other places in town—"

"If you don't mind my interjecting, I hope you'll be distributing at my new restaurant at the hotel as well."

I turned to see Julian Grenier, one hand in a pocket, the other checking his watch, standing just a few feet from the table.

"Oh. I—"

"Maybe you should talk to her about that during working hours?" Warrick said, eyes narrowed on the enigmatic man.

"Julian, how are you?" Calla rose from her seat and greeted the man with a kiss on his cheek. He returned it in a kind of rote, robotic way that told me he was entirely immune to Calla's charms.

That had to be a rare thing. Calla was beautiful enough that looking at her was mildly painful sometimes. She had the kind of features that jumped out and shook you until you looked away, only to steal another glance because they're just so pleasing. Paired with her stardom, few people received her so calmly.

So Grenier's total lack of concern for her was borderline shocking, except he'd been enigmatic, to say the least, anytime I'd witnessed him.

Even with all that understated reaction, he did mumble something like *"pleasure,"* and then shifted his focus right back to me.

"I'd be happy to talk with you sometime, Mr. Grenier."

"Good. I'll have my assistant set up a meeting."

"Please do," I said, meaning it.

Without another word and only a curt nod, he moved past us to enter the main restaurant.

Warrick grumbled next to me. Before I could ask him what that was about, Wyatt laughed a low, taunting sound.

"I'd forgotten how much he gets under your skin."

Warrick sent him a glare of such disdain, I chuckled.

"He's not under my skin. He's on the bottom of my shoe," he replied, the closest to sneering I'd ever seen.

Wyatt laughed in earnest at that, and Calla ducked her head, though I saw her smile before she hid it.

"Warrick Saint, that's nasty," Jane said, though the warmth to her tone gave away the laugh she clearly held back.

"He's rude, coming over here to interrupt a family dinner for business. The guy needs boundaries. Plus, he just maneuvered a deal that put Quinn in a tough spot. I don't have to like him," he grumped and nestled into his seat.

Family dinner sent lovely little waves of something warm and hearty through me.

"Sorry about that. He'd asked to talk at *A Night in Bloom*, but I haven't heard from him since, and I'd forgotten about it. I'm sorry to hear about Quinn—I didn't realize."

A flash of satisfaction crossed Warrick's face before he wiped it clear. Calla interjected into the odd moment. "Well, that'll be a great addition to your lineup, right? The new restaurant at Silver Ridge Resort is fine dining, I thought I'd heard?"

Warrick nodded. "Yeah, should've opened last summer, actually, but they've had a heck of a time finding a chef. Almost like the position is cursed, though if you ask me, working with Grenier has to be its own sort of repellant."

I pressed my lips together to keep from laughing. I'd never seen Warrick so crusty about something, other than Julian Grenier. And though I wouldn't ask right now, especially since the waiter had arrived to take orders and deliver waters, I made a note to find out what he had against the man. It was so unlike Warrick to be negative about someone, especially someone who kept to himself. Everyone in town knew the name by now, especially after the hotel had been built and it'd become clear that without Jonas Bauer and Julian Grenier, Silverton would've dried up like a little mountain spring in July.

"What's everyone doing for the twenty-fourth?" Jane asked, blessedly refocusing the table on something other than Grenier.

"Are there fireworks this year? Seems like it's been years," Wyatt said.

Amazingly, I knew the answer when no one else seemed to. I made a point to calm myself before speaking. I felt comfortable here, but speaking in front of a group without nerves, even a small familiar one, was still a developing skill.

"I heard there would be, but they aren't permitting individual fireworks again. The county will do a show, and I think the dreaded Grenier is rumored to have donated to the firework fund."

I'd made it to another planning meeting last week, and though it'd knocked me on my butt for hours afterward and I'd had a ridiculously early bedtime, I was so glad I'd attended.

"Come to my house, then. It's decided." Jane smiled at me, particularly.

"Oh, I don't—"

"We'll be there." Warrick cut me off, then gave me a look I couldn't quite decipher.

We'd talk about it later. The twenty-fourth of July was a huge holiday in Utah, focused on the pioneers who'd come across the US and settled in Salt Lake City. Silverton's settlers had come a few decades later, and not in July, but the whole state celebrated the state's history. Liam Morrison's brewery always did a huge Pie and Beer day party, and though I'd never been, I'd always wanted to try it.

Maybe Warrick and I could go check out the party and then go to Jane's? Would he even want to do that? I could ask him, but I didn't want to push.

"Whatever you're thinking, the answer is yes. Or no, depending on what you're thinking." His voice came in a low whisper, his breath brushing my ear.

My neck prickled, and goosebumps broke out over my skin.

"That doesn't make sense," I said, turning to find his face shockingly close to mine since he hadn't backed away.

"All I'm saying is, stop worrying. We'll work it out."

And then, he took my chin gently between fingers and drew me closer. My breath caught in my throat, my mind spun out so the only thought was less logic and more feeling —the feeling of his fingers on my chin, his nearness. Then he pressed a light kiss at the corner of my mouth—so close to my lips, but not quite there. Not *quite*.

When he pulled back, the look in his eyes turned me liquid. I couldn't have put it into words, but it felt something like falling back into a featherbed—those moments where you're falling but haven't met the resistance of the cushion.

My stomach jumped from the high dive, and I didn't look away until Jane asked me a question. The rest of the night, my mind stayed on that kiss—that near-miss, or near-hit—and how much I hoped he'd do it again soon.

CHAPTER TWENTY-THREE

Warrick

My mom hadn't left me alone since dinner last Friday, so her text message now wasn't a surprise. I shouldn't have been surprised, but her level of enthusiasm outmatched my expectations. I had ten minutes before this workout was done and everyone would take off for the day's festivities.

The twenty-fourth had arrived on the tail of five days of pestering from Jane Saint, and it hadn't come a moment too soon.

It'd started at the family dinner last week. Taking Sadie was admittedly notable. I didn't bring dates or even friends to family dinners. Wasn't my thing. And since Tracy, I hadn't been in a relationship where I'd even considered it.

So me showing up with Sadie was significant—I understood that. I'd chosen not to overthink it and just *do* it, but the second I saw their faces—Mom's, Wyatt's, and even

Calla's—I knew I couldn't pretend it meant nothing. It meant something, and as we settled into our seats, I felt only happy about it.

Happy Sadie was next to me. Happy she seemed to calm at my touch. Happy she seemed as affected by being close to me as I was her.

If I was confused by the whole thing—me wanting to be around her, wanting something from her despite having sworn off those kinds of feelings—I gave myself a pass in the name of our fake date we needed practice for. I sank into the cushy comfort of that as a shield for any real feelings, and just went with it.

Turned out, it felt both natural and new. I'd nearly kissed her—I'd been so damn close to doing it right at the table, but luckily, logic had me steer to the side and give her an unkiss—not quite the lips, but definitely not the cheek.

Heat shot through me at the memory of her eyes after that—pure *wanting*. Damn if a look like that didn't belong on Sadie's face, and especially when she looked at me. I officially could not pretend I was only in this for friendship, but I wasn't about to admit that to her. Maybe she'd want more too, if she knew... but this had an end point. No escaping that.

So going into tonight, when I'd take Sadie out as my date to Silver Ridge Brewing's party and then back to Mom's, I'd relax into the convenient shield of our larger plan—that we needed to be convincing for her family.

And sure, part of me did chafe against lying to my family, and especially my mom. She wanted me happy and settled so she could be cradling her grandbabies as soon as possible, but she tried not to push. Deep down, I knew she tried, even if her excitement over me and Sadie felt like pressure.

The problem with Jane Saint was that she knew me too well. And she wouldn't be thrilled if I told her about my arrangement with Sadie, nor would she pull her punches. So for now, I was placating her with as little information and response as possible to keep her from being suspicious.

"What time will you and Sadie arrive?" Her text made my phone buzz for the sixth time this afternoon.

"Your mom again?" Pete asked as he cranked through push-ups next to me. My shoulder had decided to cooperate today, but it was about at the end of its rope.

"Yep. Wanting to know when I'm showing up to her house tonight." I pushed up and took a rest at the top, rolling my shoulder back just a bit.

"What's going on there? With you?"

He didn't have to say *with you and Sadie.* He'd already asked, and I'd said we were friends. But it wasn't fair to keep telling him that when evidence suggested more. Plus, I wasn't a man who walked around holding hands with women who weren't something special—physical affection beyond a basic hug or high five with a friend who was a girl just didn't happen. He'd see us tonight at the brewery, and he'd give me grief for it if I kept denying it.

"We're trying something out," I said, then called out a warning for the final thirty seconds of the circuit.

"I guess I thought—"

"Push," I urged, and we raced to the finish. When my alarm trilled, I called it. "Good work, everyone! Don't forget to record your reps."

Bodyweight circuits for time proved to be an excellent measure of progress. Far more than pounds or inches lost, it gave people a boost to see they could grit out five more push-ups or pull-ups—whatever.

After chatting with a few people, waving them off and

assuring them I'd see them tomorrow for our usual times after being closed this afternoon, Pete cornered me.

"So, seriously. Are you with Sadie now?"

I nodded. I was. He didn't need to know that it wasn't real, and I didn't feel like telling him that because it made me an idiot. It made a cement ball drop in my gut, but I couldn't be sure that was purely from knowing we weren't together.

Because weirdly, it might've been from regretting that we weren't.

"And it's good? She treats you right?" Pete narrowed his eyes, crossed his arms, and studied me like he might discover the hidden side to my relationship with just that action.

It warmed me straight to my core. Pete had lost it when I'd told him about Tracy, how we'd broken off the engagement. He'd promised he'd go confront her and Gord on my behalf, which of course I'd refused. But the fact that he'd even offered—that he felt so upset for me it made *him* upset to that degree—had always been a small gift.

His protective tendency was kind, but unnecessary on several levels here. "She's great, man. No worries."

Probably better he had no idea I was still a little messed up over her.

"Good. Better be."

I chuckled. "She is. Now go get cleaned up and I'll see you tonight. You bringing a date?"

He shrugged a shoulder and grabbed his keys. "We'll see."

He never committed to anything, kind of like our buddy Danny Morrison used to be. Now Danny was a married father of *four*—dang, what a crazy few years.

I waved him off and glanced to my right, hoping for

some amount of subtlety, but also completely hoping maybe Sadie had made it to her kitchen. Anticipation shot through me, mingling with my dropping heart rate to cause a dizzy haze to descend. The lights were on, but I couldn't see her. She could be around the corner where the sinks were and I couldn't see.

I could just go knock. But what would I say? *Yipes*, time to grab some calories.

After practically inhaling a protein shake and an apple, I peeked out of my office to see the kitchen lights on, but still no Sadie. Maybe she'd decided not to come in today. A lot of businesses closed early on the holiday. Though that didn't quite fit with what I knew about her since she'd be taking the weekend off for the engagement party. I'd imagined her working away in here for the rest of the day until I came to pry her loose and take her to the party.

But... *no.* No, no, no, that was *not* Julian Grenier walking through the door that led to the outside. And there came Sadie, her lips moving, but I couldn't hear a word. I cursed the thick-paned glass. Usually, I was glad for it since it kept the clunky gym sounds out of her space, but just now?

Just now, I needed to know what she was saying. Why Grenier was giving that spare nod. Why he was inspecting the space with squinted eyes like he knew anything about a professional kitchen. Why she was smiling at him.

My feet were moving before I could stop them, my hand banging on the door in an unnecessarily loud knock. Seconds later, Sadie emerged with a light smile.

"Hey! It's good to see you. I'm in a quick meeting, but can I come find you after, or are you heading home?" Her blue eyes were bright, her cheeks pinked with normal, lovely color. She didn't seem upset or particularly anxious, despite Grenier's lurking.

"Uh, any idea how long it'll be?" I asked like an idiot, because I was one.

Before she could speak, however, Grenier stepped closer and held the door open above her head. Something lit on fire in my gut and burned to a crisp.

"I have twelve more minutes allotted for this meeting." He blinked at me, but as far as I could tell, his face held no expression.

Sadie startled. "Oh, wow, okay, let's get to it then. Warrick, I'll find you in just a few?"

"Yep. Yeah, I'll be here." Taking a giant step back, I held up a ridiculous hand to... wave goodbye? Who knew? Certainly not me, because my body had decided to act without my permission. The calories hadn't reached my brain, and my weird fit of fury at seeing Grenier had fizzled.

The door swung shut behind me and I forced myself inside my office so I wouldn't troll around the gym and spy on them through the window. Though I wanted to. Badly.

Instead, I organized every file in my office, responded to the three e-mails that'd come in, caved to another text from my mother and told her our plans for the night, and clicked back and forth between windows on my browser at a pace of about seventeen per minute.

By the time Sadie came to knock on the frame of my office door, I'd worked myself into a weird spiral of anxiety, anticipation, and jealousy.

"Well, that was an interesting conversation." She rested her head on the frame and sort of sagged against it.

I wanted to tell her to come sit in my chair, or better, sit in my lap. I would hold her and comfort her in the wake of horrible Julian Grenier, and yet, I needed a shower, and she didn't seem as traumatized as I would've guessed after twelve additional minutes with the man.

"Everything okay? Did he do anything weird?"

She made a face. "Not like *that*. He was just... unexpected."

Hmm. The way she said that wasn't nearly disenchanted enough. And I wasn't an idiot—Grenier was frustratingly good-looking, especially for a man who didn't seem to have the requisite muscles it took to form a smile. He was severe and odd and pushy and greedy and, oh yeah, a freaking billionaire. Yep. With a b. Several b's, if the last *Forbes* article had been accurate.

I couldn't compete with that.

Wait. Am I trying to compete with that?

I swallowed hard, then grabbed my water and chugged it down before asking, "What does that mean?"

She entered my office and leaned her backside against the edge of my desk. My pulse immediately shot through the roof. Was I having some sort of episode? Everything that'd happened in the last twenty minutes had felt heightened and intense.

Maybe it was all the extra adrenaline jetting through my veins? Her choice to move closer to me, and not stay glued to the door, seemed good. That was good, right?

"Well, first he asked if he could buy Rise and Shine and hire me to run a state-wide expansion." Her blue eyes flicked up to me.

"Whoa."

"Yeah."

"And you said..."

She gave me a look like I was ridiculous. I couldn't fault her.

"I said no."

I nodded. "It's a good offer. He'd probably do it well."

"Yeah. But that's not what I want."

I nodded again, and some of the bands of stress strapped across my chest loosened.

"Then he asked if I would consider working with him on some exclusive offerings for the restaurant at the resort, which he assured me the new chef, whoever it ends up being, would be thrilled about." She widened her eyes as if to say she found that hard to believe.

"That sounds good."

"I told him I'd come up with some ideas, but that ultimately, I should work with his chef to find a flavor profile that fits their vision. He seemed pleased by that and told me he'd have the new hire contact me for a meeting."

"Huh. Sounds good."

Her face changed—cheeks brightening and neck flushing from the collar of her white shirt all the way to her chin. "Then he asked if he could take me out."

I tried not to react. I swear it, I did. But that was exactly what I'd known Grenier was after. Yes, the bread, but also, the woman. Because she was a freaking delight, a treasure, and the fact that people had left her alone so long was only because that was what she'd wanted. Now that she'd opened herself up to the world, even the bit that she had, it was open season.

"Interesting," I gritted out, arms crossed tight over my chest.

"Think so?" she asked, dipping her head to the side.

I nodded, sure whatever words on my tongue would not be okay to say out loud.

"Well, I told him no. That I was with you. I hope that wasn't the wrong—"

I shot to my feet. "That's good. That's right."

Our eyes locked.

"Okay. Good." Her lips pursed just slightly, like she hid a smile.

"We still on for the brewery later?" I asked, my chest feeling a little like the sun was shining directly on my soul, brightening it by degrees with every second we stood in that small space together.

"Yep."

"I'll swing by at six."

She smiled and sent more delicious sunbeams into me. "See you then."

I watched her go, shaken. By everything. My response to Grenier in her space. To her. To her being asked out by that sneaky little billionaire, and by her refusal of him *for me*.

It might not be real, but everything that'd just happened felt completely authentic.

And I had to face it... I'd broken all my rules, and by the time this was over, I was going to be a mess.

CHAPTER TWENTY-FOUR

Sadie

Warrick's hand in mine had a dual effect.

First, it did calm me. Walking into Silverton's other mill building, home of Silver Ridge Brewery, felt significantly less terrifying than gearing up for *A Night in Bloom* had weeks ago. At the same time, I walked a tightrope. On one side was the simple threat of falling a thousand feet—apparently, this tightrope was stretched between buildings in New York, not Silverton. On the other was a metaphorical fall into crazy big feelings for Warrick.

And so while yes, his hand calmed me, it also sent little sparks from my fingertips up my arm. More pleasurable than pins and needles, and yet just as concerning. We'd touched before, and every time, I'd had a similar response. I'd expected to become inured to it like I'd gotten used to singeing my forearms on the oven over the years. Alas, no such luck.

"We don't have to stay long. You just give me the word and we'll bounce." He squeezed my hand, no doubt in a move to reassure.

"Okay. Sounds good. I don't know why I'm nervous." My skirt swished around my legs and I had the fleeting wish I was home in my sweatpants.

The familiar longing frustrated me. Shouldn't I be doing better with this?

"Honestly, I'm a little nervous too."

I glanced at him, my eyes huge, no doubt. "You are? Why?"

"We're walking in, publicly together as far as anyone in there knows. Plus, as social as I am, sometimes I get nervous too. Excited nervous, usually, but still." He squeezed my hand again.

"I wish it was just excited nervous for me. But there's some of that," I said as we approached the brewery's entrance, where a handful of people stood and chatted.

He tugged and we stepped off the path and out of the way. He faced me, disconnecting our hands for a moment before he set both of his palms gently on my shoulders. As though a reflex, his thumbs stroked over the bare caps of my shoulders, and I mentally congratulated myself on the choice of the silky royal blue tank top to go with the white skirt.

"We don't have to go."

"I want to. I can do this. I don't know why it's different this time, but it's way better than before, I promise."

I could honestly say I wouldn't have walked into this event last year even if someone paid me. Group events could be easier in some ways because I could stay on the periphery and not have to deal with small talk, but I also had no one to talk to. I hadn't started my shifts at the register back then, I hadn't made any friends, and now?

"Good. But also promise me you'll tell me we need to leave at any time, whether that's five minutes after we walk in there or two hours from now, yeah?" His handsome face was so insistent, all signs of humor absent as he spoke in that low, sincere tone.

"Yes. I'll tell you." Meeting his eyes directly made my stomach swoop low before I gathered myself, cleared my throat, and nodded. "Let's go. I think it'll get better once we're in and I'm not anticipating. Sometimes, waiting for something is worse than the thing itself."

"That's absolutely true."

He held out one of those giant, warm hands again, and I took it. A minute later, we'd entered the brewery after Warrick handed over tickets at the door, which I hadn't even realized were necessary, and the crowd pressed in on me.

My heartbeat echoed in my head, which typically didn't bode well. I must've slowed my walk because Warrick's head whipped to mine, and he immediately led me to the side of the room, feet from any of the tables and where no one else had camped out to chat.

"Let's take a minute. Adjust to the noise and everything," he said.

"Yeah, the space is good," I said, slowly exhaling, willing away my racing heart and straightening my fingers where they'd curled into an odd fist on the hand he didn't hold.

He dropped my hand and moved to step away, but I grabbed his shirt, a soft short-sleeved button-up plaid with red, white, and blue. "Don't leave me."

He froze. "Not leaving. Just giving you space."

I kept my hold on him and closed the distance between

us so we stood, bodies almost touching, but only connected by my hand gripping his shirt. "I don't need space from you."

His mouth twitched into a smile even as his brows bunched. "All right. Good."

He took the hand still clutching the plaid material and pressed it flat against what I could now feel and knew from more than one visual confirmation at the gym were firm, tight ab muscles. He did it like he meant to reassure me *he* didn't need space either. And certainly, he did it without imagining what it'd do to me to have my hand on his ridiculous stomach, a place I'd only touch on another person with a level of intimacy that was absolutely more than friendly.

My tongue tied itself into a knot, maybe from the aforementioned abs, or maybe simply the sweetness of the gesture. I couldn't remember why I'd been nervous before, especially not with his eyes locked on mine and blocking the rest of the room out. Somewhere in my mind, I could hear the band in the background, but it wasn't pressing in on me anymore. The mingling of music and chatting didn't seem so insanely overwhelming.

"Let's grab a drink." Warrick curled his fingers around mine and pulled our hands away, then knitted us together and waited for my response.

"Yes. Good." And apparently, I'd be speaking in monosyllables the rest of the night.

"Are you up for a beer? Something else?"

No. I didn't want a beer, but mostly because beer made me feel full and I wanted to eat more than I wanted a drink. "Could I just have a glass of water?"

His face did that half-smile, half-perplexed look and he stopped walking, so I did too.

"You can have whatever you want whenever you want it."

"Okay."

"You gotta own it, though. None of this wavering. You want water?" He snapped his fingers. "Done. You want beer?" Another snap. "Done. You want me to do a back handspring while I hold sparklers?" One last snap, then he pointed at me with a mock seriousness that killed me. "Done."

I burst out laughing. "What? Why would I want—*wait*. You said that like you've definitely done that. Please tell me first, can you really do a back handspring still, and second... *sparklers?*"

He chuckled, and the sparkle in his eyes paired with the charming way they crinkled and showcased what innate good humor he had made my heart do its own little back handspring. Then he sobered and brought our hands up, kissed the back of mine.

"I've got so many moves you haven't seen, Miller. Your mind is going to be blown."

He kept our gazes locked for a beat, then burst out laughing.

I followed suit, of course, because no one could resist that broad smile and beautiful laugh, but inside my chest, my heart thundered from the contact, the kiss, the words. I believed him. He might be joking, but I bought every dang line.

"Come on. Let's get you that water. After that, we're going to talk to a small handful of people, eat some pie, and then we're going to blow this popsicle stand and go hang out in my mom's backyard and watch the fireworks, maybe with some additional pie. Good?"

I nodded, the warm glow of his actions and care for me cocooning me in the moment.

He didn't need to do anything to charm me more than he already had, or to put me at ease, but he did. Outlining the plan, even though it was exactly what we'd already talked about, went a long way toward keeping that anxiety from rising in me as we continued walking.

We both had waters, and then we moved around the room in a counter-clockwise circle. We each had pie—I had blueberry and he had lemon meringue. Bites of pie helped me escape feeling like I had to make conversation, plus Warrick did almost all the talking, except when we found Calla and Wyatt. And, of course, when Julian Grenier approached.

"Thank you for talking with me earlier," he said to me. Then he turned to Warrick and gave him a tight nod. "I apologize if I overstepped."

The scowl on Warrick's face softened, and he extended a hand, which Grenier immediately accepted.

"Not at all. And I'll admit, I can't blame you." His eyes flickered to me, then back to the rigid man in front of us.

"Have a good evening," Grenier said, then slipped away as I'd come to expect from him.

"Are you coming down to the gardens for the fireworks?" Sarah asked, wandering up with Dahlia in tow.

Warrick greeted them both, then inched toward Pete Perry with a gentle squeeze to my shoulder before jumping into a conversation with him.

His eyes caught mine, and he winked before he turned fully to his friend. My stomach flipped, but I focused on the women, my new friends, in front of me. "I think we're going to Warrick's mom's house. I guess she's got a big backyard on a hill that has a perfect view of where they shoot them off."

"Ooh, I've heard Jane has gorgeous roses and an amazing vegetable garden." Dahlia clasped her hands together and hugged them to her chest.

Sarah chuckled. "I love that your first thought is of her garden, and not of how romantic it's going to be to sit under the stars and watch fireworks."

She wiggled her brows at me. I swallowed, glad at least Sarah knew the truth. Calling her before going out with Warrick's family had been an impulse I didn't regret. I'd been desperate to talk to her, and it felt like a load off even now. I was all the more grateful someone else besides me knew things with Warrick weren't what they seemed now that we'd gone out so publicly.

And in response to her comment, of course I'd thought about how romantic it would be, but I'd put it out of my head. Overthinking the romance wouldn't keep me calm. Plus Jane, and Wyatt and Calla, would be there. We'd all chitchat, just like dinner the other night. I'd been looking forward to it.

"Fair point, but yeah. It is super romantic. You guys look pretty cozy as it is..." Dahlia trailed off, eyebrows raised.

"He's great."

Too true, and I wasn't about to get into details—first because there weren't really all that many, and second because, well... all the little things about our relationship, even if it was friendship with a side of pretend-romance, were mine. And while I'd longed for friends, I hadn't gotten used to sharing everything yet.

It felt like a first rise. Something only I saw, but we'd end up molding it, shaping things, and what everyone else saw would come after a lot more work—a second rise, the bake, the cooling. They hadn't seen what I'd had all along. And while that didn't take away from their opinion—I loved that they thought we were "cozy" together—they didn't understand everything behind it.

And I supposed, in this silly metaphor, they didn't know that this ornately scored little loaf of earthy, chewy pain de campagne was actually a hollow, plastic replica more useful for a stage prop than consumption.

That's just dark. Maybe a tad dramatic. But so was the image of our relationship as a loaf of bread, and honestly, so was my heart, which felt dangerously close to hungry for something real with Warrick.

Sarah squeezed my arm and dragged me from those edgy thoughts. "Well, have fun. I think we're going to run over and set out blankets before all the young families and high schoolers steal all the good grass. Dahlia has a secret spot we're using."

"Give us the update on all the juicy details since you're the only one who's getting any, will ya? Oh, I see John. Gotta run. Have fun, Sadie!" Dahlia practically skipped away, high on the energy of the night, I supposed.

I waved as she moved away, then my eyes shot to Sarah. She gave me a soft, commiserating look and I nodded. "Thanks. I'll see you next week?"

She beamed. "Yes. But you better send me pictures and updates all weekend. Promise me."

Her genuine kindness and insistence washed away some of the nerves that'd been twisting in my gut, only for them to return as soon as I realized what she wanted pictures and updates of—the engagement party. But I did want her to know how it went, so I'd do that—for her sake, and mine. "Promise."

She blew me a kiss, then swirled around to talk to someone else just as Warrick stepped back into my sightline.

"Ready?"

His deep voice and warm hand on my arm made my stomach flip for the nth time tonight, and I nodded. He steered me by a high-top table and we left our glasses there on the way out of the building.

Out of the corner of my eye just before we left, I saw Julian Grenier standing against one wall, eyes glued to someone across the room. I wasn't tall enough to see who he had his focus on so intently, but it looked like maybe he was watching the band. Maybe he'd been captivated by Quinn's voice like the rest of us, though picturing him being *captivated* didn't quite click with my impressions of him thus far. That said, now that I thought about it, this was the first time I'd ever seen him standing still aside from being in conversation with someone.

Huh.

"War! Hold up."

Wyatt came jogging up. "Sorry to shout. Wanted to let you know we're heading home—back to the ranch."

Warrick's brows bounced up. "I thought you were coming to Mom's."

"Yeah, sorry. Change of plans. But she's definitely expecting you guys. She gave me an earful when I talked to her." He held up his phone and widened his eyes.

"I see. Got some of your own fireworks to make, huh?" Warrick made a ridiculously goofy face and winked.

Wyatt rolled his eyes.

"You're gross." He glanced over his shoulder at Calla, who was chatting with Wells and Liam Morrison. "But yeah, we do."

He hit us with a broad smile, startling both for its beauty and rarity, because I was fairly sure I'd never seen him do that before, then jogged back over to his date.

"Well then. We just got ditched. I guess it's just you, me, and my beloved mother. Just how I like my dates with a beautiful woman." He winked, mouth open in a wide smile.

"You should probably stop winking. I'm a little worried you think it's cute, considering you just did it twice in the span of two minutes."

He gasped and pressed a hand to his chest. "What? Moi? I don't just think it's cute, I *know* it is."

He winked one eye, then the other, and then a grin spread across his face.

I laughed and rolled my eyes, but followed him to his car. The reality? It *was* cute. Somehow, this big tower of a man could make sarcastic winks adorable. And frankly, even when goofy, he was devastatingly handsome.

He rolled the windows down once we were settled into the seats and took a deep breath, then let it out as he stared out the window at the oak tree in front of us. Something about it hit me low in the stomach, like he was bracing for what came next. With me? His mom?

So unlike the jaunty demeanor of seconds ago.

Before I could ask him if he was okay, he turned and gave me a small grin.

"Alright. Ready for a hot fake date with my mom?"

CHAPTER TWENTY-FIVE

Warrick

I pulled up to my mom's place right as Sadie's phone buzzed in her little purse. The sound drew my attention, but I immediately jerked away since her purse was pinned between her bare knees and her skirt had slipped up to midthigh.

Don't get me wrong—great freaking view, but I couldn't be sitting here ogling her legs. The reality of this situation felt heavy enough. Being close to her, having her at the brewery with what felt like the whole town seeing us together, had sent my mind and heart chasing their tails.

"I'm sorry. I think I need to get this. It's my parents." She held up her phone, a regretful tent to her brows.

"No worries. I'll give you some privacy."

Outside the car, I eyed the house my mom had called home the last few years. She'd bought it off an older couple, and I'd helped her fix it up. It'd started the renovation bug in me, and I'd ended up getting certified in all kinds of stuff in the process. The front porch had baskets of bright red, pink, and white geraniums hanging at intervals. On the ground, little pots packed to the brim with carefully chosen plants and flowers flanked the door. Just around the corner, several of her famous roses peeked from their north-facing bed.

"Oh! You're here already." Mom slipped out the front door, purse over her shoulder and Tupperware of something in her hand.

"Yeah, we are. I texted you we were on our way." And why did she look like she was leaving?

"Of course you did. I'm a little scatterbrained. When I got Wyatt's call, I decided maybe I should go out and be social. So you and Sadie can have the yard to yourselves. It'll be fantastic."

She gave me one of her broad, *everything will be fine* smiles. I knew it well because it was the same one I gave to someone I was letting down easy.

"You don't need to go. We're here to spend time with you, Mom. I don't want you to leave just so we—" I cleared my throat, a bucket of nervous anticipation dumping over me.

"Oh, you'll make the best of it, I'm sure." She winked at me, but didn't stop walking, clickety-clacking on her sparkly sandals, which, come to think of it, seemed fancy for the twenty-fourth, but matched her dress...

"Were you ever going to be here? Was Wyatt?"

Her head turned to me and those blue eyes, exactly like Wyatt's, blinked back at me, all innocence.

"Of course I was. You'll see I've got everything set up. But my friend Carol is having a rough year, and she's alone tonight, and I just thought it'd be nice. She and I will have some quality time and you and Sadie can enjoy the view and, you know, a little privacy." She winked.

I realized how annoying that must've been for Wyatt and Sadie only minutes ago and vowed to never wink again unless my aim was to irritate someone.

"This is pretty rude, Mom. You invited us, and now you're bailing. Sadie's going to—"

"Sadie's going to be just fine with you here to keep her company. Plus, from the look of it, she just got bad news. See to your woman. I'm off." She wiggled her fingers and slipped into the front seat of her car.

Irritation crawled up my spine until her car door slammed and her words about "my woman" sank in. I turned just as Sadie was leaving the car, a determined look on her face. Not sure what my mom had seen, but she looked okay. Unless she'd overheard our conversation and realized my mom was ditching us.

"Hey, sorry about that one." I nodded to my mom's car as she sped off, a hand waving wildly from the driver's side window as she went. "She's got a friend in need, so it's just you and me."

"Oh. Sure. No problem."

Her response wasn't all that small. It shouldn't have raised a flag, but it did. A big, fat red one. Something was wrong.

"Please don't take this personally. She's being weird, but it's nothing new, honestly. Jane Saint lives by the beat of her own drum, and I suppose she's earned the right." And I knew for a fact this was her trying to force me and Sadie into a romantic situation. Fireworks on a warm summer night?

Yeah, that had Jane Saint all over it.

Before we got in too deep with my mom's scheming, I had to ask. "Everything okay with your folks?"

She shook her head, evidently not ready to talk about it.

"I'm here. If I can help, or you just need to vent." Or maybe I was reading this all wrong, but I didn't think so.

As we rounded the house on the stone pavers I'd laid years back, I chuckled as the view came into focus. *Yeah, real subtle, Mom.*

"Wow."

Sadie's soft exclamation made me want to reach out and take her hand. Pull her to me. Reassure her she had nothing to worry about with this.

And another part of me? Wanted to sink into the moment. Take what my mom had done and run with it. See what might lay here under the surface of this agreement we'd made. Because every minute I spent with Sadie made me like her all the more. Our relationship had moved from cordial strangers to close friends, and I couldn't pretend I didn't want more of it. Of her.

"Yeah, she's mildly obsessed with her backyard," I said, directing my attention to the matter at hand. My mother's beloved yard.

She really was obsessed, but with good reason. Aidan Wallace had designed the space, one of his first small jobs back to landscaping after everything that'd happened with him. He'd created a masterful mix of wildflowers, drought-resistant plants, and perennial blooms, though tonight, with the sun nearly fully set, we couldn't see those details as well. There were terraces of grass that the natural spring running through the north side of her property helped to nourish. On the patio directly outside the back door of the house, she had a large grill, glass bulb lights strung at angles across the space, and a fire pit surrounded by extremely comfortable chairs.

She loved her house, but it was tiny. She'd snagged this property because it gave her something to do *and* enjoy. I had to admit, it was a killer setup. Someday, I'd buy a house for myself that I intended to keep, and I'd go to town like we had on her place.

"This is magical. Gorgeous." Sadie clasped her hands together and held them to her chest.

I'd seen her do this before, and it got me today just like it had the first time.

Crap, I like this girl.

"It is pretty magical. We'll have to come back in the day so you can see the garden better. I'm sure she'd love to give you a tour and tell you the name of every single plant she has in here."

Sadie laughed, still that understated, soft sound that made me study her. It wasn't that she was normally loud, but more like someone had thrown a blanket over a speaker. Something obscured her, and it'd changed since we'd left the party.

She wandered around the patio and lightly touched the chairs seated at a large round table made of stone. She glanced up through the strung-up lights, took a deep breath, and her shoulders dropped low as she released it.

That was it. I couldn't pretend I didn't see she was visibly deflating right in front of me. "Ready to talk it out?"

She turned to me, lips pressed into a firm line. "That was my parents on the phone."

I nodded, remembering that tight tone in her voice when she'd seen the call coming through. "How'd that go?"

Based on what she'd told me, probably not well.

She swung her little purse up onto the table and let it

plunk down, her eyes everywhere but on mine. "Oh, just great. They told me they're so excited to meet you that they've decided we should come up tomorrow instead of Saturday and stay over. They'll send a car. We can stay in a guest room they've already had made up, and it'll be *lovely*."

Her tone belied her panic. She must've been parroting words directly from her folks.

And me? My mind had stuck on *guest room*. Guest room, singular. Just the one room. Just one bed too, no doubt.

A fist clenched in my gut as pure wanting gripped me. I'd kept those thoughts away relatively successfully, had forced them out of my mind every time we hung out, or when I thought of her during the day, and especially at night. I didn't go there mentally, and I'd trained myself to stay away from that line of thinking.

Now here it came, running back on a breakaway streak through my befuddled brain. All I could do? Open my mouth and let something fall out. "Oh. Okay."

She whipped around. "Okay?"

"Yeah, I mean... we'll do it."

Her eyes doubled in size—perhaps in direct proportion to my insanely chill outward response. If she had any inkling about the weird can-can panic dance going on in my chest, she might not be so incensed.

Her mouth parted, then pressed into a grim line. "You can't mean that. An engagement party surrounded by vaguely familiar strangers is one thing, but a night and an entire day before that being peppered for details about our relationship and how soon you plan to propose and set me up in a nice mansion somewhere closer to a major international airport? No. Just... no."

She'd been wringing her hands together, but when I noticed, she quickly tucked them under her arms.

I dared to step closer, and she didn't take off, so I took that as a good sign. "I want to understand. You're upset, and I get it on one level, but I'm confused by your reaction on another."

She swallowed with effort, then sank onto a chaise lounge next to her. "I'm sorry. I'm overreacting."

She sighed and dropped her face into her hands. I moved to sit by her and didn't shy away from placing a hand on her back. I needed to show her I was with her in this, even if I didn't totally get it, and this was one small way.

"Can you tell me?" I asked.

She straightened a bit but didn't move away from my touch, so I kept on, my hand smoothing over the silky fabric, not quite riding high or low into any interesting places—the bare skin at her neck and shoulders, or her lower back. Just small soothing movements.

"Because apparently, I have no backbone when it comes to them. I know this is an issue and I've actually spent a lot of time on this in therapy. And by a lot of time, I mean, like, *years*. So answering a call thinking it'd be a quick question about when we plan to arrive Saturday and getting roped into more, and not telling them no? I'm just so mad. At myself."

"That sucks. I'm sorry."

"It does suck. And it's worse because I'm dragging you into this. And I realize that to solve this problem, I could call them up and say no, we won't be coming. Or better yet, I don't have a boyfriend and you're just a friend coming to help me out and be a fun date. But I can't do that because I don't want to disappoint them, and far more than that, I don't want to ruin this day for Marguerite and anything I do other than show up with you and a smile will be construed as causing problems."

When she looked up at me, a strand of hair slipped in front of her eye. I tucked it back behind her ear, then lifted her chin so her gaze met mine head-on. My hand slid to her cheek, and I cupped it in my palm as I said, "I'm not worried. We'll go, we'll have fun. I'll see your childhood home and put to rest all of the questions I've always had. Then we'll return to Silverton and get back to our lives."

Her lashes fluttered and she leaned into my hand like it brought her comfort. Then her gaze dropped to my lips, and my stomach dropped through the floor.

The summer night's breeze whispered around us, stirring up something like magic or fate. The moment stretched and heated, and when her eyes met mine again, the look of sheer desire I saw there made all other thoughts evaporate.

There had never existed a woman more beautiful or compelling. There had never been an instant filled with such an obvious way forward.

So I kissed her.

CHAPTER TWENTY-SIX

Sadie

I didn't mean to grab hold of the shirt at his shoulders. I didn't intend to lean into him or deepen the kiss at a new angle when he made a soft, surprised groan. But I did it.

Nothing had felt so good. Ever. His lips were firm but gentle. Kind of like him—muscle covering what I knew with certainty was doughy softness at his soul. And though I wished he would've, he didn't press for more. Didn't open his mouth or demand. He seemed to simply savor the connection between us, which lit up like fireflies in my belly.

The kiss lasted for too-quick minutes, and far sooner than I would've liked, he pulled away. The dark had closed in, only Jane's patio lights casting a glow over us. That was enough, though. Enough to see his face change and his eyes darken with concern and regret.

"I—"

Pop!

A sharp crackle spread over us, interrupting his words. Then a second later, a bang that echoed in my rapidly hollowing chest.

"Guess it's starting. Where should we sit?" I asked, silently begging him not to apologize for kissing me.

It'd been too sweet. Too perfect. After consoling me, listening to me without judgment, he'd brought me comfort and pleasure in a moment I never wanted to forget, and certainly didn't want to erase with apologies and regrets. Of course, we'd have to talk about it. At some point. But not tonight. Maybe not this weekend.

Soon enough, the lines between us wouldn't be blurry. They'd be painted a foot thick and leave me stranded on one side and him untouchable on the other. So for now, I didn't want to talk about the kiss or how it couldn't happen again. I didn't want to review what good buds we were or be reminded we had no future romantically. He didn't want marriage. And I, ostensibly, wasn't ready for a relationship.

Though that had become less true by the minute the more time I'd spent with Warrick. Problem was, obviously enough, I wanted that with him, and he couldn't give it.

He spread out a blanket on the grass of the terrace farthest from the house. It was only about a hundred feet back on a slight hill, and that little incline gave us a clear view over Jane's house and out toward the fireworks now popping in earnest. They set them off quite close to her house, and I realized we must've been closer into town than I'd thought.

I stood at the edge of the blanket and looked at him, my heart still sprinting from the kiss and the loud explosions overhead. His long legs were bent, and he looked big as always, but a little unsure. Like I might not join him after what he'd just done, as though I hadn't willingly participated. He patted the space next to him and I quickly dropped to my knees and took my place, wanting to make sure he could see I wasn't hesitating to be near him now.

If he only knew how much I liked this—even just sitting by him, feeling heat radiating from his golden skin, he'd probably be freaked out. Well, probably not, since he's Warrick and very little seemed to bother him.

"I didn't realize we were so close. It felt like we drove a ways out of town." The booms of the fireworks arrived at regular intervals, and now that we were both sitting on the blanket, just inches apart, there was no need to yell.

"The road is a little windy, but it cuts back on itself. It's like a ten-minute walk to town, but the drive is the same because of the road. My house is about five minutes from here. It's kind of weird, but it works perfectly for fireworks since they shoot them off on the east side of the high school's football field."

A series of coordinated explosions went off, one after another. We craned our necks up to see until he tipped back and rested his head on his bent arm. *Goodness.* He looked ridiculously appealing all stretched out like that, the muscles in that arm on full display. He'd worn a short-sleeved button-up shirt, so it didn't fit to that magnificent chest quite as well as a T-shirt would've, but he still looked nothing short of mouthwatering.

I shifted my eyes back to the sky, then felt his hand tug on mine. With a glance—a short one, so I didn't singe my retinas with his hotness in that laid-back pose—I saw the invitation. And despite the little prickles of warning telling me this might be too much for my already-fluttering heart, I laid down next to him on the blanket.

My head sank into the fabric on top of Jane's soft grass as bright lights exploded overhead. I didn't think about how good it felt to know Warrick was right there, his shoulder brushing mine. If I thought about that, I'd think about how easy it would be to rest my head on that same shoulder or roll to my side and set a hand on the ripped stomach I'd touched hours ago. Or how much I wanted to kiss him again.

"We should probably talk about—"

"Can we not?"

He turned his head to the side, and I did the same so our faces were inches apart. "We should."

I sighed. "I know. But can we just not for tonight? Maybe in the car tomorrow. We'll have a long drive and tonight, I just want to enjoy the show and being here with you."

His gaze skated over my face and though I couldn't see him perfectly, I could've sworn his eyes dipped to my lips.

"Okay. Tomorrow it is."

The next day, we were silent in the car for the first ten minutes. He'd walked up to the rear exit of my building just as Martin, my parents' driver, messaged he'd pulled up in front. Warrick grabbed my small suitcase when I showed him the text, and my stomach had twisted itself into a pile of knots large enough I didn't even attempt to protest.

And so, here we were. Ten minutes into the forty-minute drive up the canyon, though a different one than he'd take to get to All Saints Ranch and his family's homestead. That little detail, that he had to drive such a long way to get to school too, had been one thing I'd liked about him.

Such a silly commonality, but almost everyone else in our graduating class had lived within walking distance of the high school. Maybe ten of us had a commute that required wheels, and Warrick and I had been the only ones who had such a slog. The county was so sparsely populated outside of Silverton, it was the nearest city and actually still the city for my parents' address despite being so far out. Granted, they didn't reside there except maybe a few weeks a year, but they maintained the residence.

"So, we going to talk about this?" Warrick asked in low tones.

I glanced to see the back of Martin's head. He'd been with the family for about a decade—he'd never been my driver while I lived at home, but he seemed like a nice person. Even so, I didn't want him to overhear this. "Martin, would you mind closing the privacy screen?"

He nodded and the little panel rose slow and steady. The modified Land Rover had this feature, which I'd always thought of as just rude and superfluous, but today, I appreciated it.

"Yes." I tilted in my seat, my knees aimed toward him, hands in my lap. "So."

Half his smile kicked up, and he mimicked me—tucked his knees together and tilted to the side, hands primly placed on his quads. "So."

A chuckle tripped out of me, and one of those knots came loose. "I'm not sure what to say."

His brows wrinkled. "You don't need to say anything. I need to apologize. I shouldn't have kissed you."

Disappointment sank into my belly like stones into

water. I knew it had to happen, but that hadn't stopped me from hoping for a different outcome.

And what would that be?

I shook away that snarky thought because I didn't know. All I *did* know was that I wanted him any way I could get him, so if friends was it, then... so be it. He'd made my life better just by being in it, and I didn't want to ruin that by insisting he not feel regretful or sorry if that was how he truly felt.

That said, I wasn't going to act like he *needed* to apologize.

"It's fine. Please, you don't even need to say that. I actually did think it might've been..." I swallowed back a tidal wave of nerves. "It might've been good practice. Being close like that."

His brows dipped and that half-smile returned. "Oh yeah? You planning on making out with me in front of your folks?"

"No. Absolutely not." I should've been horrified, but his eyebrows wiggling and the fake lascivious grin he gave me made it impossible.

"Bummer. But maybe better for my first impression." He winked, that ridiculously cheesy look making my shoulders relax a touch.

We rode in silence for a while—more than a while, since I only snapped out of the motion-induced trance when Martin steered the car into the steep drive of my parents' home. My mind had been a muted mess—no clear thoughts, only dread, anxiety, and an aching sense of wanting mixing together to make me wordless.

Warrick had stayed quiet, which had to mean he was lost in his thoughts too, or maybe he could just tell I was. Now that we'd reached this point, anything in me that'd relaxed knotted up again. Still, I needed to make one thing clear before we walked in.

"I need you to promise me something."

"Anything," he said, completely serious.

My stomach swooped low as I looked at his handsome face. He'd trimmed his beard and hair in the last few days and he looked so appealing, it almost hurt to look at him. Instead of placing a hand on his cheek like I wanted, I twisted my fingers together.

"Promise me that you won't do anything you're uncomfortable with. And swear to me that if you're upset or this gets... I don't know, if anything gets weird, you'll tell me, and we'll go. I don't care when—just tell me, and we're gone."

His eyes flickered back and forth between mine like he could read something there. I wondered what. Dread at spending the next thirty-six hours with my parents? Gratitude for his being here with me? Fear that I'd do something stupid that pushed him away and I'd lose him, even the little that I had of him?

"I promise I won't do anything that makes me uncomfortable. And"—he glanced out the window as Martin stopped the car and exited—"I swear I'll tell you if I need to go. But Sadie, I don't anticipate that. And I want you to promise the same."

I chuckled, though it was the very definition of a humorless laugh. "I'm positive you won't do anything that makes me uncomfortable. And I'm bracing for whatever's next in there, but I am doing my best to stay positive and not lean into the rather stark gloom gathering on my horizon."

His face softened into a look full of sweetness and concern.

"We'll be fine. I'll protect you." Then he squeezed my

wrist in a comforting gesture and slipped out of the car. Martin opened my door, and I slid out too.

It should've sounded like a joke or a throwaway statement, but he hadn't made a face. He hadn't been wearing that joking, silly mask he donned when he was teasing. This was purely him, and I knew he would do his very best to protect me, even if he didn't fully know what he was protecting me from.

But as I smoothed my dress and took a deep breath, I could feel it down to my toes. As much as I dreaded all of this and the ocean-sized bucket of emotions spending this time with my family would unearth, I knew one thing with a sparkling, blade-sharp clarity.

This weekend, things would change. Between me and my parents? Maybe. But Warrick would see into just how small I became, how I folded myself up and tucked me away. He'd never look at me the same way, and I'd thought that would be just fine when all this started, but I hated the reality of it.

He wouldn't need to protect me from anyone else, and he couldn't protect me from myself.

CHAPTER TWENTY-SEVEN

Warrick

Generally? I liked people. Other than a small handful I'd disliked fairly immediately for one reason or another, I gave new faces a shot. And while technically Sadie's parents, Randall and Arianna Miller, weren't *new faces* as I'd seen their literal faces in a few Miller State Alum publications Wyatt got, I could easily say I thoroughly disliked these two jerkwads.

"Warrick, tell us. What do you think of the developments in Silverton?"

Arianna tilted her head to the side, brows raised in expectation. She had blond hair pulled into a low, stylish ponytail. Every part of her was polished, and she was strikingly pretty, even in her late fifties or whatever she was.

I bought time while I chewed and resisted the urge to slam my fist on the table. The question was innocuous enough, though even it had a whiff of superiority. Like they weren't currently technically in Silverton, and their daughter hadn't been living there for years. Like it was some quaint little slip of a township instead of a city that'd grown exponentially in the last decade, and particularly the last few years.

But the fist-pounding motivation came from the fact that the question had been directed at me. Not that I couldn't answer or didn't have thoughts, but they had addressed exactly one question to Sadie since we'd arrived two hours ago. *One.*

"Leave the poor man alone, Mother. Let him eat in peace."

Marguerite caught my eye with a meaningful look, something that said maybe she wasn't as awful as her parents, though the jury was out thus far.

"Fine, fine. Of course, Warrick, dear. I didn't mean to pester you." Arianna's voice had started to grate.

The only voice I wanted to hear was the one that hadn't spoken a word since we'd sat down for dinner. Even when Marguerite had asked Sadie a question only she could answer—about her bakery expansion—someone had interrupted and she didn't get to talk.

"Has Sadie told you about the expansion plans for her business?" I asked, trying to circle back and give her an opening.

She stiffened next to me but kept her focus on her plate.

Marguerite smiled. "I want to hear—"

"You need to be careful about these kinds of things. Expansion can be the quickest way to failure if it's not carefully planned." Randall spoke for the first time since the very beginning of the meal.

Mostly, he sat at the head of the table, looking for all the world like he wished he had a newspaper he could sink his teeth into and transport himself away from the table surrounded by his two daughters and their men.

"Sadie's actually brilliant with the business part of things. She mentioned a subscription service she's getting off the ground in the fall the other day. Have you let your devotees know about that?"

Okay, so Marguerite was maybe a good egg. *Maybe.*

Sadie set down her fork and gripped the napkin in her lap, which only I could see since we sat next to each other.

"I haven't put it out yet. I wanted to make sure I know what demand I can handle with the obligations I have from restaurants. I—"

"Is this wise? Should you be committing to things like this?" Arianna's voice had never sounded more shrill.

I clenched my jaw, wanting to jump in but hoping Sadie would. And this time, she did.

"It's fine. This is what I do." Her blue eyes weren't hiding or downcast. They were directly meeting her mother's.

A small surge of pride filtered through me. *Atta girl!*

"Is it? You've just said you're expanding. You don't know about your demand yet. You may not have enough of a customer base to need expansion. You may be jumping the gun here, sweetie."

Randall's tone was more infantilizing than I could've imagined. My molars were in danger of being ground into dust based on the way my teeth were crushed together to keep me from speaking.

"Dad," Marguerite said in a low, embarrassed tone.

"I'm just saying, she's going to overextend herself and end up in trouble."

Next to me, Sadie took a deep breath and set her fork on her plate. Then, in a move I couldn't have choreographed better, she stood, and spoke.

"With all due respect, you know nothing about my business. You've never tried to understand it, or me for that matter. I've been sought after by no fewer than thirty restaurants in the state. This week, I had a billionaire beg me to sell him my company for seven figures. And while yes, it's a small operation I'm only just now, after years of long hours and hard work, figuring out how to scale up, I'm proud of it, and I should be. And you should be too, but you refuse to see it because it's not something you're interested in. And thanks to a lot of therapy, I'm relatively okay with that. But please don't try to advise me on a business you know nothing about."

She pushed in her chair and cleared her throat. "If you'll excuse me, I woke up at three-thirty this morning for work, so I'm going to head to bed. Thank you for dinner."

Her eyes found mine, and I popped out of my seat faster than a top dollar running back. "Yes. Thank you for dinner."

Sadie took my hand, and out we went, the table still stunned into silence behind us.

We didn't speak until I shut the door to our room, a place we'd spent approximately five minutes before Marguerite had texted to say it was time for cocktails.

Sadie kicked off her shoes and crawled onto the bed, still fully clothed in her dress. She flopped onto her side and I could see her blinking back tears.

"You okay?" I asked, coming to sit on the edge of the bed next to her.

"Yeah." It sounded watery, but sure.

"Want to talk it through?"

Her eyes hit mine, and I died a little. She was so damned beautiful, even now, but no one should make her feel like this.

"Not really. I think I used every last bit of energy I had in reserve to get that speech out."

I smoothed a hand along her head, all of her sunshine hair still neat in its low bun she'd likely been wearing since three this morning. "It was a damn fine speech. I'm proud of you. Are you proud of you?"

She loosed a big sigh. "I don't know if *pride* is right, but I'm relieved. I didn't become a shriveled up little raisin of myself in there like I used to. But I'm not sure any amount of time will free me from the regret over having to say any of that in the first place."

"I get that. Ideally, you wouldn't need to."

She nodded and tucked her chin down into where her hands were curled close to her chest. My hand fell to her shoulder, so I left it there but let my fingers gently trail over her trap until I registered the tension there.

"Good grief, woman. Your traps are like steel."

She chuckled silently. "I may or may not have been a little stressed these last few days."

I pressed into the muscle, not too hard, and her eyes closed like it felt too good to keep them open. "Can I give you a back rub? Please? I think my back is crying out on your back's behalf."

One eye peeked open. "Your back is very opinionated for a nonverbal body part."

"Tell me these shoulders haven't been talking to you. I bet your neck is too." My hand slid down the curved line of her spine.

She exhaled a slow breath. "I admit nothing. But please don't stop touching me."

Then it clicked. I was sitting here pawing at her, and until that exact moment, she hadn't given me permission. *Yikes.* I'd already kissed her without warning yesterday, and here I was feeling her up? *Get ahold of yourself, idiot!* Granted, I was genuinely massaging her, and not trying to coerce her into something else.

Touching her, consoling her, felt so natural, I hadn't even stopped to think. But that wouldn't work. *You have to stop and think!*

If touching her like this sent all kinds of ideas into my head, that was my problem. "I won't stop. But roll onto your stomach so I can use both hands."

She glanced up at me and our eyes locked. It might've been heated or sensual considering we were sitting on a bed and I was massaging her, but all I saw there was exhaustion and that she felt safe here. We'd come out of the crapstorm of her family dinner and into this quiet place, the space between us so comforting, she could relax. Rest. Recharge before we had to dive into the fray again tomorrow.

I wanted her to know she was safe here. She always would be with me. And that she was awesome. And so beautiful it made my stomach hurt.

Then she rolled over, before I said something stupid to ruin the moment. And I got to work running my thumbs into the muscles lining her spine, those fist-tight sections of her shoulders, and even along her neck. At one point, she leaned up and took her hair out, and then seemed to truly relax. After another few minutes, her breathing evened out and she'd fallen asleep.

I'd like to say I didn't sit there and watch her sleep, but I did. I let my fingers play with her hair a while longer, just in case it wasn't like this again tomorrow. I had to admit I hoped it would be—not with her sad and recovering from a confrontation, but with us close.

Closer.

CHAPTER TWENTY-EIGHT

Sadie

A knock on the door woke me at seven the next morning. I lay curled on my side, still in my dress.

"One sec," I said, and hustled to the bathroom to find my eye makeup looking like I was heading to an Alice Cooper impersonation contest—probably best Warrick was nowhere in sight.

Warrick. Just thinking his name made my stomach flip. Maybe that was him at the door, though I doubted he'd knock after spending the night right next to me. Or, so I assumed.

The fact that I'd slept so hard for ten hours meant I had no idea how our first night in a shared bed had gone. Maybe that was for the better, since it had the potential to be so charged, at least on my end.

He'd been so heartbreakingly sweet last night. He'd tried hard to make my parents acknowledge me, and I hadn't thought to warn him about that—maybe because I'd hoped it wouldn't be necessary this time.

And it did feel like heartbreak this morning, especially after finding him gone. Heartbreak over the burgeoning, unignorable feelings I had for him, and that all-too-familiar rawness of facing the reality of my relationship with my parents.

The knock sounded again and Marguerite's voice came through the door. "I just need a minute, and I have coffee."

Bless her. I needed caffeine since I typically had my first cup around four a.m. A dippy little part of my brain had hoped it might've been Warrick, but again, it made sense it was Marguerite, I supposed. Not that I expected to roll over and see him sleeping soundly next to me, but... well, I kind of had. I'd looked forward to seeing what a sleepy Warrick Saint looked like, so sue me.

I shuffled to the door and swung it open to find Marguerite, steaming mug of coffee in her hand, smiling gently at me. Her hair fell a few inches below her chin, the locks the same bright blond as mine. Her makeup was perfect, her dress stylish and perfectly pressed, and her nails manicured. I never let myself paint my nails for fear of nail polish chips in bread, so this was the only real point of envy I felt.

Had I been any less well-rested, I would've felt far more irritated. This was the smile she used when she was afraid I was having an *episode*. And she didn't always treat it that way consciously—she was genuinely concerned for me. I would never stop thinking of her as my helper and beloved sister, but sometimes, this tendency to treat me like a wounded animal chafed worse than whatever it was actually bothering me.

"How are you?" she asked, brows tented in concern.

"Come in, sit down." I took the mug from her and cupped it in two hands as we moved to the sitting area of the room.

Two high-backed chairs with a small marble-topped side table between them occupied the corner of the room nearest the window, so we each took a seat.

"Thanks for the coffee." I took a sip and sighed, grateful for the fuel.

"Of course. I figured you'd be exhausted this morning after last night, and when you didn't come down with your man, I thought maybe you weren't well." She swallowed and pressed out that thin smile again.

"I was exhausted, for sure. I've definitely been dreading the weekend, but not surprisingly, dinner took it out of me, too. I can't believe I slept this late."

Her eyes flickered over me. "You look pretty rough."

I chuckled and shook my head. "Thanks so much."

"You fell asleep in a silk dress." She wrinkled her nose just a little.

"Yeah."

We sat in that awkward stew for a minute before she took a deep breath that drew my attention back to her.

"Listen. I feel like I need to apologize. I know I make excuses for them a lot, but last night, they were extra awful."

I laughed. "I'm not sure I've ever heard you say that outright."

She shrugged. "Well, it's accurate here. I'm sorry. I haven't known how to talk about you with them because they're so *weird* about you. Like they don't want to acknowledge your anxiety, and yet they don't know how to treat you normally either."

Wow. Okay. She'd gone for it. We'd never fully talked

this out, but I guessed now was as good a time as any. "That's pretty accurate too. But you kind of do the same."

She reared back. "What?"

"Not that you ignore it, but you seem to worry that talking about it will make it worse or something. I don't know. You've been my biggest champion at times, and then at others..."

Her face dropped. "I'm sorry. I—I admit I don't know how to. And we've never been all that close, so it's always seemed like something I should know, but I don't."

"How would you know without asking?"

Did she really expect to understand how to talk to me about something sensitive, something big, without learning more about it *from me?*

She let out a breathy, mirthless chuckle. "Yeah, fair point. I'm used to just doing what I need to, making decisions, and I think after New York, I felt like, 'okay, I did what I could to help her, now it's up to her.'"

My face must've shown the mix of disappointment and hurt swirling in my gut, because she reached out and grabbed my hand. "I get that was wrong. It was."

I nodded, crushing my mouth closed against the rising emotion. I didn't need tears to muddle things even more here.

"Can we use this weekend as a starting point? A new start? I'm on Team Mercedes, and I love you. I want you to get to know Doug and *me*, and I want to help you with our very thick parents. If you want my help."

I smiled at that, and she reached out and pulled me into a hug. I got ahold of myself and told her that I liked the idea of a fresh start. We spent an hour chatting until I couldn't put off getting ready for the day any longer. We hugged again, planned to have breakfast together tomorrow morning before we all dispersed, and she remembered to leave me with a final thought as she snuck out the door.

"Can I just say, well done with him?" Her mouth dropped open, eyes flared wide, and she gave me two thumbs up—a gesture I couldn't imagine she had ever made before.

I didn't disagree. Warrick was a dream, all except that whole no serious relationship or marriage thing. But as I stepped into the shower, it wasn't Warrick on my mind. It was Arianna and Randall.

I'd said what I needed to say to my parents, yet I'd failed to mention one essential part. Maybe it'd been my pride's rallying cry to skip this part, but I wanted them to be proud. I wanted them to see what I'd built and marvel at it. I didn't want to be counseled or warned about how bad my choices were. They wouldn't even know what my choices were because they'd never stopped long enough to consider them. But they could be proud of what I'd done—and even without the help of a husband to pat my head and send me to bed at the right time.

It'd taken the entire cocktail hour and dinnertime to summon the words, the calm, and the ability to speak. Warrick had tried to loop me in by mentioning me, asking me, referring to my life in Silverton, and still, they'd always shifted it away—back to themselves, Marguerite, or Warrick. And to her credit, Marguerite had tried more than once to direct questions to me or bring attention to my expansion, which we'd texted about. But the focus simply hadn't shifted, not once, until the end.

I didn't envy any of them the attention, though it'd cut deeper than I'd expected to sit there and be invisible to them.

I'd made peace with this aspect of our relationship, and

yet here it cropped up again. Healing wasn't a one-time deal, and I knew that well enough. Still, for some silly reason, even though I'd been dreading the weekend, I'd hoped it'd be more about me and Warrick and less completely ignoring *me*.

My heart felt bruised this morning. A little less so after repairing things with Marguerite, since that conversation had been years in the making. Maybe she knew how crappy her way of talking to me about coming to this event had been, or maybe she'd been struck by how messed up the dynamic surrounding me was in the family as a whole. I was thankful at least she and I were in a better place.

But my parents? I needed to find them and talk to them, make sure things were smoothed over before tonight. And hopefully, close the gap between what I'd said and that I did still care. Probably far too much.

Most immediately, though, I needed to get cleaned up and get food, and then find Warrick.

Finding Warrick sweat-soaked and chugging water wasn't an entirely unusual occurrence, but finding him in that state in the kitchen of my childhood home chatting football with my father? Jarring.

Like, swapping sugar and salt in a sweet bread recipe. No. Just... no. I had things to discuss with each man, and I wasn't about to have either conversation in front of the other person.

"Hey, how are you?" Warrick said, attention shifting fully to me the second he saw me.

"Good. Hungry." I glanced at my dad, whose eyes carefully tracked Warrick's hand coming up to slide into place and cup my jaw and cheek.

"I won't kiss you, because I'm gross. But... you know." He winked, and my stomach tumbled down a previously unforeseen stairwell.

"That's—okay." That lovely reply ended with a swallowed half groan at the way his thumb swept over the apple of my cheek.

"Warrick was just telling me about his recovery after surgery on his shoulder." My dad nodded to him in this way that made me know he wanted to get back to that conversation.

"Great to talk with you, sir. I should probably go get cleaned up." Warrick ducked his head and spoke right to me. "Come find me when you're done."

His silken, rich tone was dark chocolate dripping down the side of a perfectly formed bundt cake. *Maybe I need to put bundts on the menu soon.*

"Okay. Shouldn't be too long," I managed.

He nodded, a glimmer in his eye that told me he might have some idea how he affected me, and then I was alone. No kitchen staff, just me and Randall.

"I would like to talk to you and Mom."

He nodded. "We suspected as much. She's in the day room."

He set down the mug he'd been using and paced away, me following just behind. My mother sat scrolling on her iPad but looked up, evidently entirely unsurprised to see me. My father gestured to the chair next to her, so I took the seat. He settled in across from us and looked at me.

Nervous energy bounced through me, and I pressed my

hands between my knees. *Okay*. Guess I'd be the emcee of this fun meeting.

"I wanted to clarify something from yesterday."

My father nodded, just slightly, and my mother's lashes fluttered, but she stayed perfectly still. Their minimal response wasn't unfamiliar, though I banished the thoughts that came barreling in. *They're not listening. They won't hear you. They don't care.*

In my heart of hearts, I knew they did care, but they didn't understand. I'd decided they didn't have to and had tried to live my life that way—knowing that they loved me in their way and doing my best to accept that it wasn't necessarily the way I needed.

Still, I wanted them to get this. I blew out a silent breath, then just went for it.

"What I said last night is important. I hope you heard it. But I also want you to know that your opinion of me matters—that's why I said anything at all. I've tried to ignore that part of myself, the part that wants your approval and recognition, even while I've been nearly desperate for it. Nothing you can say will change me or make me whole—I know this. But I do want you to be proud of me, to try to understand me, at least a little."

My mother jumped in. "We are proud of you, Mercedes, of course—"

"How can you be? You know nothing about my life or business, as last night's discussion exemplified." My heart clattered in my chest, but what should've made me feel nearly ill with anxiety—a feeling I'd felt no small handful of times when even thinking about talking to my parents about important things—miraculously didn't. I felt clear-headed.

My father cleared his throat. "Well, you've had your say?"

I stood, knowing that response signaled a hard end to this meeting. "For now, yes."

Because I was reserving the right to talk about this again, if needed. And I hoped I'd get something a bit more from them, but if not? Yes, I'd had my say.

He nodded, not exactly stern, but unsurprisingly not showing any real reaction to my words. "We'll see you to greet people at five, then."

A dismissal if I'd ever heard one.

So I returned his nod with a small one of my own, gave a similar gesture to my mother, and walked out.

"Mercedes." My father's voice stopped me before I reached the door and continued the second I turned back toward him. "You've done well with Warrick. He's good for you."

I searched my mind for a response as my feet carried me away without one. Those words, of all the words. Of everything they could've said after what I'd shared with them, how I'd tried to make them understand, it was *him*. It all came back to me needing someone else to take care of me, even when the very point I was trying to make was that I didn't *need* someone.

But I did *want* someone. For years, I'd been resisting that, almost like a Pavlovian response to their insisting I'd be *fixed* if I just had a man. Now I could parse that out more clearly than ever. While I didn't need Warrick, I did want him—even if I couldn't have him.

And so, it was time to find Warrick and drown out these feelings of disappointment and pride and confusion. Time to focus on him, because he was good for me—my father was right about that.

CHAPTER TWENTY-NINE

Warrick

Sadie entered our room ten minutes after I'd left her. Thank goodness I'd made my shower quick or she would've caught quite a show since I'd failed to take my clothes into the bathroom with me.

I eyed her as I approached. Her cheeks were flushed, hair so shiny it practically sparkled, and I grabbed the wood beam that made up the corner of the bed to keep my balance. Looking at her made the room tilt.

"How'd it go?" I asked, running a towel over my hair with my spare hand.

Her gaze cast around the room before landing on me. When our eyes met, I was glad I hadn't let go of the bed frame. *Good grief, she's beautiful.* I pushed off from the bed and moved to stand in front of her, where she'd leaned back against the closed door to our room.

I didn't need to be sitting here mooning over her. I needed to help her. Support her in some way that would erase that serious expression.

"It went okay, I think."

"You think?" I widened my stance, settling in, and the bonus was also that it made me a bit shorter.

"Yeah, I mean, they didn't respond to the most important stuff, but I didn't *really* expect them to. That's not how they seem to process things. But my dad did say that I've chosen well with you and that you're good for me. The Saint charm wins again." Her smile was fleeting but warm.

And though I wouldn't have blamed her if there had been, there was no trace of bitterness in that statement. The fact that her dad had declared his approval of me when I knew for a fact the whole point of the conversation revolved around how little they knew her... my hands curled into fists where they tucked under my arms.

"Seems like he may have missed the memo."

She huffed. "Yeah. Well... we'll see. Maybe it'll sink in."

My feet carried me forward before I thought better of it, and I stopped inches from her. "If they can't see how remarkable you are, they're idiots."

Her eyes flicked back and forth between mine, blinking rapidly, and then she grabbed hold of the shirt on either side of my waist and dropped her forehead to my chest.

My heart kicked at the same time my arms came to her shoulders.

"I don't want to cry about this," she said to the ground.

Only the tips of her fingers in my shirt and her forehead touched me, but my body buzzed from the contact and closeness. From the intimacy of this moment and her choice to share so much. It felt heavy in consequence, but not in weight. Not like a burden I had to carry for her, or if it was heavy, I'd been training all my damned life for it.

Not to be too dramatic, but it felt like this—exactly this kind of tenderness and care—was what I'd been missing for too long, and also what I'd been made for.

"Then don't. But it's okay if you need to, too." I rubbed my hands on her upper arms for a minute before I caved to my impulse and urged her closer. To my satisfaction, she came willingly, wrapping her arms right around my middle and pressing her whole body against me.

I had to close my eyes against the crush of heat and tenderness that rushed through me. I was ten feet tall and a puddle of mush all at once.

"You're amazing, Sadie. I don't know how long those things have needed to be said, but I hope you're proud that you did it. Whether they get it is on them."

She tilted her head so her chin rested on my chest. "Thank you."

"Anytime."

"Especially thank you for this hug." She squeezed me tighter.

"My hugs are at your disposal anytime you want one. Always."

Saying that aloud caused the truth to punch through me. I had feelings for Sadie—far from friendly feelings. I'd known this since the beginning. Hell, I'd had non-friendly feelings for Sadie since the day I saw her in tenth grade and she'd given me that nervous smile before we walked into Mr. Halyard's history class. But these feelings... these were the kind that could pull me under or run me over.

Even knowing that, I stayed there in an embrace so perfect it made my heart feel like it was double-beating. I didn't pull away because I didn't want to, and she wanted me. So I wasn't going anywhere.

Sadie flopped down on the huge blanket some poor sap had laid out under the tree not far from the tennis courts. *I know, right?* The estate had at least one of everything, and tennis courts were no exception.

Eye-hand coordination was squarely up my alley, so when Marguerite came knocking on Sadie's door a few minutes into that hug earlier, I happily agreed to a game of doubles. Sadie's sister and her fiancé, Doug, versus me and Sadie.

I hadn't expected Sadie to be an absolute beast. It took her a few minutes to warm up, but it turned out, she had incredible coordination and had played tennis all growing up. Never on a team, which I discovered she regretted, but she'd had a coach give her lessons at the house for years. *Fascinating.*

We'd only gotten ten minutes into the game before Arianna had come to steal Marguerite away for something related to the party tonight, so Doug begged off and Sadie and I played one on one for a few minutes before the heat of the day caught up with us. Fortunately, we were high enough in the mountains that simply shifting to the shade made a world of difference, and Jeeves, or whatever the butler's name was, had facilitated that.

"I think he packed us a lunch too, but we can go inside to eat if you're too hot." Sadie said this from the blanket where she lay exactly how she'd fallen down, eyes closed and her body unmoving other than her lips and the rise and fall of her chest.

I smiled to myself, enjoying the realization that this was what she did. She fell down into bed, the couch, or even a blanket and she just *stayed*. Didn't readjust to get comfortable, like she'd run completely out of fuel.

I hunched down and took a seat so I could lean against the tree and nudged her leg with mine. "I'm always too hot."

She chuckled and shook her head, though she didn't open her eyes or move otherwise. A thrill shot through me knowing I'd made her laugh and that she'd liked my lame joke.

"It's nice here. There's even a breeze. Jeeves picked the perfect picnic spot." I glanced in the direction where whatever his name was had disappeared after setting things up out here. Back inside to the AC, and probably to set about a long list of tasks before the party tonight.

Her laugh recaptured me, and I looked down to see her beaming back at me.

"His name is David. He's a very nice man."

I narrowed my eyes. "Should I be concerned about you running away with David the Butler?"

She popped up on one elbow to look at me. I couldn't read the expression there.

"Would you be concerned?"

I leaned forward so I could say, in a low, gritty voice, "My woman running away with the butler? Yeah, I'd be concerned."

Her grin spread slowly. It grew and grew until she dropped back onto the blanket and laughed. I couldn't help but smile along with her, my mind dizzy with the pleasure of winning that sound from her.

"I think I need to feed you, if that was so hilarious." I winked, playing it cool, but let my fingers capture a lock of hair that had spread out close enough to me to reach when she'd fallen back just now.

"I guess you do."

Her soft agreement did something new to my heart—maybe tenderized it. Because for the rest of the meal, every look or laugh or smile felt like she'd booted me down a hill and I was Westley in The Princess Bride yelling "Aaaas yoouuuu wiiiiiish" while I tumbled down, head over feet.

By the time we'd finished the sandwiches and fruit David had packed, and each sipped a glass of champagne along with ice-cold water, I felt drowsy with the afternoon heat and completely relaxed. No idea how it happened, yet eventually, we lay underneath the tree, her head on my stomach, chatting about nothing.

After a few minutes of quiet, she pulled my hand into hers and held them up to inspect. She pressed her much smaller palm to mine and measured the difference. We'd held hands before, and we were laying in a fairly intimate pose even now, but this purposeful comparison, the brush of my calloused palms against her soft skin, made my stomach clench.

"I always wondered what it'd be like to have such big hands." She slipped fingers between mine, and my hand instinctively closed around hers.

"The better to catch a football," I said, and if it sounded a little darker, grittier, who could blame me? She was essentially seducing me with her caresses.

Instead of accepting the joke, she sat up and set her free hand on my chest. Her fingers squeezed my opposite hand, and she licked her lips when she looked at me. "The better for a lot of things."

The air, already thick with summer heat, electrified between us. Our eyes locked, and I said something like, "Yeah, they are." Pure poetry, really, considering my brain had stopped functioning when her hand pressed into my chest and she'd said those words.

Maybe the champagne had loosened her up. Maybe I'd gotten heatstroke and hallucinated this whole thing. Either way, I sat up as she leaned down and the contact of our lips made wanting coil in my chest as a kind of relief washed through me.

I laid back slowly, urging her down with me. She gripped my shirt with one hand and leaned on the other next to my head, her upper body pressed to mine.

She'd kissed me back before, but it'd been so light and quick in the scheme of things, I'd convinced myself her response was a fluke. A matter of momentum and timing more than natural interest or need.

This kiss was far different than the last. I'd kept it chaste—closed, dry lips, and gentle presses. This time was night to that first kiss's day. It set fire to the memory of the other kiss and burned it up with a frantic, ravenous sensation of lips and tongues, teasing and tempting, drawing each other in until a bell rang and we pulled apart, breathing heavily and eyes blinking back at one another in a blurry disbelief.

She'd kissed me like the world was ending, and I'd kissed her right back. I didn't remember the last time I'd kissed someone with any intensity, and I couldn't think of a single kiss so purely pleasurable without rushing to something more. There was heat and need, no destination but simply kissing on this grassy hill under a tree. No ulterior motive here but a kiss.

Sadie bit her lip and smiled down at me, looking almost

shy, then her hand came up and she traced an index finger over my eyebrow. "You have good eyebrows."

I chuckled, though the sound was amazingly deceptive since it masked the dazed sensation that'd hit. "Thanks. I like yours too."

That might've sounded like a line, but I'd noticed her eyebrows. Honestly, I had. And despite the warning bell in my mind and the actual bell ringing somewhere on the property, I had to say something. I couldn't ignore the kiss like she had the other night. "So... that just happened."

She ducked her chin to her chest, though it didn't hide the evidence of her smile. "Yes, it very much did."

She sounded pleased, maybe even happy about it. She wouldn't have kissed me back like that if she hadn't been, and I saw the opening. I'd take the rushing yards and see where I could get. "Honestly, I'm glad. I feel like—"

But she'd started saying something too. "I think my mother was scandalized."

"Your mother?"

How did that relate? *Why* were we talking about that woman when I was just about to do something I didn't do?

She raised her head, humor in her eyes as she met mine.

"She was calling to me. Wasn't that why..." she faded off, and her expression dropped, slackened into what I now understood was a perfect imitation of deer in headlights.

She'd just made it clear. She'd kissed me, and maybe all of that hand-on-chest sweetness, because her mom had been watching. Her mom, who liked that she was with me and whom she wanted to make proud.

But for me, no. I hadn't kissed her because we'd had an audience and, idiot me, I hadn't been aware that was why she'd kissed me. I'd kissed her because it had been necessary and she'd leaned into me. She'd had that look. She'd...

No. She'd kissed me because her mom had been calling out to her. Because it'd been an opportunity—not motive-free. Not pure. Not at all.

I cleared my throat and sat up, which forced her to do the same. "Ha, no. Or, yeah, yes, of course. But, you know, I'm just saying. It was good. We make a good team, Miller."

I added a wink, just to make sure it felt light and easy—to make sure I hid the bit of me that tumbled down the hill from a great height, no Princess Buttercup falling after me.

Her frown deepened, but she nodded. "That we do."

Then we both busied ourselves with cleaning up the picnic and packing up the blanket. We walked side by side back to the house in silence, though my mind was screaming at me.

I'd thought we were getting closer. And we were—I wouldn't accept any claim to the contrary. But maybe that emotional connection I felt to her was different on her end. Maybe the way she viewed all of this—the personal conversations, even the cuddling and taking comfort in each other —maybe it was just part of what friendship looked like for her.

That shouldn't make me go cold in the middle of this July late afternoon, but it did. Because Sadie was soft and genuine and everything, I'd come to terms with the fact that Tracy wasn't. But she also wasn't for me.

So tonight, I'd put on the best show of my life. I'd fawn over her, make her look good—not that she actually needed my help to do that—and we'd end the night in the same bed again. I'd ignore the intimacy of that, the stupid anticipation that coursed through me *even now* as I thought about it, and I'd wake up tomorrow with my heart intact. It'd all be fine.

And when we got back to Silverton? I'd keep my

distance for a while. We needed space, after being crushed together so often lately. Eventually, I'd get my grip back, or build up callouses to this part of me that felt so ready for something she didn't want.

No way around it—I had to.

CHAPTER THIRTY

Sadie

Smoothing my hands down my cornflower blue silk dress, I shut my eyes and tried to calm myself. Normally, I'd be working to do that very thing before an event like this, and yet tonight, the only nerves had to do with the man twenty feet away in the bathroom.

I'd ruined the moment in a spectacular way earlier. I'd replaced bread flour with talcum powder, or something else disgusting and horrible.

And we'd hardly spoken since. I'd stopped to help Marguerite with something on the way in from the picnic, and Warrick had disappeared somewhere. He'd arrived at the room forty minutes before the party started and hopped in the shower without anything more than a "Be out in a few."

I'd hurt him, and it was the very last thing I wanted. More than making peace with my parents or even making sure the night was perfect for my sister, I wanted him to understand that *yes,* I'd kissed him because my mom had been there and some part of me had panicked. I'd thought, *What if she can tell?* and moved. But the second I'd felt the pull of him, and met his molten eyes, thoughts of my mother had fled.

And the kiss. Holy *wow.* I'd heard the phrase *bone-melting* before, but I'd never understood what that meant. Now I did. Warrick Saint had melted my bones with his insistent mouth and warm hands.

And then I'd shoved him away with a crack about my mom watching to hide my real feelings. He must've read them on my face, I was sure, and I panicked.

Before we went into this night, I wanted to make sure he knew. I wanted to stop and talk about this before we were shoved into a room with people I barely knew and was expected to play doting, delighted sister. Fortunately, after our talk this morning, I felt far more like one in real life, but the crowd would make that hard. Warrick by my side had been the thing buoying me since he'd agreed to come, and I couldn't face the night if this dampened distance lingered between us.

I missed him, and it'd been hours since we'd last talked. What was I going to be when this little fantasy was over and we returned to real life? What would happen when we were back to strictly friends and had no excuses to "practice" being more?

I exhaled and emptied my lungs, then pulled in a slow, calming breath just as the bathroom door opened and he stepped out, towel around his waist and gorgeous chest, shoulders, and arms on display.

"Sorry. I thought maybe you would've gone ahead," he said, not looking my way.

I blinked, reaching for what I needed to say, and finding that Warrick in a towel was what I'd call a brain blitz. Just completely annihilating to my ability to think clearly. I'd seen him shirtless, of course. Plenty of times. But the context here, the towel replacing his usual workout shorts, the little drops of water still sparkling on his shoulders and in his hair... *mercy*.

But words. I needed to respond. "Uh, no. I wanted to wait for you."

"Okay. I'll just, uh, be back in a sec." He turned, presenting me with a view just as glorious as the previous one. Still, I forced my focus to his head to avoid another mind melt and hustled toward him. "Wait, please."

He turned to me, those muscles in his back shifting as he moved—fine, I didn't successfully keep my eyes on his head because *seriously*. He was art. He was stunning, and three feet from me now.

With one hand where his towel tucked in on itself, the other holding the hangers donning his suit, he turned to face me but didn't give me his eyes. As a man I'd come to know as direct and open, this evasion made clear that the wall erected between us was no small thing.

"I'm sorry," I said, weirdly breathless despite standing perfectly still.

His gaze finally met mine, and he smirked—one of his casual, playful looks that had no hint of anything I'd sworn I'd been seeing from him in his posture and demeanor. "For what?"

"Oh, um, earlier. With my comment. I—"

He waved me off, one big hand swiping through the air between us. "Nah, don't sweat it, Miller. We're good. I'm glad she saw us."

"No, I didn't mean it the way it sounded." I huffed a

frustrated breath. "I wanted to kiss you. I'm glad we kissed. I liked it. I—"

"Seriously, Sadie. It's fine. We kissed, it was good, your mom saw—all good. Let me get dressed and we'll go continue the show for everyone." He held up his hangers and one brow notched up.

I floundered around for the right thing to get through to him. He started to turn, but I rushed forward and grabbed his arm. "Please, Warrick."

He whipped around, face unreadable, yet said nothing.

The words were so close to the surface now, almost ready to slip out and change things between us. *Really* change things—more than a kiss, for sure. But I couldn't edge them out. They wouldn't budge. And I knew in my gut if I let him go without saying something, or doing something, we'd have this wall between us indefinitely.

So I launched myself into his space and hugged him, pressing my hands flush against the warm skin of his back, my front to his. It took some amount of time—a minute or a decade, I could hardly be sure—before he tossed the clothes onto the nearby bed and closed his arms around me.

I exhaled in relief even as heat coiled in my belly and warmed my cheeks. I was pressed against Warrick and he was in nothing but a towel. I could hear his heart beating under my head, and I had to order my head not to turn into the smooth curve of his pec and place a kiss above his heart.

But that would be just shy of the confession I wouldn't let escape me, so I stayed still, resisting all urges to stroke up and down his spine with my hands or nuzzle even closer. Another relieved sigh escaped, and finally, he set me away with hands on my shoulders.

"We're all right. I promise." His voice was low and reassuring. No joking or smirks or brushing past my apology, though it wasn't the conversation I wanted to have.

Something told me if I pressed, maybe I could get us to that point, but then what? What was I expecting him to say? That he wanted me? He'd throw his plans to avoid marriage out the window because I was so uniquely special to him?

I could've laughed, or cried, because *yes*. That was exactly what I wanted. But pushing him to tell me that he *didn't* want me would be foolish, and especially right now, before we went to the party. Marguerite and I had made our peace, and I believed it would last. Still, I didn't want to show up and be even more awkward all night because my heart was broken.

"Okay. Good," I finally said, stepping fully out of his space.

"Let me go get dressed, and then let's do this thing."

I nodded, and he disappeared into the bathroom to change. If I hadn't spent an hour on my hair and makeup, I'd lay on the bed and scream into a pillow or something. Or more likely, let myself cry. Because this situation had me shaky and unsure, and I hated it. One thing I loved about being with Warrick was that he never made me feel like I didn't belong. And now, I had the nails-on-chalkboard feeling I didn't belong in this friendship with him.

"You can do this. You can do this." I chanted it low under my breath, my perpetual mantra for new situations applying more to standing next to Warrick and pretending to only be pretending to be in love with him more than face the party and social challenges therein.

Because I couldn't pretend with myself anymore—I loved Warrick. Was in love with him. It'd been seeping out of my locked-up heart slowly, a leak from the filling of a jelly-filled pastry during the heat of baking that had now spread over the whole pan. No denying its sticky, sweet substance anymore—it coated everything. The way his words hit me, how my body responded to his nearness or touch, the tenderness I felt for him when he joked or tried to soothe me. His goodness. His insistence on helping people and his brutal sweetness.

And more particularly, the hopeless, anxious, desperate longing to cling to him, call him mine, and somehow change the inevitable trajectory between us. The soul-deep *need* to hear him say he wanted me and his former refusal to marry meant nothing anymore.

I pushed out a breath, releasing the tension just thinking about the end barreling toward us, and mentally promised myself to enjoy the evening. "You can do this."

Minutes later, Warrick emerged fully clothed in a dark blue suit and white shirt, and just as compelling as he'd been in the towel.

Well, maybe not just as *but close.*

"Ready?" he asked brightly.

I nodded, and off we went. Down the hallway and past the kitchen, into a library filled with leatherbound books and high-backed chairs and a small gathering of early-comers.

"There they are. Here's Mercedes and her Warrick." My mother herded the couple a few feet to stand in front of us. "Sadie, you remember the Joneses?"

And so it begins.

Hours later, my father held up his champagne glass one last time. "Thank you for joining us to celebrate Marguerite and Douglas. We're thrilled to have you here, and we hope you'll get home safely. We'll see you at the wedding in a few months. To Marguerite and Douglas!"

The crowd of approximately a hundred people raised their glasses along with my father and echoed the refrain. We'd heard it no fewer than ten times during speeches or during the passed hors d'oeuvres when someone commandeered a small fork and tinked it against their glass.

The constant toasting had finally ended, and I'd decided Warrick and I would be leaving. Or at least I would. He seemed perfectly at home here next to me, making conversation with one hand lightly on my lower back or running across my shoulders. He'd been an anchor every time someone had sidled up to introduce themselves and remind me of how they'd seen me in diapers or knew me from something or other.

In the end, much like my therapist often rehearsed with me, nothing bad happened. We moved through the night side by side. I talked to far too many people who pretended to remember me, some of whom I vaguely recognized. And now, I could give Marguerite a kiss and go to bed.

"Looks like we made it," Warrick said low into his glass of champagne as he polished off the drink, then set it on a passing tray of empties.

I didn't drink more than a sip here or there—since I'd had a glass earlier, any more wouldn't be wise with my medication, which I most definitely had carefully taken every day this week to ensure I was as prepared as possible. Miraculously, other than a general nausea and dread as we'd approached the party, I'd had a decent time.

That was due to Warrick, one hundred percent. He had

not left my side at any moment. He'd even accompanied me to the bathroom at one point and waited outside the door. Maybe he was super worried about me, but it felt more like that was the role he'd promised to play tonight, so he did it.

That clarity and faithfulness felt so… good. Honestly? Everything with him felt good. Meeting strangers and having them tell me they remember when I ran around the yard naked at an aunt's wedding left us laughing and his eyes sparkling with such sweet amusement, I couldn't worry about being anxious over the memory. As Warrick reminded me, I was four, after all, and shouldn't my nanny have been watching me?

But more than any comments from guests, it was spending the evening next to him. I'd known he'd soften the blow of this overwhelming social event, yet I hadn't realized I'd be able to have fun.

"I think we have." I turned to him and grabbed his hand. "Thank you."

He smiled down at me, eyes tired. "My pleasure."

We'd held hands for a few minutes here and there tonight, but his large, rough palm against mine still made my stomach flip. Having his full attention on me still felt like a gift, even after months of it, and I hated the thought of not having that anymore.

"You survived!" Marguerite said, approaching with arms outstretched and a wide smile.

I chuckled, feeling less stung by the comment than I might've before our talk today. Because yes, I had survived. I wanted to sleep for a week after this, which I wouldn't be able to do, and I couldn't wait to get home and back to the routine, but yes, I had.

"It was great, and you seem happy. I'm so glad to see that."

I'd believed her when she'd assured me she truly loved Doug a year ago when they'd come to a rare family dinner. They'd seemed happy, but the fact that Doug had tons of money and our parents had set them up made my skin crawl. Not that either way was bad, but it'd made me wonder. That was a perfect example of what might've been different if we'd managed to be closer in the years since I'd left New York. I'd know her well enough to know she really did love Doug, and she'd know me well enough to know I wasn't trying to make her feel bad by asking.

"I'm glad you could see for yourself." She squeezed my arm, then turned to Warrick. "And thank you for being such a willing participant. I don't know why anyone would sign up for a night of sort of hosting an engagement party for a bunch of people they don't know, but I suspect you're good people."

He chuckled, then presented her with his sunrise smile. Or maybe it was a normal thing for her. For me, it hit right in the gut.

"Glad Sadie asked me, and so glad I could be here. Congrats to you guys again."

Marguerite beamed just like she had every time someone had said as much and I had a flash forward to her wedding, her wearing a longer white gown and smiling just the same. I could look forward to that event with a little more enthusiasm now that we'd patched things up, and now that I'd proven to myself I could do this.

My heart sank with the reminder that Warrick wouldn't be with me then. I could still handle it, of course, but it would be a thousand times less fun.

And that sinking heart would be something smaller, pieces missing.

I exhaled slowly, calming the tripping sensation in my

chest at the thought of being without Warrick. I needed a way to hold on to him—to this partnership we'd created. *To this feeling I have standing next to him, like he's mine.*

"Go ahead and sneak out—the parents will be busy a while yet and you've more than done your duty." Marguerite ushered us both away from my parents.

"Are you sure?"

Her gaze softened and she nodded, then pulled me in for a hug and spoke into my ear so only I could hear. "I promise. Go. Enjoy the rest of your night with your man."

My cheeks burned as she released me to Warrick's care, twiddled her fingers in a quick farewell, and a woman I thought might be a state senator swept her up in conversation.

Warrick and I were already moving out of the room, down the hall, and after a few more minutes' walk, into our room. I shut the door behind us and leaned against it, wondering what to say. Each step leading us here had felt like a strange combination of freedom from the party and nerves ticking higher at the time alone in here.

Last night, I was so preoccupied with my speech, I hadn't let the gravity of sharing such an intimate space penetrate my otherwise disconcerted brain. Of course, I'd thought of it nearly nonstop, but the time dressing together before the party had been fraught with worry over hurting him. So now... this moment was the first time we'd shared the space with nothing between us.

And more than nerves or anxiety over doing the wrong thing, I wanted to be here with him. Now. Alone.

CHAPTER THIRTY-ONE

Warrick

I heard the door shut but focused on hanging my jacket back on the hanger. As much as I didn't mind dressing up, I'd had enough of this suit and its constraints, and I wanted it off.

Also, I wasn't sure how I felt about watching Sadie close the door, effectively shutting out the rest of the world and sealing us in here together. We'd recovered from my insanely misguided understanding of her kiss, and then her sweet attempt to make me feel better. She'd seemed to have a good time at the party, too—at least as much as she could. I wouldn't have blamed her for downing a few glasses of champagne, but that wasn't Sadie. She didn't want to numb herself to the situation. She wanted to live without needing to.

As far as I could tell, she'd done remarkably well. Her hands had been cold and clammy much of the evening, but instead of finding that off-putting, it had made me so damn proud of her. She'd faced the dread of this night head-on, and though I'd bet she'd say I had a hand in keeping her relaxed and not focused on her fears, it was all her.

But fast forward through several hours of conversations, her kind words about me and the way she'd touch my arm or smile over at me, and my heart felt nearly pulverized. Between the kiss this afternoon, the generally intense attraction between us, and that closed door?

Down, boy.

"Who was your favorite person to talk with?" I asked, tugging at one end of my tie that seemed to be twisted in a sailor's knot of no return.

She zeroed in on my struggle and glided over, so smooth she practically floated. I'd only had one glass of champagne, right?

"Here, let me." She reached up and set to work unknotting the mess a few inches from my throat.

I froze, one hand off to the side awkwardly while she worked through the knot. Seriously, what had I done there? A quadruple Windsor or something?

"So?" I prodded, needing the distraction of conversation so I wouldn't put my hands on her waist and drag her into me. Up close like this, she was nothing short of devastatingly beautiful. Her eyes were dark blue in the low light of the room, and she bit into her bottom lip as she concentrated on her work.

"I'd say all the cougars. What about you?" One brow raised.

"Cougars?"

I'd never seen Sadie smirk, but here it was, a little side smile and another brow pop.

"All the older women hitting on you?"

I frowned. "Not my favorite."

I would've loved to pretend it hadn't happened, but there was no downplaying it.

"Did the one lady actually give you her number?" She pulled on one end of the tie and slipped along under my collar until she held it up, knot-free and blessedly no longer around my neck.

"Thank you." I unbuttoned my top two buttons. "And yes. Supposedly to talk with her husband about football."

I frowned again at the memory.

Sadie chuckled, seemingly enjoying the same.

"Why is that funny? I mean, I get it, I played ball, that's alluring for some. But it's been years, and they're *all* married except that one, Silviana whatever." I continued unbuttoning and did my best to focus on my righteous indignation over the topic of conversation instead of how she'd toed off her high heels and taken out her earrings.

She laughed brightly. "Silviana Randolph. Yeah, she's always been eccentric. But you're on point. They were objectifying you." Her brow furrowed then. "Sorry. I guess I've done that too."

"Totally different. We have a relationship, and you weren't talking about getting with me right in front of your partner, or in front of mine." The gall of those women, seriously. Again, it'd happened before, though never so overtly and never in front of someone I was with.

Granted, I hadn't had someone at any kind of event like this since Tracy, and she gave off a *look but don't touch* vibe that scared most people.

"True. That is messed up. I'm sorry for finding it amusing."

Her tone was serious enough that it made me turn back

to her from where I stood staring into my suitcase, wondering what I should wear at a time like this.

"Don't worry about it, really." My voice sounded a little gritty, so I cleared my throat. "Do you need help?"

She held her hair in one hand, and the other was fiddling with her zipper in the back of her dress with no progress. And me being the consummate gentleman, I offered to help.

"That'd be great," she said, padding over to me.

I saw the moment she registered that my shirt was fully unbuttoned, nothing beneath it. Her eyes slipped over me like a hand skimming down my abs, then jumped back to meet mine. I swallowed hard.

"Come here," I said, all gruff and low.

She stepped in front of me, facing away, and held her hair to the side. I pinched the material at the top of the dress and slowly unzipped. Inch by inch, the material parted just enough to show her bare back. Based on the way her body moved, she had to be breathing about as hard as I was.

Was she feeling this magnetic pull between us? Did she want me to kiss her again? To slip my hands inside her dress and feel her warm skin with mine? Would she welcome it, or would it become another moment banished under the guise of our fake relationship? Would it be one more thing I had to bury when this weekend was over?

When the zipper found the bottom of its track, none of those worries stopped me. It wasn't my head that drew me closer to her, but my heart—the one she'd roped in and tied to hers without knowing it.

I crowded her and dipped my head. "Done."

Her body jolted, but she didn't move. "Thank you."

The tone of her voice made my lower abs tighten, and

all the more considering she didn't move away. She still held her hair to one side and, *there is a God*, she tilted her head in the same direction, leaving the smooth line of her neck bared all the way to the cap of her shoulder where her silky blue dress hung by one stitched line.

"Sadie." I breathed it, more than said it, then bent to press a kiss where her neck curved into her shoulder.

Her breath hitched at the contact, and she arched into me. Her hand dropped her hair and reached around the back of my neck. I held her at her waist and met her lips with mine when she turned her head toward me. My height gave us the advantage—I could lean over enough that she didn't have to strain. I swear my knees went weak when she dropped her head to my shoulder and moaned.

Good glorious grief, this woman turned me into magma. I moved us then, shifting so we faced each other. Her hands locked around my neck. My fingers slid into her hair on either side of her face, tilted her chin up, and I kissed her again.

She moved against me, like she was desperate to get closer, and my mind could only think *more*.

More

Everything.

"Warrick..." In between kisses, her eyes flashed open to find mine.

But that was what I needed. That slip of reality to ground me and remind me this was only two-sided in *this* way. And while we clearly weren't doing this for anyone else's benefit but our own, I needed to pump the brakes here. I wanted her—everything with her—way too much to rush into this.

I pressed another kiss to her lips, then when she leaned

in to deepen the contact, I pulled back. "I'm going to go get ready for bed."

Those beautiful lips parted, but she didn't speak. I sidestepped to my suitcase, grabbed the pile of pajamas, and walked directly to the bathroom, shutting the door between us and wondering what I'd just done.

CHAPTER THIRTY-TWO

Sadie

He just... left.

Mid-kiss. Or as close to mid as one can get. He didn't seem happy about it, but he also didn't seem all that happy about the kissing.

Okay, fine, he seemed very pleased with the kissing, though you can't really say that about someone when they walk away in the middle of the hottest make-out session of your life. Embarrassment grabbed me by the shoulders and shook mercilessly, dropping my confidence, my excitement, and any plans for what would happen in that bed on the plush carpet underfoot.

Instead of running from the scene or curling up and crying just to have him find me, I moved robotically through changing my own clothes—he'd already partly undressed me anyway. My stomach dipped at the flash of his hands running over mine, even as my cheeks heated all over again.

I had to ask him. I couldn't spend another minute in the room with him and pretend that hadn't just happened. So, I pulled on my sweatpants and T-shirt, sat on the edge of the bed, and waited.

Six minutes later, because yes, I did watch the clock, he emerged, fresh-faced and evidently completely ready for bed. He hung his suit pants and shirt, then widened his long legs, crossed his arms over his broad chest, and pinned me with his gaze.

"You seem to have something on your mind."

He said this like he hadn't just walked away seconds after having his tongue in my mouth. Maybe I shouldn't be thinking of it that way, but in those six minutes of waiting, I'd gotten more and more frustrated.

"Yeah, just a bit."

He raised his brows, signaling me to go ahead. This small gesture sent a flash of irritation through me. How dare he stand there acting like he had nothing to do with me getting worked up—on more than one level.

I returned his look, hoping he'd acknowledge whatever had just happened, but now, he did that thing I normally found adorable and settled into his stance even more. I stood, no longer able to contain the energy building in my chest and sizzling out my fingertips.

"I'd like to talk about what just happened."

His eyes shot to the side, then returned to me. "Okay. Go ahead."

I groaned in frustration and nearly stomped my foot but managed to contain myself. "I get that something changed. I just don't know what. And I'd like to know."

His lips thinned into an unhappy squiggle.

"So, uh, let's recap. You unzipped my dress and kissed

my neck, and then me. And then..." *Now's the time to fill in the blank, buddy.*

He lifted one brow. I clasped my hands together and willed them not to strangle him. For someone effusive and typically chatty, he'd clammed right up.

"And then you... ran away? Freaked out? Changed your mind and remembered you don't actually want me?" My heart pounded an aggressive beat in my chest. "Please, Warrick. It's okay if you don't—"

"I didn't change my mind."

His brown eyes found mine, and my sucker of a heart flipped. He looked serious. That was good—that he wasn't trying to evade the conversation anymore. But what did that mean?

"Okay. Can you help me understand?"

He dropped his hands, then set them on his hips. It was a gesture I'd make in the corner of a crowded room and which struck me as completely foreign on him. He never looked anything but completely at home in his body, yet right now, he was as close to ill at ease as I'd ever seen him. I didn't know whether that was a good thing or a really bad one. Probably bad, considering I loved that he had that security in himself and occupied every gorgeous inch of himself with confidence.

One hand rose to his forehead, and he rubbed there, his chest deflating. "I'll try to explain it."

My stomach twisted at his tone. He sounded defeated, which made me nervous. What about the last ten minutes had felt like defeat to him?

"Come sit by me," I said, and backed up until I sat on the bed, then patted the space next to me.

He took the seat at an angle, so he was mostly facing me

and our knees bumped. Even after far more intense contact not long ago, the skin where he touched me felt warm.

"I like you." His eyes searched mine.

"I like you too."

He exhaled in what sounded like a dejected sigh, though I couldn't say how I knew it sounded dejected—it just did.

He focused on his shorts, fiddling with the hem as he spoke. "I know we're friends, and I'm glad. But this attraction between us is intense. And I don't want to get swept up in it and then try to go back to the way things were—weekly lunches and such. I don't think..."

"You don't think...?"

He swallowed, his throat working like it didn't come easy. "I don't think it'd be enough for me. To go back to how we were before this weekend."

I sucked in a breath, praying that I was understanding him. "As in, you want to be more than friends? You want... something with me?"

His handsome face stayed serious, and he nodded. "I do. I understand if that's not what you want. I know you mentioned you aren't looking for anything, and that's probably—"

I grabbed his hand and pressed it to my heart. "I do. Want that."

"You do?"

I laughed, disbelief and hope and joy and anticipation shooting through me. "Yes. I—I have for a while."

Something like awe took over his features. "You have? Why didn't you say something?"

"Why didn't *you*?"

Though that was my response, what echoed through me

was something far more specific. *Other than the fact that you very clearly stated you don't want to get married?*

What we were talking about wasn't that. I had to remind myself of it. Him saying he was attracted to me and wanted *something* with me wasn't him saying he wanted everything. Still, this was an incredible development, far beyond what I had hoped for even earlier tonight.

He squeezed my hand. "Touché."

I chuckled quietly. "So?"

His smile was small for a Warrick Saint smile, but it still sent a wave of heat through me to see it pointed directly at me.

"So now, you go brush your teeth and do whatever else, and we go to bed."

"Okay," I said dumbly, and stood, letting our hands fall apart.

Without another glance, I moved to the bathroom and through my nighttime routine, a buzzy energy keeping any solid thoughts from nesting in my mind.

But any number of little fragments flitted through as I brushed and washed. Did *"we go to bed"* mean get in bed and sleep or...?

Did him wanting more mean beyond tonight? I thought so, but now that I'd stepped away from the moment, I couldn't be sure.

And did I trust myself to be with him in any significant way and then be able to step back when what was between us came to an end? We may have decided to date, but that looming reality that he didn't want the same thing I wanted in the end—marriage, a family—that meant it would end.

The realization landed like a punch to the gut. Imagining an ending before we'd hardly gotten started felt cruel and unfair, and yet, I'd be an idiot not to factor that in. Wouldn't I?

With those cheery thoughts swirling around my mind, I exited the bathroom to find Warrick lying on his side, head in hand, watching me. My pulse increased at the sight, especially since I could see his chest peeking out from the blankets, unobstructed by a T-shirt. I shuffled to my suitcase and stripped off my sweatpants, which left me in a soft T-shirt and sleep shorts. I assumed he wasn't actually naked under there since, well, I mean, that would be a bit much, but who knew?

"I'm pretty sure I could hear you thinking through the door."

I huffed out a breath and flipped off the light. Then I approached the bed and my stomach felt like it was being tossed like pizza dough. Tugging back the covers and slipping in to face him, I admitted, "Not surprising."

He reached out and laced our hands together like we were comparing palm sizes. Moonlight filtered in through the huge windows, casting enough brightness on the bed that I could see him fairly clearly. I loved how big his hands were—how big *he* was. Mostly because as powerful and skilled as that body was, he was gentle. Sweet.

"What are you worried about?" His thumb arced over the back of my hand.

"I'm not sure what all this means. I'm excited, but nervous. Shocker."

His eyes flickered between mine, then he pulled at my hand where we were joined. "Come here."

I moved, a little unsure, until he had me tucked against him, big and little spoons. My head rested on his bicep and his other hand traced up my arm, then slipped under and rested flat against my chest. I inhaled sharply, the warmth of his hand on the cool skin of my collarbone scintillating every sense. I couldn't help but want his hands to wander, to touch all of me, and yet, being nested together like this felt good.

It felt right.

"Let's start right here. Let's rest. And if anything develops between us, let's let that happen somewhere other than at your parents' house, yeah?" He pressed a kiss under my ear, as though that would do anything to calm my racing heart.

"Fair enough."

So we lay like that, quiet and relatively still. Warrick's weight was comforting, and he was amazingly warm, but I couldn't sleep like this. After some amount of time, his breathing deepened, and I was sure he'd fallen completely asleep, so I slipped out of his arms.

"Done with me already?" he mumbled, not opening his eyes.

"No. Definitely not. But I can't sleep like that, and I figured I better get some rest."

His eyes blinked open, and he watched me a minute, then another. Seemed like he was looking for something— some answer or piece of information that would solve a riddle he'd been trying to puzzle out.

Before I could ask him what he was thinking, his eyes shut again, then he said one last thing.

"Don't break my heart. Okay?"

My throat tightened, but I nodded. Then I realized he wouldn't see that, so I found the words. "I won't."

With a sigh, he relaxed into his pillow, evidently fully asleep. Had he been asleep that whole time? Did Warrick sleep-talk? It had seemed perfectly lucid.

That was the only reason I kept myself from answering, "Please don't break mine."

CHAPTER THIRTY-THREE

Warrick

My arm and shoulder tingled. *Crap.* Never a good sign for the day. Usually, my shoulder gave me less grief in summer, but waking up with it already tingling and feeling more like the hinge of a phantom limb than an existing part of my body? Bad start.

"Mm, sorry I ended up crowding you." Sadie's sleepy voice drifted to me as though in slow motion.

Sadie. I could hardly process the events of— *wait.* "Sadie?"

"Yeah?"

I cracked my eyes open and finally saw her. She blinked back at me from where she lay tucked into my side, head on my shoulder. *Ah.* It wasn't a bad day. It was a freaking fantastic one.

"You can crowd me anytime." I kissed her head and breathed in the clean scent of her hair.

She sighed and tucked her face into my side. Her lips were *right there,* and if she kissed me, this sweet little wake up would combust. It was a mark of maturity or maybe straight-up heroism that we'd only snuggled after our conversation last night. We both seemed to agree we didn't want the progress of our relationship to happen here at the Miller Manor.

That said, if her hand kept skating over my abs, slowly tracing the shape of me, I was going to lose my mind.

"I thought I couldn't sleep close to you, but seems like my subconscious knew better."

I could hear the smile in her voice. If I looked down and saw her lips stretched into a smile against my skin, I'd definitely throw all that level-headed caution to the wind. Studying the ceiling, I prayed for self-control, then regretfully stopped her wandering fingers.

"Baby, you've gotta stop that."

Her head popped up. "Are you ticklish?"

She brushed her palm up and down the midline of my stomach.

I coughed when she reached the waistband of my shorts. "Not particularly."

Our gazes locked, and it clicked for her. Fire entered her eyes, like it just now occurred to her that her touch might be turning me on. Might be setting me on fire. I suspected when I sat up, I'd leave a Warrick-sized outline singed into the sheets.

"Oh, right. Yeah." Her words were a little husky, and her shoulders rose and fell like she was breathing heavily.

"We should get up. And maybe have this conversation again soon."

She tucked her lips between her teeth to hide a pleased smile. "Good plan."

Half an hour later, we'd dressed, packed, and one of the many staff had deposited our bags into the car we'd take home. We entered the dining room to find Sadie's parents sipping coffee, plates half-full.

"Are you staying for breakfast?" Randall asked.

Sadie glanced at me. "Actually, we're going to head out. That way, Warrick can have a few minutes before his Sunday evening session."

"Of course. Well, don't forget what we'd talked about, son." Randall rose and offered his hand to shake, then patted my arm with the other.

He'd given me a long talking to about appropriate staffing, outsourcing, and making my business replicable. All absolutely in the plans, but also not really something I suspected he'd dealt with in the last twenty years—or potentially ever. I'd been looking for more trainers and had a few good options. My goal was to have them in place by end of August so I could focus on a few other things come fall.

I didn't need the trainers until I had other projects lined up. I liked being busy. I needed to be busy, and I could accept that. Maybe it wasn't the best business practice, but I was doing just fine. In fact, I couldn't wait to get back to work. Now that the end of the weekend approached, I felt the pull to think about the long list. I wouldn't, though. Not until I got home. But I'd taken more than enough time off lately, and it was time to get back to it.

"Thanks, sir. I'm on it." I gave him my charming smile, the one I used more for networking than for people I cared about. His use of *son* seemed premature, but I honestly didn't know what else to say and I certainly wasn't about to address that.

"Thanks for coming. You did well." Arianna directed

her comment to both of us, though it was obviously for Sadie.

"I'm glad we could come."

Sadie's response sounded completely genuine and clear. Pride swelled in my chest. She'd confronted at least two things I knew she didn't want to do on this whirlwind trip, and I couldn't have been happier to have witnessed her in action.

"Thanks for having us," I added with a nod to Arianna.

With a few more quick comments and farewells, Sadie grabbed my hand, and I turned to lead us out. I entered the kitchen just as her mom said something to her, and she stopped to hear it. When she turned around, she had an odd look on her face, and my ire shot up immediately.

"What's wrong? What did she say?"

She shook her head. "Nothing important. Let's go home."

Despite my concern over whatever Arianna had chosen as a parting shot to her daughter, I followed her out to the car with more anticipation than I'd had for almost anything in recent memory, except maybe other interactions with her.

This was different. I didn't know exactly where we were headed, but this was real. We weren't pretending. We weren't spending time together as a form of *lessons* or teaching her to date or even grow friendships.

And it certainly wasn't pretend for me either. If I let myself be completely honest, it never had been pretend, or just about friendship for me. But that couldn't be my focus, because whatever was happening here, we needed to go slow. Sleeping together—and nothing else—last night had been the right choice. It'd felt amazing to wake up next to her, especially once I realized my arm was asleep thanks to her head on my bicep and not my shoulder.

We held hands the whole way home. As Silverton neared, my heart sank. I'd gotten used to being around her all the time. I'd been spoiled by her presence the last few days, and I didn't want to go back to the once-in-a-while meetings.

"We're almost home."

She glanced at me, her gaze sweeping over my face before she nodded. "That we are."

Tension knotted between us at her acknowledgment, like our arrival in Silverton would tear away all the progress we'd made. But it wouldn't. The quiet car ride hadn't been a sign of disaster approaching with every mile we passed—no. I refused to buy into this low-key dread tripping through my gut.

I squeezed her hand. "When am I going to see you? How are we going to do... whatever it is we're doing?"

And maybe that was part of it—what *were* we doing? We liked each other and wanted each other. We hadn't spelled out anything. In the light of day, I could've kicked myself for not being explicit last night, but it'd felt clear. Or, clear enough.

She smiled. "How about I see you tomorrow afternoon? I could do lunch, but then I have to catch up on some things. I could do an early dinner too."

Disappointment must've showed on my face, and I couldn't pretend I liked her answer. "Either. Both."

I didn't ask what she was doing tonight or why I couldn't see her. I had an invitation to family dinner tonight anyway, and I should be a good son and go. I'd avoided responding in hopes maybe Sadie would either give me an excuse not to, or go with me.

"I had fun. A lot of fun," she said, eyes stuck on mine.

It felt like there was a *but* coming, yet I couldn't figure out what it was. Was she already regretting things? Or... *crap*. I hated this doubt, and the feeling of not knowing what she thought. I hadn't missed this part of dating and getting close to someone. The last time I'd done it, I'd been so foolish and confident. I didn't know if I'd ever be certain about someone else again, yet in this moment, it occurred to me that I could ask.

The driver pulled up to the entrance to her building on Main Street. She'd asked if I wanted her to drop me at my house, but I didn't want to go to that half-finished space and feel all the more alone. Because that's how it always felt, and leaving her after being so close—*yeah, no.*

"So, see you tomorrow?" I said, adjusting the strap of my bag on my good shoulder.

She dropped her bag at our feet and slipped her arms around my waist, hugging me to her. I soaked in the contact, breathing in her nearness, her scent, and this last moment.

What is wrong with me? Why did I feel like this was the end of something instead of a mutually agreed upon beginning?

It had to be the lack of clarity. I didn't do well there, even though I'd tried my best to live in that land for the last few hours. But no, it wasn't sitting well.

"You seem a little upset, maybe." She pressed her palm to my cheek.

Looking down into those blue eyes settled me, as did her comment. Not that I wanted to act out enough to get her attention here, but I didn't want to push her. The last thing I wanted was to pressure her about all this, and I figured maybe she was doing the same for me.

"I was hoping we could spend time together tonight, and I'm being a baby."

She chuckled, seemingly delighted. "How can I reassure you I feel the same way? I would love to see you tonight, but I think I need a little time to internalize everything. Not just us—me and Marguerite, my parents... everything. Does that make sense?"

I cupped the back of her neck and dipped my head. "Absolutely. I wasn't trying to whine you into submission or make you feel bad for needing space. That's why I wasn't going to say anything. I want you to process and relax and get a good night's sleep."

She leaned up on her toes and pressed a soft kiss to my lips. My stomach did its usual swooping *Sadie Miller is touching me voluntarily and liking it* thing, and I kissed her forehead one more time.

"Off with you. I'll see you tomorrow."

I held out her bag, which she took, and then I pretended to boot her toward her door with my foot. She rewarded my stupid pantomime with a genuine laugh, and my heart swelled for the nth time today.

Hours later, after a brutal workout, finally unpacking, doing laundry, and cleaning up, I scrubbed post-dinner dishes in the sink at Wyatt's house. Used to be mine too, but now, it'd become his. Someday, he'd have his own family here with Calla. It was only a matter of time.

And in the last few months, I'd thought about wanting that for myself again. I'd pushed aside that plan after Tracy, and I hadn't really even been tempted to review my policy on marriage until very recently.

Until the last week or so, honestly.

I'd never imagined loving someone again. I'd felt like that part of my heart had been irrevocably broken by Tracy's betrayal, so coming to this point...

"Where are you tonight, man? Seems like Sadie did a number on you."

Wyatt's voice cut through my thoughts.

"Not really past tense. *Is doing* is more like it. I'm rethinking a lot of stuff." I scrubbed at the plate in front of me, despite its being clean and destined for the dishwasher.

"Like?"

I glanced at Wy, who regarded me with his usual calm demeanor. He'd been the one in a romantic upheaval not long ago, so maybe he'd have some extra special wisdom from the inside. I plunked the dish down into the dishwasher and caught his cringe, which I ignored.

"I've always assumed I'd never do this again. It about killed me before."

He nodded, knowing exactly how bad it'd been for me since he'd nursed me through some of the physical and emotional fallout after.

"But... she's already got me messed up over her."

His brows furrowed. "Is she jerking you around? Misleading you?"

I loosed a gusty sigh. "Not purposefully, I don't think. *Not really*. But I worry she doesn't know what she wants. She told me, flat-out, that she didn't have the space for working on her relationship skills before all this fake-dating started."

His eyes widened, but he asked quietly, "Fake-dating?"

Crap. I hadn't planned on sharing that, though he probably needed to know. "Yeah. We've been 'practicing' dating. We were together for her sister's engagement because—well, long story short, she needed a date, and it needed to seem settled and steady, not a first-date kind of thing. And we agreed—she didn't have time or desire, and I have this whole 'I don't date' thing going on, so why not?"

Wyatt waited for the punchline, patient as ever.

"And obviously, the *why not* is I've always liked her. I've been falling for her since the second she gave me the time of day, and despite several conversations in the last twenty-four hours establishing that we both want this to be real, I don't know where I stand with her. I'm not sure I'll ever be able to trust my perceptions."

He nodded. "Understandable. You've got a history with her, but a history of discovering you can't trust the person you should be able to trust the most. That's not an easy situation."

"Yeah." I dried my hands on a dishrag and tossed it on the counter.

He grabbed the rag, folded it, and hung it on the hook next to the sink. "I take it you don't want to ask her straight out? Like, 'Do you like me? Check yes or no' style?"

I forced a chuckle, searching for the lighthearted version of myself and finding it conspicuously absent. "I mean, I know she likes me. I do. But what I don't know is to what degree. What's ahead for us, if anything? Am I just a practice boyfriend, warming up for the real thing?"

And what eventuality would make that become clear? I didn't have a professional football career to lose, but what else might it be contingent on?

Wy's hand on my shoulder felt both familiar and grating. He shook me a bit until I met his eyes.

"You are the real thing, brother. You're it. Whether

that's for Sadie, I don't know, but don't you settle for being practice for someone. You deserve more than that. Maybe you should take a step back? But I'll tell Sadie Miller to her face if—"

"Whoa, whoa. Simmer down there. You don't need to talk to her. I'm not sure I do either. I think I just need to tuck away my feelings like a real man and wait until she breaks my heart."

Wyatt snorted and rolled his eyes. "False."

I set a hand on his shoulder and shoved him away. "*I know.* I'm joking. I'll figure it out. Maybe a step back is a good call."

Nothing in me wanted to do that. I wanted to sprint forward. I wanted to rush every bit of this. I also knew I couldn't trust my ability to read her. That wasn't her fault, but I'd been had before. I'd been blinded by this very feeling —or, a shade of it. And that scared me. If I'd tripped over myself for Tracy, I couldn't possibly trust myself around Sadie.

He nodded, giving me one last stern big brother look before floating over to his woman. I stared out the window at the land and mountains in the distance, a mess of emotions mixing into poison in my gut. I hated feeling like this—this weak, unsure version of myself. This was why I didn't do relationships. I'd vowed I'd never feel like I did before, and here I was setting myself up for pain and seeing it coming this time.

But nothing Sadie had done hinted at some devious plan to hurt me. If she did, it wouldn't be cheating on me with one of my best friends. One, she wouldn't ever do that. And two, Wyatt was taken and Pete had his eye on someone else, nor would either of them take a second glance at a woman I liked.

So maybe I'd just wait. I'd ratchet-strap down this whole topic and keep my mouth shut. I'd enjoy what came, and see what happened. Totally doable. I'd dive into work—I needed to anyway. I had a list a mile long, and more to add to it. So it'd be fine.

Totally fine.

CHAPTER THIRTY-FOUR

Sadie

Warrick ended up canceling our lunch date and dinner plans. He didn't ghost me or anything, but he seemed to have slipped into a vortex of busyness. He'd made a million calls Monday morning, which resulted in meetings with contractors for his current house project, and an interview with a trainer for the gym. We finally landed on Wednesday lunch, which he'd promised he wouldn't bail on.

I did my very best not to take this as a bad sign. He'd been so sweet and almost needy on Sunday, wanting to spend time together. But I'd needed space. Honestly needed the time and space to come back to myself and process all that'd happened with basically my whole family and the person who was rapidly becoming the most important person in my life.

And now, he was giving it to me in spades, and I just wanted *him*.

If we could get in the same room, a room not separated by glass with him on one side making people squat until their quads melted and me trying not to watch while I half-heartedly supervised my bakers learning the equipment, we could figure this out. At least the *now* part of this, and I refused to think about the later.

I'd had two training sessions with new apprentices after my time at the bakery this morning, working through some complex techniques I specialized in with my experienced assistants while covering basics with a handful of new hires who would be starting full time in a little under five weeks. Tomorrow, I had a full roster of interviews to add to the people I already had, all working toward the expansion which was coming up quickly. Now that I didn't have Marguerite's event hanging over my head, my official expansion was the next big thing on my list.

It felt *fantastic*. I was ready—or I would be, once I hired a few more people.

I waved the assistant bakers off and let the door swing shut behind them just as Warrick burst through from the gym. I was hoping he'd be up for a longer lunch break and a little baking.

Goodness, he looked so handsome. He had to have gotten better-looking since I'd last seen him, but how was that possible? His hair was short on the sides and spiked up at the top—getting a little long there, yet still stylish and clean. His brown eyes sparkled, and he gave me one of his Warrick Saint specials.

"It's been like a month since I've seen you," he said, rushing to me and hoisting me up into an embrace.

And somehow, like we were in a movie, I knew just

what to do. I wrapped my arms around him and hugged him with all my strength, then tilted my face and kissed his cheek three times before releasing him.

"It has been. Have you been avoiding me?" I didn't want to pretend it hadn't felt like it.

"What? No. I just... I felt weird after taking so much time off lately. I'm behind on a few things and, uh, I needed to get my head back into things." He nodded toward the gym as I slid down his front to my feet.

"I get that. I do. I can't tell you how relieved I am to be focused on work instead of the impending doom of Marguerite's engagement party." I made a face, and he chuckled.

"Was I supposed to pick up lunch?" He glanced around the kitchen, eying two bowls sitting in the middle of the counter.

"Actually, I was hoping you'd have time to make it with me." Something about him seemed off. "Are you okay, though?"

He sighed. "Wilder tried to call me. And I missed it. I called him back, but no answer, of course. I—" He shook his head once, like he was trying to dislodge his brain. "You know what? Never mind. I really am fine. Just busy and weird. But I'm over it."

"You don't have to be. We can talk about it."

He shook his head. "Nope. I'm good."

Watching him force away the wrinkle in his brow, smoothing out his face, and tacking on a little half-smile made my stomach drop, and not in a good way. He'd papered right over whatever was actually going on, and seeing him stuff it back in was all wrong.

"Seriously. I don't mind—"

"I'm good. Tell me the plan."

Okay. Message received. "Uh, well, I thought we'd make pizza."

His answering grin lit me up from the inside out, quelling some concern since he seemed genuinely happy. "I am yours to command, m'lady. Are we going to knead some dough?"

I chuckled. "Just a bit, and then shape it. Why?"

"Any chance we can turn this into a *Ghost* pottery wheel-type situation?" Eyes bright, he looked so excited by the thought.

I burst out laughing. "Um, no?"

"Why not?"

I couldn't stop laughing as I rinsed my hands and responded. "Well first, because you're alive. And second, because I don't think I could get my arms around your massive torso enough to properly help you."

"Semantics. You could do it if you tried."

I uncovered the dough and let it drop to the table. "A sensual dough-kneading *Ghost* reenactment is a fantasy of yours? Should I be concerned?"

He was drying his hands on a towel when he stopped on the other side of the prep table and caught my eye.

"It's not so much the kneading as what happens after." Then a wink.

Oh. I laughed again, a little breathy and nervy in response to that retort. If very vague memory served, what happened after Demi and Patrick failed at pottery-making was fairly steamy.

My stomach twisted. *Maybe I wouldn't mind...*

"We're just going to make some pizzas, if that's acceptable for today."

"Fine then. I can be patient."

I could feel the heat from his gaze without even looking,

so I bit my lip and focused on dividing the dough and sprinkling flour out so it wouldn't stick. I talked him through kneading and shaping into a ball, then rolling it out. He made me promise I'd let him learn to toss pizza dough, which I had no idea how to do either. Something told me Warrick would figure it out if I gave him a steady enough supply of practice dough.

Thirty minutes later, our pizzas emerged. Mine was artichoke, spinach, and chicken, his a buffalo chicken. He must've been starving by the time we ate, because he devoured the pizza in less than five minutes.

"That was amazing." He balled up his napkin and tossed it into the trash can.

"I'm glad you liked it." I took another bite of my slice.

Leaning his elbows on the table across from me, he watched me eat.

I resisted the urge to hide my mouth behind a hand, a habit I often still resorted to when eating in public. "What?"

"You're just so pretty. Even when you chew. It's stupid."

Pleasure washed through me at the compliment, given almost unwillingly. "Sorry?"

He shook his head, all seriousness. "I'm not. At least not about that. I *am* sorry that I need to head out. I have a personal training session at two."

"Okay. I think Sarah's coming over tonight, but could I see you tomorrow?" I eyed the rest of my pizza, wondering if I could bring it back to life enough tomorrow to have as leftovers for lunch.

"I'm slammed tomorrow. Friday night? Are you baking early on Saturday?" He leaned over the table and slid his hand in the hair behind my ear, his thumb resting in front of it.

My heart sped up, thrilled at his suggestion and close hold. "I am, but not until six. My assistants are opening."

He dropped a too-quick kiss to my lips. "Good. I'll be at your house by five on Friday. We'll eat and relax, and we'll at least have a few hours before I have to leave you to your baking sleep."

"Baking sleep?" I asked, charmed and weirdly sad to see him leave, though happy we had plans.

"You don't need beauty sleep, obviously. Baking sleep is the power-up sleep you need before a big baking day."

"I like it. And I'll see you Friday. I mean, I'll see you a bunch, but I'll get to, uh... *see* you Friday." *Cringe.* Way to babble him out the door, Sadie!

He gave me one last parting grin, then jogged out the door to the other side of the gym where his client awaited.

Now I had the choice. Did I stay and pretend to work while secretly just watching him and feeling this weird sad-good feeling? Or did I leave a little early and go wait impatiently for Sarah?

I wouldn't think about the way he'd showed his upset, then shoved it away, and me in the process. He didn't want to talk about Wilder, and I couldn't fault him. I'd made an art out of avoiding talking about my problems, sometimes even avoiding them with the person I paid to help me sort through them. The unease that hit me when I witnessed how he'd hidden it wouldn't leave anytime soon, but we'd recovered. I knew some of the flirty *Ghost* references were to shift us far from the heavier topic of his brother, but I'd enjoyed our time. I hoped he had too.

He squatted low with a bar overhead, his back and other fine assets showcased marvelously to my view, and my pulse sprinted yet again.

Uh, yeah. Time to leave. No sense in standing here like a creeper. I'd be doing that the next two afternoons anyway.

Sarah had been at my house for close to an hour before she finally asked. We'd talked about her work, my work, the expansion, Loaf Monthly—the latest tentative name of my bread club—and Marguerite's engagement, all without addressing the giant ex-pro-footballer in the room.

We sat on opposite ends of the couch, her sipping a beer and me sipping water. Being with Sarah felt blessedly natural. Even though we were five years apart in age, I often felt older than my thirty years. Or maybe she was younger than her thirty-five years. Or more likely, at this age, the difference just didn't matter as much as it would've earlier on in life. Whatever the case, I felt an overwhelming thankfulness for her being here.

"So? Are you ever going to tell me how the weekend was?" She tilted her head to one side, blond hair piled into a bun on her head just like mine.

"Uh, short version?"

My stomach fluttered. Recounting this was something I'd anticipated. I *wanted* to hash through things, get her perspective. But I also worried what her impression of everything might be.

She bounced in her seat. "Any version. I'll take anything. I'm *so* curious."

With a reluctant laugh, I told her everything. About my parents ignoring me and my rant at dinner and making peace with Marguerite. About sleeping in Warrick's arms the second night after kissing so heatedly. And then about how odd this week had been—seeing him from afar through the window into the other building but not talking. Knowing he was busy, but worrying. Facing the reality that though we'd said we wanted to build something here, something real, it didn't feel like that was actually going to work out.

"You guys had lunch today though, right? Was he weird then?"

"I can't pinpoint it, but kind of? He was joking and playful. He even made a joke about, uh—" I swallowed down the specifics of the *Ghost* joke as my cheeks heated.

"Ohhh. Say no more. So yeah, he wasn't pretending like you guys are buddies or anything."

"No. Definitely not. And maybe it was the call from Wilder, or—"

"*Wilder?*" She sat up, pin-straight.

My heart sank. *You idiot!* I didn't know exactly what their story was, but I knew it had ended up badly. I shouldn't have mentioned it. "Oh, yeah. Sorry, I didn't mean to upset you."

She pasted on a too-bright smile. "No, no. Just... surprised me. I should know better when you're dating his brother. I just... I was thinking people didn't hear much from him and, yeah."

She waved it off, brushing her hands through the air like that would erase his name from the space.

"I don't think Warrick does very often. So, that was a part of it, for sure."

I watched her sink back into the couch, my stomach knotted with the dread that I might've hurt her. I mean, Wilder was a person, but he was so far out of sight and mind, I couldn't remember much about him. He'd been older than me, then took off to the Army and... that was that.

At least, for me, that was that. Obviously, there was more to it for Sarah. Something told me pressing into that wouldn't be right tonight. So, I refocused on Warrick.

"Well, whatever's going on, I hope Friday will be good." That thought wrapped around my heart and squeezed. I so wanted to feel connected to him again. To feel like we were on the same page, reading the same book.

"I'm sure it'll be fine. But, can I say something potentially a little tough?" She folded her hands in her lap and waited. I could just imagine her patiently waiting for the little kids she taught to respond.

I inhaled slowly. "Yes. I mean, I think? Be gentle?"

I squinted to lighten the mood, though my insides trembled. I didn't know how well I could take tough things having to do with Warrick right now.

"You mentioned he doesn't want to get married. I don't know where you want this to go, but one thing I've learned the hard way is to believe what a man tells you. If this is his conviction, then believe him on it. Don't expect that to change. I worry that maybe, with all of this intimacy between you, that's dropped by the wayside." She offered a kind smile.

Oof. "I know you're right. I haven't let myself think that far ahead, but I'm pretty sure that was part of what had me so unsettled about everything. This feeling like it's fleeting, and when we reach a certain point, whatever that is, it'll be over. Like a larger version of pretending this weekend. Maybe not pretending to date because we both have admitted to feelings, but more like we're pretending there's a future together instead of some undetermined end date he knows about but I don't."

She nodded, understanding radiating from her though doing little to calm my thrashing heart.

I didn't want an end with Warrick, and it felt like we were there already. Maybe what my parents had so insanely suggested as their parting shot last weekend—that Warrick and I get married—maybe it wasn't so insane after all. It would keep the end from coming, whenever that would've been. He didn't want a *real* marriage, but maybe I could keep him close, keep him as someone special, if we did get married. No expectations of him having the same feelings I did, but it might free him. Wouldn't it? It'd give him the freedom not to have to worry about letting other people down. And I could...

I could hold on to him a little longer. It would let me stave off the day when he'd had enough of me. Whenever that might be coming.

Okay. *Wow*. No. Just... *No*.

That was insane. I knew it was, and yet, part of my grabby little heart couldn't stop a lowkey beat on that drum. I had to remember that what that heart wanted didn't dictate what happened in real life. I could daydream about being with Warrick, but thinking like that wouldn't help the situation at all. It could make it worse, in fact.

I wouldn't know anything until we talked about it, and I wasn't going to be someone who lived in fear of hard conversations. Not anymore.

Friday night, I'd ask him. Straight out. And we'd get to the bottom of this, once and for all.

CHAPTER THIRTY-FIVE

Warrick

Walking to Sadie's on the hottest day of the summer thus far was probably not my best move. The heat of this day felt as close to thick as the air got in Utah. The semi-arid and desert climate made even the hottest summer days dry rather than humid and horrible like the south. I'd missed the lack of humidity during my time away, so I tried to enjoy the oppressive heat. Fortunately, rain should arrive late tonight, and when living in a desert with drought conditions, everyone talked about the forecasted rain.

When the storm front moved in, it'd cool right down. And I could walk home in the rain—in fact, that sounded kind of nice. *Or, you could* not *walk home.*

My stomach tightened with longing for that version of the story, but I'd said I would leave her early so she could get to bed and not be too tired tomorrow. So we'd know there was no pressure. Therefore, I hadn't packed a bag.

I'd had an off week, to say the least. I hated thinking of it that way—it did nothing for my mental health or my ability to face each day with determination and focus, but I had to call it what it was.

After talking with Wyatt last Sunday night, I'd backed off with Sadie. I'd decided I needed space, just like I'd originally planned on when she and I went into the weekend and I realized I was in over my head. But *man*, was it hard to stay away. I'd filled my schedule down to the minute. Then came Wednesday.

Wilder's missed call had thrown me. Then she'd been so typically sweet and concerned, it had made me ache. But once I let in the doubts about her, about us, I hadn't been able to shake them. I'd also had more than one setback this week—one of the trainers I wanted to hire had broken her ankle, the contractor working on my current house was behind, and I'd caught a glimpse of my mom on a date last night that'd made me cringe so hard my eyes nearly glued shut.

I didn't begrudge her dating. Truly. But did I want to witness it? Did I want to see some salt and pepper-haired charmer brushing the hair back from her face at a romantic little table in the window of Basta?

A thousand times *no*.

Add in the heat. Add more than a dash of sexual frustration, because let's be honest. Add in a heaping pile of *I have no idea what we're doing, and anytime we talk about what we're doing, then I get freaked out and second-guess everything I thought I understood.* A lovely little recipe.

So I was tromping up the stairs to Sadie's apartment in an off mood, wishing I could just get rid of all these crappy feelings and enjoy being with her. Just enjoy being around someone I cared about and not worry about the future. Couldn't I do that?

Times like now, it seemed hilarious anyone thought I was laid back. It was almost funny how I had them all fooled.

"Hey. Come into the AC." Sadie opened the door with a big smile and waved me in.

My heart was doing stupid things in my chest. Things like saying "There she is!" and "Let's just stay here a while," and "Take a load off, we're home."

Shutting the door behind me, she turned and leaned against it. There it went again, that leaping recognition and joy in my chest a little drumbeat soundtrack to the moment.

"I missed you," she said without moving to touch me.

"I missed you too," I said automatically.

Because I had—to a frustrating degree. Which only added to my foul mood the last few days. Seeing her through that little glass pane between us made it feel like we were still separate. Two people orbiting around different planets that would never meet.

I'd never been more thankful we'd finally started talking —actually talking, not just the polite crap we'd exchanged out of obligation for so long. And yet, I'd never been more pained by my inability to just take her at her word. It made seeing her running the big mixer and rolling out different doughs far more painful than it had been before.

"The food beat you here." She nodded toward the kitchen.

"That was fast." My throat felt dry and tight. Stupid dry climate. Stupid week. Stupid heart. *Dammit*, I did not like this version of myself. "Can I—"

"Is it okay—"

We both stopped, smiled. I held out a hand in a *you go ahead* gesture.

"I wanted to know if I could hug you."

My heart flipped and I reached for her. She pushed off the door and wrapped her arms around my neck. Our bodies met, our heads curved around each other, and something tangled and raging in me took a breath.

Without releasing me, she spoke into my neck. "I think we should eat, and then talk."

My mood must've been obvious. I should've released her and moved away. Being close like this made it impossible to think clearly. Why had I stayed away this week?

My hands tightened at her small waist, and I inhaled a slow breath, savoring her nearness for another second before releasing her. "Sounds good."

So we did. We doled out the food from Guac and sat on her couch with something on the TV. And even though I wouldn't have chosen to sit and not talk, taking a beat to get some calories in me did do a bit to calm my inner beast. Sitting next to her and being in her space might've helped with that too.

When we'd both destroyed our meals, leaving only scrapes of sauces across plates, she took our dishes, left them in the sink, and sank back onto the couch facing me. I held out a hand palm up and she took it in hers.

"I feel like everything's messed up, and I don't know why. I'll be the first to admit I don't know how to do this. It's been years since my last relationship, and I don't think that one was a very good practice round."

I internally winced at her use of practice. But she wasn't saying *I* was practice. She was referring to her past, that trashpile of a chef who'd hardly noticed she'd left the city.

"Same. I've avoided this."

She blinked. "*This* as in relationships?"

"Yes."

She pressed her lips together, her eyes focused on nothing. "So, would you rather not be doing this? Trying something with me?"

"No, I want to. I just... I'm struggling a bit. Kind of like you said, I guess. I don't know how to do this."

My stomach churned at the admission. I didn't want her thinking of me as damaged goods, but that was me, wasn't it? In reality, my past was affecting my present negatively enough to officially be called baggage.

Her brows knitted together, she nodded.

"I really do understand. I—" Her phone chimed and she glanced at it, then shoved it under her leg. "I feel like we both like each other. And we both want to try dating. But I'm not sure where it goes after that."

My heart sank like someone had tied rocks to it and tossed it in the river. There it was. I *was* practice if she didn't see a future together. My pulse sprinted, but I forced myself to ask, "Does that mean you don't want anything beyond dating?"

Her phone chimed again. She pulled it out and silenced it, then tucked it back out of sight.

"Sorry. My parents." She reached for her water and gulped some down. "I do want—I mean, eventually, I want a husband and family. And I know that doesn't line up for you. I—"

Her phone buzzed, and she whipped it out, looked at it, and her eyes widened. "I'm sorry. It says it's an emergency and I need to answer. Do you mind?"

"Go ahead."

She brought the phone to her ear and answered. After a minute, her jaw clenched, and it was clear she was not happy. "Okay. Come on up. Warrick's here, and we're—Sure. Okay."

My heart hadn't stopped its jackhammer beat since this conversation began, and now seeing her upset by her parents only increased that frantic pace.

"They're here and they're coming up." She pushed off the couch and smoothed her hair away from her face into a low bun. A form of armor, maybe.

Alarm bolted through me. "Were you expecting them?"

"Definitely not. It's been years since they've come here —I don't think they've ever even been inside the shop."

The knock sounded on the door seconds later. I stood, thankful I hadn't gone full grunge, but I wore only shorts and a T-shirt. Sadie had on shorts and a tank. I liked that neither of us had dressed up, but suddenly, it felt weird, which made no sense.

"Mercedes, you really should be aware of your phone. We've been waiting ten minutes."

Arianna breezed in like she owned the place, followed closely by Randall. His eyes skated around the room, likely not seeing it based on the speed, then held out a hand to me before he ever said a word to Sadie.

"Good to see you, son."

I shook his hand. "Thanks, sir. Nice to see you."

Though I did my best not to lie, sometimes social niceties demanded it. I couldn't very well say, "I could live a lifetime without seeing you again," or "Thanks for interrupting the most important conversation of our relationship," or even, "I was about to confess my feelings to your daughter and then take her to bed, thanks so much for interrupting."

That last one was wishful thinking, but since I wouldn't say any of that with them here, what did it matter?

"We're on our way into the city, then heading to California. I wanted to make sure you've got the dates for Marguerite's wedding clear. I know you like to plan." Her mother sat primly on the edge of a bright yellow upholstered chair and tapped at her phone, then began listing dates.

Sadie stood, arms crossed, face unreadable. Since I'd known her, I'd realized her face was almost always readable in stressful situations, so this must be more of that armor. Whatever progress they'd made over the weekend, for some reason, this was hurting her. This was potentially *harming* her. It made me want to throw them out into the hallway.

Arianna finished listing dates, then looked at Sadie like she should have a specific reaction to the news.

"Good to know." Sadie's tone rang hollow.

"What's essential here is that first, you realize we'll expect you at all events. And second, we'd love to be able to announce your engagement soon, too." Arianna's face brightened prettily, her brows rising on her wrinkle-less forehead.

And my heart stopped.

"Engagement?" I asked, sure I'd heard wrong.

"We know it's early days, but you've known each other for years. We're a good family, and though I don't know your parents, I know you're from good stock. You've done well for yourself, and you can support our daughter."

My mouth dropped open, but too many things were competing for the exit.

"Dad." Sadie's admonishing tone was far less shocked than I would've anticipated. In fact, she didn't sound all that surprised.

"I'm sorry. I—my father passed when I was a baby. My

mom is the best. And Sadie doesn't need me to support her. She's—" My throat involuntarily swallowed. "She's fine."

Out of the corner of my eye, I saw her stiffen. Where was the Sadie from dinner last weekend who'd put her parents in their place? Where was the woman who stood up for herself? What the hell was happening?

Before I could say anything, or she could, Arianna rose to standing.

"Well, we've taken enough of your time, though we consider that it's good for both of you. It'll make things easier on everyone. You won't have to worry." She moved to the door while Randall nodded at Sadie, shook my hand again, and they left.

No response to my statements, no more words for their daughter. They just walked right out.

Silence filtered in like fog. Sadie stared in front of her, and I tried to be patient. But what just happened?

"What just happened?" I closed the distance between us, yet she still stood there, off in her own head. "Sadie."

Her head jerked and she met my eyes. Her arms were crossed tight against her, and it felt like she'd shrunk up the minute her parents said they were coming.

"Sorry. Uh, so yeah, they think we should just go for it. Get married. I guess you really charmed them, and they like the idea of us."

My eyes widened, and I searched the room like there'd be a clue to make sense of this. "That's just... so out of left field."

She mumbled something.

"What?"

She sighed. "Not all that. They mentioned something to that effect when we were leaving last weekend."

"You didn't say anything." How had she not mentioned that little tidbit?

"I was embarrassed, and mad. I didn't want to sit down in their suggestion since we were on the way home. But..."

"But?"

How was there even a *but* right now? What alternate universe had I dropped into where Sadie was this person again? This cowering woman who apparently forgot how she'd stood up for herself and pressed her parents to do better only last weekend?

"But it might work." Her eyes shot to mine, and she took a breath. "It would solve problems for both of us."

Someone had poured mud in my ears. Someone had lit a fire in my chest, but not the good, hot kind that meant fun, sexy things were happening with Sadie. No, it was the black smoke of a plastic fire, all opaque, poisonous air and danger.

"What?" I managed, trying and failing to guess at what on earth she meant.

"It's crazy, yes, but then p-part of me thinks, is it? It gets them off my back, makes them stop insisting I need a man to help me function, and since you don't want to actually get married anyway, it kind of takes you off the market without the real-life consequence." She squinted at me.

My chest constricted and threatened to collapse in on itself. I coughed, reaching for breath. "How would us getting married not have real-life consequences?"

"I mean, if we did it as f-friends, and we just, you know, like, uh, last weekend. We have fun together, and we like each other."

A laugh of pure disbelief shot out of me. "Wow. Yeah. Just... get married, huh?"

"I know you don't want to *really* get married, obviously.

But this would be different. It'd be okay. We could even—I mean, we could work out the details later."

She'd taken my heart in her strong little hand and squeezed until nothing but bloody pulp was left. She had no idea how much this suggestion felt like a whack-a-mole game with only one hole starring me and her holding a sledgehammer.

This was worse than being a practice run. At least practice ended at some point. Marriage... that was for life. 'Til death do us part. A life of committing to be with someone who saw me as a way to solve a problem.

"I don't know what to say." My voice sounded far away, and I knew I had to get out of here. I was about to lose it, and no way was I going to cry in front of my apparent fake future wife. I paced to the door.

She shuffled after me, grabbing for my arm, her voice urgent. "I didn't mean to upset you. It's crazy. We don't need to keep talking about it, we—"

"It's fine. I'm just—you've gotta get up tomorrow. It was a weird night. I'll catch you—" My stupid voice cracked, and I cleared my throat. "I'll talk to you soon."

She sucked in an audible breath but nodded. And I was gone. Out. Down the stairs, out the door, into the street, walking until I gave up and started jogging, thankful I hadn't kicked off my shoes in her place, because I absolutely would've left without them.

I didn't want to think about what just happened, but her words pelted me right along with the rain as I ran. "*It would solve problems for both of us.*" Like marrying me would be a fix for something, not a choice she wanted. Not something she'd dreamed about or couldn't imagine *not* doing. It'd solve my problem of not wanting to be married and hers of, what? Her parents bothering her? Thinking she always needed a man when she clearly didn't?

I made it home in record time and stomped through the half-finished house to my sad little room. Once there, I let it come. I hadn't realized that I'd wanted her to choose me—not just as a boyfriend, but for more. Not until tonight, when she'd made it so clear she'd choose me as a friend, as a convenience, but certainly not as a husband.

"I'm not sure you're husband material."

Tracy's words came echoing back to slap me in the face. Here I was again, but worse. At least Tracy had left. She'd lied and cheated first, sure, but she'd left.

Now, the woman I loved wanted to *use* me. And I couldn't pretend I didn't love her anymore—not with this shoved in my face and my response. If I didn't love her, this wouldn't hit so hard—not *this damn hard*.

I wanted to love her, cherish her, comfort her—to be with her. Sadie wanted to use me. Not just to get somewhere and leave me, but indefinitely. To keep herself comfortable, and supposedly to do me a favor too.

I'd been looking for clarity. I'd wanted to know where she stood, and she'd made that clear. I didn't have to guess at this any longer or second-guess my own perceptions.

I should be thanking Arianna and Randall about now, shouldn't I? I got exactly what I'd wanted out of the night, in the end.

CHAPTER THIRTY-SIX

Sadie

Sarah, Quinn, and Dahlia knocked on the back door of Rise and Shine as I was wrapping up my clean-up around eleven the day after what had to be marked as one of my most idiotic moments ever.

They'd vowed to be here the minute I was ready to go after I'd sent a text to Sarah. Apparently, she'd looped in Quinn and Dahlia because they were working on something or other when she got my text earlier, and now here they were, smiling at me with care and concern. Those were generous expressions, considering the text: *I proposed to Warrick last night. It didn't go well.* That was reductive, but in the end, also true.

"I can't talk about this here."

"Let's go to my shop. I have a wedding order and I need to finish some ribbons. Come on."

Dahlia waved us after her, and I followed gratefully. I

didn't want to go home, and I didn't want to go to the big kitchen and try to ignore Warrick, who would most definitely be there all day because that would be just my luck. Plus, he was normally there on Saturday afternoons.

Sarah hooked her elbow with mine and nudged my shoulder. "It'll be okay."

Throat instantly tight, I swallowed. "Sure."

I couldn't say anything else because I didn't believe her. And she had no idea how deeply I'd messed up. How wrong everything had gone.

In minutes, we were stepping through Bloom's doors, off the Elk Street sidewalk and into a life-sized fairy house. I loved this shop, and just entering the space soothed. We followed Dahlia through the charmingly crowded space filled with interesting bird feeders and chimes, other home décor, and peppered with huge vases of flowers people could take single stems from to create their own bouquet. The check-out counter had an old-timey register with those big metal buttons, and behind it was a cooler of the "prissy" flowers, as Dahlia called them.

We entered the back room, which seemed positively empty compared to the main space. A huge worktable sat in the middle and the walls were lined with cabinets and countertops. Every bit of it was covered with boxes and containers of what looked like finished bouquets.

"Is the wedding today?" I wondered aloud.

Dahlia had already started adjusting the ribbon on a bundle of perfect pink roses in front of her. "Yes. And she has twenty-two bridesmaids."

"Whoa." I didn't even have that many people I spoke to willingly, let alone would want to be a bridesmaid.

And then, there it was. Bridesmaid. Wedding. Me proposing to Warrick, my mouth saying the words and my mind too jumbled to stop it, and the look on his face like I'd stabbed him in the back. His speedy exit, and the ensuing total silence since he'd left. I steadied myself on the table to keep from hunching over against the feeling.

Sarah was right there, her hand between my shoulder blades. "Please tell us what happened. Can you tell us?"

I blew out a breath, summoning courage. I hadn't imagined sharing this with Quinn and Dahlia too, but that didn't bother me. What was chipping away at my insides was the very real sense that I'd damaged something I couldn't repair.

"Yes. I can tell you. But I'm going to sit down." I'd been working since six and hadn't slept *at all* last night, so between the adrenaline-fueled baking this morning and the general misery, I felt utterly poured out.

"Sit on this stool," Sarah said, pulling up the seat. "And let me give them a quick recap?"

I understood her question. Could she tell them about the fake-dating-turned-real last weekend, and everything? If I was going to share my newest misstep, then yes. She might as well. I nodded, and off she went. Hearing it from her made it sound almost sweet and comical. We became friends, and then I branched out and made friends. I asked him to help me, and he agreed. We had a great time, had insane chemistry, and decided to try for real.

And then it all went belly up. He backed away, and I basically clobbered him in order to keep him from running away, though they didn't know about that last part yet.

"Dang. So you have all these feelings, and you're obviously adorable together, but then he flips his lid? What's wrong with him? I've always liked Warrick—he seems like a good dude. But this is not a good look for him." Quinn made a disgusted face.

"I mean, it wasn't clear between us. We were going to

try, but I'll admit I was thrown by him on Wednesday because he totally papered over his upset with his brother and that just gave me this feeling like he was doing that with us. Like there was something else going on. So yesterday, I decided I'd come out and ask. But just as we were getting to the heart of the discussion—the *where are we heading and what do we want* part of things, my parents showed up."

Dahlia looked up from her work. "Wait. I thought you guys didn't really talk to or see each other."

"We don't. It's been more than a handful of years since they've bothered to swing through Silverton on their way to the house when they visit. I guess it was their olive branch after the engagement party and my talks with them. In some twisted way, I should be glad they came. But they mentioned how nice it would be if Warrick and I went ahead and got engaged and then they'd have two daughters ready to marry."

Quinn's expression would've sent me into a fit of laughter if I could've found any humor in the moment.

"Wait. What? Why?"

Sarah waved her off. "That's not important right now. What did you say? Did Warrick freak out?"

I scrubbed a hand over my face. "I think the fact that I *didn't* freak out in response put Warrick in a weird spot. Because I barely reacted, and I think he could tell they'd mentioned it before. Which they had, as I was leaving last weekend. And honestly, it'd been nagging at me. This idea that we'd arrive at the end of our relationship, and his dislike of marriage would cost us everything. In that moment..."

Regret swamped me all over again at the memory of his face. At those words he'd said to my dad—"*She's fine.*" I recapped all that, telling them how certain he'd been I'd be fine without him.

"That's good, though. He was making the point that you don't need him, and they shouldn't want to pressure you into marriage," Quinn said.

"Yeah, but how did that sound to her? Like he didn't want her. Like, 'Oh, no, don't sign me up for that horrible job, she'll be just fine.'" Sarah's imitation Warrick voice made us all come to a stop in our movements and then break out laughing.

Well, Dahlia and Quinn laughed, and I didn't try to hide my smile. In the midst of this insanity, it came as a welcome relief.

"I panicked. I fully admit it, and after a lifetime of panicking, I can't say it's a shock. So they left and instead of saying they were crazy and I just wanted to date him and if we got to the point where we wanted to be married, that'd be amazing, I proposed a marriage of convenience."

"No!" Quinn's voice came clear and sharp.

"Oh, no. Oh, honey." Sarah's hand on my arm did nothing to calm me now.

Dahlia made a face right in line with the others' comments.

"Yeah. I said if we got married, they'd get off my back and let me do what I wanted without badgering me about getting married. And he could be married in title, but not have people wondering why he didn't date or women asking him out and him having to let them down easy. I made it seem like it had nothing to do with *him*, and everything to do with just... convenience."

No one responded for what felt like long minutes but was more likely only seconds. Finally, Sarah spoke gently. "No mention of your feelings?"

I bowed my head, the tears coming. "No."

They gave me a moment to collect myself, which I did

in miraculously quick time considering how exhausted I was, and then she continued.

"So then he left? Just walked out?"

"He said it'd been a weird night, and he didn't know what to say. But he practically teleported out of there, and he was clearly upset. I'm not sure I've seen him that upset."

Ouch. Just thinking of hurting him like that made my heart squeeze.

"Okay but wait. *Do* you have feelings for him? Is that a factor here? Or is this a case of a friendship gone off the rails?" Quinn crossed her arms and eyed me.

"I do. I do have feelings. Big, terrifying, make-me-do-stupid-things feelings." And I hated that I'd bent to my parents' sudden appearance like their opinions mattered more than Warrick's. Like their opinion mattered more than how I felt about Warrick.

Quinn nodded once like I'd given her the right answer. "Good. Okay then. We're dealing with friendship and love, and unknown feelings on his end, but based on every time I've seen you two together, both for him too. Plus, he looked rode hard and put away wet this morning at the eight o'clock workout."

My heart jolted. "You saw him? Why do you say that? Was he okay?"

Her face broke into a broad smile. "He was miserable."

"Why are you smiling like that?" I asked, nearly shrieking, which was completely out of character, and yet, I couldn't seem to control the volume of my voice.

"Because, my sweet little introverted friend, I guarantee he was miserable over *you.* Not because you said something wrong or whatever nonsense, but because you didn't share all those big scary feelings."

Dahlia nodded, and Sarah grabbed my arm. "I think

she's right. I mean, who knows, but Warrick is sensitive. If you guys were on the verge of figuring things out and then you backed off like that, he was probably really upset."

I pressed the heels of my hands into my eyes. Thank goodness I hadn't bothered with makeup today. "He was. I saw it."

I breathed slowly in through my mouth and refused to let my breathing get out of control. I felt that drag in my brain, like it wanted to fold up shop in the face of what felt too big to get my arms around. Thankfully, instead of shorting out and sliding into a panic attack, I had help. These women were with me, and even if I couldn't fix everything with Warrick, I wasn't alone.

I wasn't going to magically be cast back to the solitude of my old life. That simple truth helped me keep breathing through the twisting heart and threatening tears.

Quinn marched around the table and set her hands on my shoulders, then dropped her chin so she was staring into my eyes. "Text him right now. Beg him to meet up tonight, beg him not to cancel, and then go take a nap. This is a problem you *can* solve. You need your wits about you because you, woman, are going to tell your parents to back off, and then, you're going to tell the man the truth."

CHAPTER THIRTY-SEVEN

Warrick

"What is my little sunbeam baby doing with that broody look on his face?" My mom frowned at me in a completely ridiculously exaggerated version of what I assumed was supposed to mimic my expression.

I'd arrived ten minutes ago—late enough that I wouldn't be moping around too long, mentally preoccupied with what'd happened with Sadie last night, but early enough I couldn't be accused of not helping a little bit, at least. They'd agreed to an early dinner because I'd told them I was meeting Sadie—no point in pretending like my mind wouldn't be completely on her and the upcoming interaction the entire meal.

Mom's spidey senses tipped her off the minute she got a look at my face.

"Really, Mom? We're still calling him *little*?" Wyatt's

question came as he set her heaping plate of salad on the table in front of her.

"Wow, Wy. This is an intense salad." It was a restaurant-sized portion—the right amount for me, if I'd had an appetite. Dark leafy greens, still-hot grilled chicken, all kinds of vegetables, and a few diced strawberries, which wouldn't normally be my thing, but I'd long ago learned to trust Wyatt's taste in salad flavor combos.

"My field greens went crazy this week. I swear it was like they knew rain was coming last night and just blew their own little minds. So here we are. Plus, I wanted there to be enough so we were all actually full." He leaned over and pressed a kiss to Calla's shoulder.

I refocused on my food and ignored the jagged, raw feeling in my gut. I ate a few bites, then decided to shovel in the chicken and call it good. I tried not to think about Sadie's messages earlier. Tried, and failed spectacularly.

She'd asked to meet tonight. I'd agreed, of course, because some part of me still couldn't refuse her anything.

What did she want? To make me admit I was upset? She had to know, but why get together again so soon? I hadn't had enough time to get past this hollowed-out feeling of pain and disappointment.

Be honest with yourself, man. It's heartbreak.

I sighed at that thought and took another bite. The hubbub around me faded away, and after a bit, awareness that everyone else had stopped making *any* sound pulled me out of my pitiful fog. When I looked up, Wyatt, Calla, and Mom were all studying me.

"Seriously, War. What's going on?" Mom reached out and put her hand atop mine, covering me with those soft palms that'd brought me so much comfort and love my whole life.

What right did I have to feel this miserable? I had an embarrassment of riches here, right at this table. I knew this. And yet, I felt like I'd been run over by a train.

I cleared my throat, wishing away the emotion that seemed permanently clogged there. "Long story short, I'm pretty sure Sadie and I broke up."

Mom tilted her head to the side. "How can you break up if you're fake-dating?"

I coughed reflexively. "Uh, what—how do you know we were?"

She raised one brow. "I have my ways. And no, your brother did not snitch on you. Why do you think I left you alone on the twenty-fourth?"

"I thought you said—" I shook my head, a smile tugging at my mouth despite myself. "Okay, well, yeah, it started that way. Then we decided we were going to try for real. Then she basically crushed me with a proposal to marry her but not out of love."

Wyatt scoffed. "Out of *what*, then?"

"To solve a problem. For both of us, supposedly."

A pause hung in the air for about ten seconds, and then they all exploded into talking, peppering questions so fast that I couldn't answer anything.

Calla was in the fray just as much as Mom and Wyatt. "Solve what problem?"

"How does marrying her solve anything?"

"Wait, was she joking?"

"What did you say?"

"What were you thinking?"

"What was *she* thinking?"

I waved my hands, clearing the questions away.

"Stop. Stop. It's fine. But it clarified things for me. I don't think she meant to use me, but it turns out…"

Damnnnn, but that reality heated my ribs to burning coals through my skin and shirt.

Mom shook her head. "No. No way. She cares about you."

"You're not going to do it, are you?" Wyatt's voice came low, but the tone said he was actually worried.

And that showed how well he knew me. Because there'd been more than a moment in the last twenty-four hours when I'd considered it. I could do it and help her. Do what she wanted and be the good guy. Or at least tell myself that while I tried to ignore that I'd be doing it just to be close to her—to take what I could get. I'd also had the thought that if I did it, she'd be grateful. And maybe someday, that would develop into something else.

It would let me off the hook for anything like this happening again—I'd only have to figure out how to live with this brutalized heart indefinitely.

But I couldn't handle that. I felt like a stranger to myself these days, at least in this area. I knew I couldn't take wanting her, loving her, and being a convenience in her eyes.

"All right, let's talk about this right here and now." Mom pushed at my good shoulder from her seat next to me so I leaned toward her.

"Me and Sadie? There's nothing to talk about."

She took a deep breath. "No, honey. Let's talk about you wanting to earn your way to love. Be the man helping people, friend to everyone, starting up businesses and then selling them for way less than they're worth. You work yourself into exhaustion, staying busy, and I want to know why."

Something in me crumpled, but I ignored it. "I—I like to work. I like to stay busy. That's not a crime. That's not me trying to *earn love.*"

My eyes flickered to Wyatt's, and his serious expression made my heart sink lower. *Was* there something wrong with me? I could be a workaholic. And I enjoyed the crap out of the occasional day-saving move like holding the door for someone as they almost spilled their coffee, or, you know, helping Sadie out when she needed me but...

But. *Bad news.*

"Is it?"

Wyatt's frown deepened. "You've been working so hard for so long. Since you left the NFL. I wonder if maybe you feel like you have to work hard to be accepted. I hope we haven't made you feel that way, but maybe it's just happened."

Mom clasped my hand in hers. "We love you, Warrick. Whether you're running a football or laid up on the couch, revolutionizing fitness in Silverton, or just laughing at your own jokes."

Everyone chuckled, including me.

"I don't do it consciously. But I definitely feel bad when I'm not working or busy. I know that."

Wy pinned me with his stupid blue eyes. "You're a good man, Warrick. Dad would be so proud. Wilder is proud. I'm so damned proud of you. And you can see Mom is basically your number one fan. If Sadie doesn't see that, then she's not it for you. And if she does, maybe it's time to think about changing your plans."

Something about the way Calla squeezed Wyatt's hand made me think they'd talked about this—they'd been concerned even before now. Then she gave her two cents.

"I haven't known you long, but you charmed me from the beginning, as you know. I haven't gotten to see Sadie much lately, but she has seemed happy when I do. And you look at each other, lean on each other, with a similar comfort and ease. I don't know how she feels, but I'd be shocked if she didn't see how wonderful you are."

I cleared my throat and felt the expression on my face mirroring one of Wilder's scowls. "I don't know."

Mom huffed. "I won't say I do because, obviously, I can't read minds. But I'm glad you'll see her tonight. I hope you'll just ask her what the deal is. Be bold, baby."

I summoned a smile, hoping acquiescing would wrap things up. "I'll try."

"Good. And as for the rest?"

Of course she couldn't let me off easy. So I played dumb. "The rest?"

"Yes, Warrick Thomas. The part where you're working yourself into the ground and not even enjoying it like you used to."

Wyatt ducked his chin to his chest and I guarantee he was hiding a smile, the traitor. Granted, he'd been thoroughly grilled enough by our beloved mother that I couldn't actually blame him for enjoying my turn.

I blew out a breath, tossing any caution or sense of self-preservation to the warm summer wind outside the ranch house because why not? "I've felt something was missing. First, I thought it was Tracy and football. Then I kind of enjoyed being focused on work and telling myself I was good, didn't need anyone but family. But honestly, seeing you guys get together combined with that feeling creeping back in after my birthday just kind of drove it home."

I hadn't even admitted it to myself, but there it was. I'd turned thirty and what did I have? A great family, sure, but nothing of my own beyond a few StayBnB projects and a small handful of businesses I'd sold. I had money, but not love. And I hadn't realized how much I'd wanted that until Sadie made it clear I didn't have hers.

"Oh, honey. That's not a bad thing, to realize you want something more."

Mom's voice was infinitely gentle, and the sound of it made me toss back a long pull of water before answering. "I know."

"You're thinking Sadie's it? What's been missing?" Wyatt didn't sound disbelieving or critical, only curious. Concerned.

"Not at first. I mean, obviously I've always been interested in her, so the friend thing a few months ago seemed like a good idea. And then the fake dating was a way to trick myself into dating her without breaking my rules about dating and looking for a future with someone. But all along, I've known that because it was her, and she was finally letting me in, it was different. And then the reality of it was —" I cleared my throat, emotion tightening across my chest. "It was really good."

Calla gave me a warm smile. "You should tell her that."

I returned her smile with a thin one of my own. "We'll see what happens."

As I passed the library, I analyzed the conversation for the twentieth time in the hour since I'd left the farmhouse, trying desperately to clear my head before I walked into whatever was about to happen with Sadie.

I'd always preferred to be busy—they'd joked about me being the busiest toddler of the family, and I'd joined every club I could in high school and college, even with athletics on my plate. So that part of me, at least on some level, wasn't new.

But I'd also taken a hit—a literal hit to the shoulder, and a metaphorical blow to my psyche when Tracy left me with the thought that I was just practice for something better. That without football, I wasn't worth sticking around for.

I'd gone to therapy for a while after that, though almost all of it had focused on losing my career. In truth, I hadn't ended up that broken over Tracy. I'd loved her and felt like I didn't want to experience that pain again, but part of me had accepted it. She'd been honest, at least after the fact, and I'd seen, in retrospect, that we probably wouldn't have made it much longer anyway.

What I hadn't confronted until my beloved mother and my irritatingly wise older brother had shoved it in my face earlier was that I felt like I was just practice. I mean, I'd felt my resistance every time Sadie used the word. So that wasn't new. And the realization that I didn't feel worthy of someone without continued wins and success, more money in the bank, and more things on my list I could show someone? There was no going back and sliding that list past my dad to show him I'd grown into someone worthwhile, someone he could be proud of. But a romantic partner? Maybe a sizeable laundry list of accomplishments would make me worth sticking around for.

I hated it. I hated the realization because the minute they pointed it out, I saw the truth spray-painted across my face. It was the reason I briefly considered accepting Sadie's offer to marry her despite that feeling like a death knell of every good thing about our relationship—I could help her. I could do something for her that she'd see as valuable. Then maybe she'd want me the way I wanted her.

I sucked in a huge breath and let it out, wishing I didn't

know so many damn people in this town who wanted to say hi or wave as I finally approached Sadie's building. I hesitated for just a second before pulling the door open and taking the stairs two at a time.

I didn't know what she was going to say, but I'd decided. I wasn't going to try to *do* something for her or be something for her. I wasn't going to try to earn her love or convince her to want me.

I was going to walk in there and show her this ridiculous mess and let her decide how she felt.

CHAPTER THIRTY-EIGHT

Sadie

Forgoing the nap and drinking a caffeinated coffee at four p.m. had not been my best move. But no going back now, right? Especially not since Warrick knocked on my door right at seven, and the time had officially come.

I yanked open the door, impatient to see him like I hadn't in weeks. Like he hadn't been right here twenty-four hours ago.

"Thank you for coming," I said, nervous energy making my voice wobble.

"Sure."

His terse response didn't sound as guarded as I might've expected. It seemed cautious, yes, but not like he'd hired a stonemason to erect a wall around his heart since last night. So there was that.

"Please," I said, gesturing to the couch.

He took his seat.

"Water?" I asked, glad I'd taken the time to set up a little beverage tray. I'd even sliced some wild raspberry whole wheat bread, just in case he was hungry. Not that he ever ate my bread, but I hadn't been at the big kitchen to experiment today, and I'd had all that extra jittery motivation, so I'd channeled it into something pretty darn good, if I did say so myself.

"Sure."

Oh, goodness. This could end up being super fun if he wasn't going to say anything but *sure*. I had to break the ice. And since I didn't have it in me to ease into this mess, I was just going to dive in with both feet.

Here we go!

"I spoke with my parents."

He stiffened. "Somehow, I didn't think that's what you'd start with."

"Well, it's a first-things-first situation, and I want you to know I told them we wouldn't be getting married. I also told them they need to stop suggesting that I need a husband to take care of me. I reminded them what I said last week and told them they needed to respect me by giving me notice before they show up. I hate to admit it, but I still need time to mentally prepare when I deal with them. And then, we talked about my anxiety, and a bunch of other stuff that's a little beside the point—"

"I want to know. What you said to them." His serious gaze didn't waver.

My heart melted like he'd turned the burner under a pan of butter to full heat. And though I didn't want to take the time now, maybe it would be best for him to know.

Running my hands over my jeans, I recapped. "Okay. So, I told them it was offensive that they keep shoving me in the direction of marriage like it'll cure my anxiety. I told them a bit about what I do to manage it—medication, sleep, routines, taking baby steps, and how I've stepped out and made friends these last few months."

He nodded. "You've done a great job putting yourself out there."

"Thanks. Part of the credit goes to you."

"Nope. You initiated our friendship and everything after that. I was just your magic feather." He smiled at me for the first time today, lighting up the entire room.

I chuckled, appreciating the Dumbo reference and feeling his words ring true. I'd been thinking I needed him to hold my hand through all this, but ultimately, I had done it myself. Having him with me for most of it hadn't hurt, though. "Maybe so."

"It's true. Don't doubt it."

Fluttering in my chest had me exhaling slowly. "Thanks. They seemed discombobulated by yet another frank discussion, but it felt good. And I think they are going to try to get back to Silverton to see the new kitchen once it's running full-time in September."

Another smile. "That's good."

I nodded, and nerves shimmied up my neck and clogged my throat. I pushed out another breath.

"You okay?"

"I'm nervous."

He seemed to struggle with that news but nodded. "Let's just get through this."

His tone sounded a little fatalistic, like he was expecting something bad. That made sense considering where we'd left things last night, but I'd hoped hearing that I'd told my parents we wouldn't be getting married just because they suggested it would've helped more than it apparently did.

"Okay. So. I messed up with even entertaining what

they said. But I had a good reason. Or, if not *good*, then maybe at least understandable."

My face had flushed with heat, and my heart felt like it might beat out of my chest. Heavy thumps nearly shook my body, or maybe that was the renewed surge of adrenaline.

My body said *Fight or Flight!* Well, tonight, I was going to fight.

Warrick shifted on the couch.

"I want to understand. But I'll admit, the suggestion that we could just get married like it was no big deal after we'd decided to give dating a genuine shot threw me. Big time. And I'll also say that some part of me wanted to say yes, just to help you. Just to make things better for you. But I'm realizing that's not a healthy way to go about things. So I'm going to try not to respond to whatever this is by offering to do anything for you. I'm just going to listen." He let out a big breath, like he'd somehow held it during his whole speech.

I scooted closer to him, finding the distance between us unbearable. I hated that I'd made him doubt himself or feel he needed to do anything but be himself. "I'm sorry. I started worrying that you were pulling away. And I couldn't escape your statement that you wouldn't marry. And I had this insane thought that maybe, if we got married and it wasn't a 'real' marriage, I could keep you."

He shook his head, not understanding. "Keep me?"

I smiled and swallowed down the rising flood of emotion. "I didn't want to date and then break up. I didn't want to pretend to be friends again and feel like we'd already ruined that with the kissing and everything. And my feelings are too strong for all that anyway. But it was wrong to even entertain the idea, and I'm so sorry I hurt you by suggesting that I could be married to you and it wouldn't change my whole life."

His face had sobered completely. Maybe like someone had punched him, or like he was about to throw up. His eyes searched mine. "Your feelings? You have feelings for me?"

I huffed a laugh and couldn't stop myself from reaching for him, setting my hand on his leg to connect us and ground me. "I'm in love with you."

His brow smoothed out, and the dawning smile on his face threatened to break my heart, except that he took my hand and pressed it against his chest.

"That works out, because I'm in love with you too."

I sucked in a breath, and tears instantly hit my eyes. No good rotten exhaustion had me teetering on the brink of tears all day as it was, but hearing that? From him? Right now? I wouldn't lie and say I hadn't hoped for something like this, but the reality of it was so much better.

"You are?" I said, my voice a teary tangle.

"I am. Pretty sure I was a goner with that first hug." He grinned, then his gaze dropped to my lips and his voice went low. "Can I please kiss you now?"

I didn't answer with words. Instead, I crawled across the couch and pressed my lips to his. Relief and thrill washed through me as he pulled me into his lap and broke the kiss to set his forehead against mine.

"I missed you."

"I missed you too."

He wiped the tears from my eyes with his warm thumbs and kissed each cheek slowly, methodically. Then my forehead, just under my jaw on one side, then the other. When he returned to my mouth, he moved so gradually, I wondered if he'd ever actually make contact with my lips.

At first, he restarted the kiss with a light press, but he then deepened it, tilting my head and sending a crush of pleasure through me.

Love welled up in me and spilled over until my tears became obnoxious and I leaned away and swiped under each eye. Warrick smiled at me, something indulgent and gentle and heartbreakingly mine.

At least for now.

"What's that face for?" His thumb came up and nudged where my brow had wrinkled.

A shy, anxious wave swept through me, but after what we'd both just said, I couldn't hide from him. Not about this.

"I'm just wondering how long I have you. I know it's too soon to be thinking like this, but what happens next?"

One brow flared up. "I would say maybe I finally get to see your bedroom, but I feel like that's not what you mean."

I chuckled and gave him a half-heartedly begrudging smile. "You'd be right. I mean, like, the future."

He reached up and tucked a few strands of hair behind my ear, then let his fingers coast along my neck and follow the line of my shoulder down my arm until he laced them with mine.

"Marriage still feels like a huge step to me. But that's not because of *you*. That's because of *me*. I'm not sure when I'll be ready, honestly. I've changed a lot of the way I think about relationships in the last few weeks and especially the last forty-eight hours or so. But I can tell you I'm not ruling it out."

I nodded, heartened.

"And I can tell you that spending another day without you seems insane. That a lifetime with you sounds perfect. And I think, in time, if it's you, I can see being ready."

He kissed me again, promising, reassuring, and I relaxed into him, breathing in his scent and loving his closeness. Loving the prospect of time together indefinitely.

Loving him.

After a few more minutes of savoring each other, he pulled back and eyed the bread board. "Can I have some of that?"

"You want some?"

His smile exploded on his handsome face, reminding me all over again how much I loved him. "If you made it? Sure I do."

"But you never eat my bread."

His expression softened, and it was like he knew a secret. "I didn't before. Now I do."

"Why's that?" I asked, genuinely wanting to know.

"I figure I've earned a slice. Plus, eating your bread now that you're *mine* won't make me secretly long for my own personal baker. Now I just have one."

I laugh-scoffed. "Your own personal baker? For a man who doesn't eat baked goods regularly, that seems entirely unnecessary."

An impish gleam in his eye lit before he said, "Yeah, but only a personal baker will help me make the dough-edition of *Ghost*."

I laughed loudly at that, shaking my head at his ridiculousness, and loving how silly he could be.

"Seriously though, I want to celebrate us. So let's toast with some *toast*."

Joy bubbling over in a chuckle, I cut him a slice, slathered it in butter, and watched him eat every bite.

I had a feeling we'd get to that *Ghost* scene, baking version, eventually.

EPILOGUE

Warrick

I breathed in and out in measured breaths, willing myself to chill out. I did not need to be losing my mind over this. This was a thing people did every damn day, and they all lived through it.

"You look ill," Wyatt said, a smug little smirk on his face.

"Shut it," I said, glaring at him.

Because sure, people lived through it every day, but they didn't necessarily do it without puking their guts out from nerves.

"She's going to say yes. She would've said yes a year ago."

He straightened my tie, and I congratulated myself for not swatting his hand away.

"No, she wouldn't have. We weren't even dating a year ago. But the first *A Night in Bloom* was the first time I really believed she might want me. Anyway, whatever, stop talking about it."

Good grief, I was a wreck. If I held my hands out, I could see them visibly shaking.

"You'll be fine, honey." Mom patted my shoulder, reassuring me like she had all my life.

"I know. On the biggest, most important level, I know that. But I might screw it up. I might totally botch the delivery or say something stupid. What if I—"

"You'll be fine." Wilder's voice cut in, stern and serious and demanding we listen.

Obediently, part of me settled. Maybe it was something about having twenty years of experience at telling people what to do, but his presence calmed me.

"I will be fine. I will be." I repeated it like a mantra.

"You will. Now let's go." Calla patted me, then led the way, belly first through the archway into the Silverton gardens.

A year ago, Sadie and I had attended separately. Tonight, we were together, though she'd showed up early to help Dahlia with set-up. I hadn't seen her yet, and though I'd been planning to propose for weeks now, being on the precipice felt a little bit like standing on an actual cliff.

I shuffled in behind Calla and Wyatt, Mom taking Wilder's hand. My heart pounded harder than it had before the Super Bowl years back—no lie. I couldn't remember being so nervous, and yet so sure about something. So completely clear about what I wanted, and what I'd do to get it.

I wanted Sadie. And what would I do?

Anything.

Just like last year, the charming little garden had been turned into a magical wonderland of blooming flowers and sparkling lights. A server passed by with a tray of champagne glasses and everyone but me and Calla took one. I already had fizz in my blood—didn't need any help there.

I didn't even try to pretend I wasn't looking for Sadie—I wanted to see her. I *needed* to see her. I'd planned on waiting until the end of the night—enjoying some food, relaxing into the evening. And when I spotted her across the lawn, past a topiary bursting with blooms and framed by an actual frame made of flowers taking a photo next to Dahlia, I realized my folly.

I couldn't wait another second.

"Here we go," I said, and Wyatt turned just in time to pat me on the back and send me on my way with a "You've got it."

I made a beeline for Sadie, barely acknowledging Aidan where he stood with John, though at some point, I'd need to congratulate them both tonight. I eased around a group watching Quinn belt out a love song that fit the moment and leaned in to kiss Sadie's neck.

She gasped and turned, then beamed at me. My heart turned to mush, and I leaned down to kiss her cheek.

"Calla warned me not to kiss your lips, so I figured I had to get creative." Her red lipstick highlighted those lips I wanted to worship, but I also knew better than to start the night that way.

"I appreciate both of those sentiments." She gently kissed my cheek in return. "You look very handsome."

Her eyes sparkled back at me as my heart flipped, then flipped again. It must've taken up on a trapeze bar and just kept on going. "And you look absolutely stunning."

With the smile, the lips, the long wavy hair, and a dress that draped over her gorgeous body in pale yellow, every kind of anticipation coursed through me.

"Thank you. How did things go with Wilder?"

"Really well. But listen, can we—" I tugged on her arm and led her down a small path that tucked us behind a large hedge and into a private little corner. "Sorry. I just need a minute, if you have it?"

Her brow furrowed, and her hand came to my cheek. "Is everything okay?"

I chuckled, mostly breath. "Yes. And no."

She swallowed, bracing herself. "Tell me."

"I love you." It came out like a burst.

She laughed. "I love you too."

"So that's the yes. But the no is that I don't think I can wait. I had planned to do this whole night and then go for it, but I can't wait. So..." I blew out a breath, grabbed her hands, and bent to one knee.

She inhaled sharply and bit her bright red bottom lip.

"Mercedes Miller. I love you more than I thought I could love anyone. You make me better, and I hope I do the same for you. I want to spend the rest of my life loving you, cheering you on, and living life with you. Will you marry me?"

Tears in her eyes, she stepped close and pressed a kiss to my lips—long, lingering, and the best damned kiss of my life. "Took you long enough."

I laughed, grateful for the break in heavy emotion so I could rein in my own watery eyes. "Yeah, guess it did. I had to psych myself up to ask."

"Did you actually think I'd say no?"

I gave her a look, and she just shook her head.

"Did you forget the part where I tried to marry you *last* year?" She scratched her fingers in the beard at either side of my jaw.

"I didn't. But I am not fool enough to think you don't

have your pick of other options." I swallowed, wondering if she had any idea how true that was.

"I don't want anyone else. I choose you. And just to be clear, yes. I will marry you."

She pressed those red lips to mine again, heedless of her lipstick, and I couldn't have loved her more.

"This isn't practice, right? I'm not dreaming, and we're not about to pretend to get married, are we?"

She laughed and nuzzled her cheek against mine. "No. It's better than a dream, and way better than practice. It's real."

Yes, it was. Entirely real.

Thank you for reading Warrick and Sadie's story! I hope you loved them. I absolutely loved writing them! If you're curious about Julian Grenier's story, you can get it today!

Back to Silver Ridge Series

Almost Perfect, Book 1

Almost Real, Book 2

Almost Sure, Book 3

Almost Home, Book 4

The Silver Ridge Resort Series

Unexpected Love at Silver Ridge, Book 1

Second Chance at Silver Ridge, Book 2

Patrolling for Love at Silver Ridge, Book 3

Fire and Ice at Silver Ridge, Book 4

The OCONUS Bonus Series

The Problem with Planning Love, Book 1

Finding Happiness in a Hoax, Book 2

Learning to Fight after Flight, Book 3

The Bright Side of Brooding, Book 4

Holding On to Hope, Book 5

The Rambler Battalion Series

Where You Go: The Rambler Battalion, Book 1

As You Are: The Rambler Battalion, Book 2

Don't Stop Now: The Rambler Battalion, Book 3

Home With You: The Rambler Battalion, Book 4

All of You: The Rambler Battalion, Book 5

ACKNOWLEDGMENTS

Thank you to everyone who was so excited for Warrick's book! I loved writing him, and I hope you loved his and Sadie's love story.

Thanks to my husband for advising on football details, and for cheering me on through every book.

Thank you to my editor, Zee Monodee, for insisting Warrick be as Warricky as he needed to be.

To my amazing Beta readers Amanda, Ashley, and Genny. Your feedback helps so much, and your enthusiasm for this book was so valuable! Thank you!

Thank you to Emma Robinson for the beautiful cover!

Thank you Amanda Cuff for catching the reallys. REALLY.

Thanks to Jamie McGillen, Julie Dobbins, and Laura Ziesel for being particularly supportive for me in regular life things while I wrote this book.

Thanks to my reader group for being so enthusiastic about reading Warrick's story and for generally being awesome! Oh! And for helping name Grit :)

Thanks to all the bookstagrammers, book bloggers, and readers who've supported this new series by reading, reviewing, and sharing! Reviews and word of mouth really do make a difference to indie authors, so thank you!

ABOUT THE AUTHOR

Claire Cain lives to eat and drink her way around the globe with her traveling soldier and three kids, but is perhaps even happier hunkered down at home in a pair of sweatpants and slippers using any free moment she has to read and cook. Or talk—she really likes to talk. She has become an expert at packing too many dishes in too few cabinets and making houses into homes from Utah to Germany and many places in between. She's a proud Army wife and is frankly just really happy to be here.

You can also join Claire's facebook reader group for exclusive content and fun: https://www.facebook.com/groups/clairecain/

Website: http://www.clairecainwriter.com

E-mail: Claire@ClaireCainWriter.com

Newsletter sign-up for new releases, exclusives, and freebies, including a free book:

http://www.clairecainwriter.com/newsletter

amazon.com/author/clairecain

bookbub.com/authors/claire-cain

instagram.com/clairecainwriter

facebook.com/clairecainwriter

goodreads.com/clairecainwriter

pinterest.com/clairecainwriter

twitter.com/writeclairecain